The Consequence

KINGS OF RUIN BOOK 2

L KNIGHT

The Consequence
Kings of Ruin Book Two
By L Knight

Published by L Knight
Copyright © March 2023

Cover: Clem Parsons-Metatec
Editing: Black Opal Editing
Formatting: Black Opal Editing
Cover Photographer: Wander Aguiar

This is a work of fiction. Names characters places and incidents are a product of the author's imagination or are used fictitiously and are not to be construed as fact. Any resemblance to actual events organisations or persons—living or dead—is entirely coincidental.

All rights reserved. By payment of the required fees, you have been granted the non-exclusive non-transferable right to access and read the text of this eBook on a screen. Except for use in reviews promotional posts or similar uses no part of this text may be reproduced transmitted downloaded decompiled reverse-engineered or stored in or introduced into any information storage and retrieval system in any form or by any means whether electronic or mechanical now known or hereafter invented without the express written permission of the author.

First edition March 2023 © L Knight

Acknowledgments

I am so lucky to have such an amazing team around me without which I could never bring my books to life. I am so grateful to have you in my life, you are more than friends you are so essential to my life.

My editor—Linda at Black Opal Editing, who is so patient. She is so much more than an editor, she is a teacher and a friend.

My UK PA Clem Parsons who listens to all my ramblings and helps me every single day.

My ARC Team for not keeping me on edge too long while I wait for feedback.

Lastly and most importantly thank you to my readers who have embraced my books so wholeheartedly and shown a love for the stories in my head. To hear you say that you see my characters as family makes me so humble and proud. I hope you enjoy Harrison's and Norrie's love story as much as I did.

Cover: Clem Parsons @Metatec
Editing: Black Opal Editing
Cover Photographer: Wander Aguiar

Prologue: Harrison

"I'm telling you I don't need a goddamn break. I'm fine." I'm lying on a couch in the shared office of Club Ruin as Beck leans over me with a blood pressure cuff. I glare at his dark head before transferring that glare to Audrey. It does no damn good. She isn't frightened of me or anyone else. It's why we work so well together. She's a force of nature, which is just as well when she owns a club with four assholes like us.

"Clearly you're not fine or you wouldn't have almost passed out behind the bar."

My skin feels tight as they stare at me, and I fight the urge to squirm. I hate being the sole focus of their attention. "I just stood up too quickly."

"If you say so. Remind me again where you got your medical degree?" Beck raises a cocky brow at me, and I sigh at his attempt to be funny.

I shrug his hand off as he moves to help me to my feet, frustration eating at me. "I can do it." He smirks and shakes his head at my stubbornness. "Haven't you got heart operations to perform instead of bugging the fuck out of me?"

He chuckles as he shoves the cuff back in his bag and I roll my shirt sleeve down. Beck Goldsmith is one of the most talented heart surgeons in the world and, because of his age and skill, one of the most in demand. If I ever do need a surgeon for anything, he'd be my pick over anyone else in the world. He's a genius, but I'd rather have a root canal than admit that.

"Nope, it's my day off."

"You don't take days off."

Beck slung an arm around my shoulder. "Lucky for you, my friend, that today I did."

"It doesn't feel very lucky." I know I'm being a prick, but I hate feeling weak.

"Here, drink this."

Audrey shoves a glass of water at me, and I roll my eyes at her fussing, but I take the glass and down half of it before thrusting it back at her. I can't believe I almost passed out like a fucking pussy.

"You should come in for some blood work and testing, but my personal and professional opinion is you have burnout."

I feel my eyes go wide. "Burnout? That's what rich, old pricks get from trying to fight time and keep up with us younger men by fucking women half their age."

"It's actually not that uncommon among our age group and especially high achievers."

"So, I'm good to go, then."

I won't say I'm not relieved. Almost going down like a ton of bricks behind the bar wasn't an experience I'd like to repeat.

"If by go, you mean a week's vacation then, yes, you're good to go."

I'm shaking my head before he can finish his sentence. "No fucking way. I have a shit load of work to do here."

Audrey crosses her arms, jutting her hip as she taps her thousand-dollar red pump on the floor. It's a look that has terrified grown men and she has the follow-through to back it up. Audrey on a tear is something to behold. She sent a contractor out of here in tears when we first started renovations on this place because he thought he could talk down to her. By the time she'd finished promising to ruin his great-grandchildren's lives, he'd run from the club promising never to do it again. He'd also never returned, and I'd been left to clean that little mess up, but that's what I do, I fix things.

"Harrison, this isn't a request."

I love Audrey I truly do. In fact, I love all my friends here at the club and while they've been christened the Kings of Ruin for the name of the club we run, together they'd die for me and I'd die for them. That doesn't mean they don't drive me to thoughts of murder sometimes. You put five determined, focused, driven individuals together and there are bound to be heads butted. "I don't have time for this."

"Make time. Because as your friend and the best goddamn doctor this world has ever seen, I'm telling you if you don't, you're headed for an early grave."

"What about my mom? I can't just leave her." I visit twice a week to make sure she has her magazines and medication, as well as take her certain items from the shops that she can't order online.

"I'll check in with her and if you die of a heart attack, you won't be any help to her at all, so listen to what I'm saying. Take a fucking vacation before I kick your ass."

My lips twitch at Beck's arrogance but I'm too shaken by his words to smile. It's been just my mother and me for so long and she relies on me. Especially with her agoraphobia and other conditions holding her hostage, she'd struggle to cope on her own. I owe her for putting up with me and sticking around when my father walked out without a second glance all those years ago. So, I guess if that means spending a week being bored to tears then so be it. "Fine, but a week and not a second longer."

Beck slaps me on the shoulder. "Good man."

I grumble my reply, hating that he's right and giving them both a withering glare as they delight in my misery.

"We can juggle the club between us for a week. I'll call Lincoln and Ryker and let them know."

Audrey is gone in a cloud of Chanel, the living embodiment of class and elegance. Beck sits back on the couch where I'd staggered after my header to the floor. When he isn't operating or reading medical journals, Beck studies law books just for shits and giggles. He has a brain that never seems to want to switch off unless he's here doing a scene at the club.

Our club is considered normal. But to a very few people who know what it really is, it's a sanctuary. Those members crave more, and we give it to them in a safe environment.

The ground floor is a normal nightclub filled with patrons wanting to dance, drink, let off steam, and pick up a hot fuck for the night. It's elite in that we only let a certain clientele grace these hallowed floors. The staff wear black denim and black Club Ruin tee shirts.

The second floor is a VIP area with table service only. The girls and guys who work that floor are all gifted with model-worthy looks and wear a very different outfit. Their uniform is more risqué, black slacks for the men with no shirts and a black bow tie, and the women wear short black dresses that show as much as they cover.

Lastly, there's the infamously secret third floor.

When Audrey came to me with the idea of a members-only sex club on the third floor, I was shocked. Audrey isn't a prude, and neither am I but neither one of us has any particular kinks as such. Beck and Linc like to share sometimes or engage in group sex and Beck has never made a secret of the fact he likes men and women, but I wouldn't consider that a kink, just a slight curve from mainstream.

Her argument had been convincing though. Why should people be ashamed of anything that's consensual and why shouldn't we capitalize on the need for privacy and discretion? That was one thing we all understood, the desperate need for our private lives not to end up in some trashy tabloid.

I'd made my first million on the stock markets by the time I was eighteen, my gift for math and analytics proving a Godsend for me and my mom. Lincoln and Audrey were cousins and part of the famed Kennedy family. Beck was a Goldsmith and had been an up-and-coming heart surgeon with a career that had no limit, and Ryker Cabot had shot to infamy when he'd established what was now the biggest social media platform on the planet. That was how we became what we are now, a club with a wealth of members on the top floor. From actors to senators and sports stars.

Privacy is important to us all, another reason we're a success. The true nature of the club is only known in certain circles, although rumors abound. The strict NDAs we make our staff and members sign keeps the mystery, bringing money to our door.

"Here, give this place a call. A buddy from work went up there last summer and said it's the perfect place to unwind."

I shake myself from my internal thoughts and take the card, seeing the logo of a little cabin and the name Pine Grove Lodges. "How come you just so happen to have this?"

"He thought I could do with a break."

"Did you take it?"

"Nah, it's not my scene."

"What makes you think it's mine?"

"You used to love nature and all that shit when we were at college."

He's right, I did. I like to get out into the peace of the great outdoors or at least I did. I can't remember the last time I walked in the park, let alone hiked a trail. It stirs an urge in me to get away from the city and see the stars at night, to feel the silence around me and just breathe again. "Thanks. I'll give them a call."

Beck nods and leaves me to my thoughts. Sitting at my desk that's covered in paperwork is usually where I feel most at home but now it's like a noose tightening around my neck, choking me. I need to get away before the choices are taken out of my hands and I let the people who mean the most to me down.

Grabbing my phone, I dial the number and wait for them to answer.

"Hello, Pine Grove Lodges, how may I help?"

The voice is overly sweet and friendly, and I roll my eyes so hard it's a wonder they don't get stuck back there. "Do you have a cabin free this week?"

"Let me check."

I hear someone scrabbling about and then a clatter before the person on the other end of the phone curses and the line goes dead. I pick up my phone and look at it with wide eyes. What the hell was that?

My cell rings in my hand and I answer. "Hello."

"Hey, sorry about that. I was trying to juggle a cookie sheet and then the damn cat knocked a glass and I tried to catch it and dropped the phone on the floor."

I smile despite myself. This woman is a hot mess and for some reason it amuses me immensely. "No worries. I changed my mind anyway."

"Oh no, don't say that. I checked and we have cabin six free for the week after a cancellation. Some big-wig city guy was meant to be bringing his mistress, but he got caught with his pants down so that's not happening now."

Again, I find my lips spreading across my face as this woman prattles on in my ear like we're friends and not strangers. If she worked here, she'd have been fired on the first day. I have no tolerance for incompetence, but I can't deny I'm intrigued by her. "It's not that."

"Good, so I'll book you in for cabin six. It's a little further away from the main lodge than the others but it overlooks the lake and has the most stunning views of the stars at night."

It's like she can read my mind and is pulling out all the things she knows will entice me. For some reason I find myself agreeing and before I know it, I'm hanging up with the promise to see her soon.

I'd hated the idea of a week away and still don't think I'll last the full seven days, but maybe a day or two in the wilderness of the Catskills before I want the bustle of home will be good for me. I pack my laptop, figuring I can probably work while I'm up there and head home to pack some clothes. Audrey texts me, promising to look in on my mom while I'm away. With that last hurdle taken care of, I hit the road for the two-and-a-half-hour drive.

I enjoy driving but don't get to do it often. Living in the city I either walk or take a car service. Getting to enjoy the open road already has me feeling calmer like I can breathe a little deeper.

I wish I could relax at the club like my friends do, take the opportunity of all the free pussy on display twenty-four-seven, but I can't. I love running the club, it gives me purpose and I'm good at it, but I don't mix business with pleasure. The club as a hunting ground for a hook up is off limits.

Linc thinks I'm crazy, but I don't want to have to deal with a woman I refuse to commit to ruining what I have there. Women always say they're okay with one night or casual, but I've learned from bitter experience that they always seem to have an angle. Wanting more than I'm prepared to give them. I have no intention of settling down with a woman or having a family. It just isn't in my future.

As the scenery starts to change, I think about the woman on the phone. She was a disaster, but she was friendly. I imagine she's homely, with kids running around her feet and a husband she adores, a little overweight but cute in the right light. It causes an ache in my chest and, for a second, I panic that I might be having the heart attack Beck warned me about.

I rub my chest as I make the last turn and the lodge comes into view. My breath whooshes out at the magnificent vista before me. A stunning wooden lodge dominates the main space, with the woods and mountains as the backdrop. The early spring means I can still see snow on the highest peaks, and my body itches to get out there and explore.

Parking on the wide gravel drive, I take a second to study my surroundings. Two paths lead away from the main lodge in different directions, and I imagine this place is a sight to behold during the holidays.

Exiting the car, I suck in the first deep lungful of mountain air. I close my eyes and tip my head to the sun that's bright and warm on my skin in the late afternoon sky. This right here is perfection. Fresh air, the scent of the outdoors, and nothing but the sounds of nature all around me for miles.

"It's stunning, isn't it?"

My eyes flash open as my peace is shattered by a voice at my side and I look down into the deepest brown eyes I've ever seen. My mouth goes dry as I take in a woman who should be gracing the covers of every magazine on the planet. Her long lashes fall to cover her deep brown eyes as she blinks at me. Her smile is wide and welcoming. Two dimples, one in each cheek, flash, and my eyes are drawn to her full pink lips that are moving as she speaks.

In my twenty-nine years, I've never felt such an instant attraction to anyone. She's heart-stoppingly beautiful in a girl-next-door way. Wholesome and innocent but when she smiles like that it's like the world slows. My body responds, my dick perking up and I wonder if perhaps this trip wasn't the best idea Beck has ever had.

"Hi, I'm Nora, we spoke on the phone."

Her voice is soft, and I detect a soft Southern twang that stirs my blood to fire. "You're Nora?"

She cocks her head. "Yep, we spoke earlier."

She's looking at me like I'm simple now, speaking slowly and it makes me want to kiss those full lips. She's the hot mess from the phone and nothing like I imagined, and I've never been so grateful to be wrong. "I remember." My eyes fall to her left hand and relief floods me when I don't see a wedding band, but maybe she took it off for some reason and I have the overwhelming urge to know. "Are you married?"

Her brows draw together, and confusion appears on her face, along with a little uncertainty, maybe even wariness. She looks back toward the main lodge and I wonder if her fight or flight is kicking in yet.

Good girl. She's scared of me, and she should be. I might look like the nice guy, but I'm the wolf.

"Why?"

I lean close and the scent of vanilla and cinnamon hits me, and I fight the urge to press her up against my car and feel her softness against my body. My lips are almost at her ear and I can see the tremor in her body, the wildly pounding pulse in her neck, and it makes me shudder with desire. "Because I don't fuck married women."

1: Harrison

ONE YEAR LATER

"Push that box out of the way, Eric, and then we can get this unit through." I wouldn't say I was handy around the house and if were up to me, I would've had people in to do this but since re-connecting with Violet, Lincoln has been like a different man. If she wanted the moon on a silver platter, he'd break his back and that of those around him to get it. So here I am, on my day off, helping shift furniture into their new home on the waterfront.

A sense of longing shifts in my belly, an ache that's becoming more and more evident with each pass around the sun. I'm happy for my friend, he deserves this happiness and God knows their journey to this point wasn't an easy one. It's not jealousy I feel, it's envy at what he's found. Especially as I know that it isn't on the cards for me. My mind goes to the woman who could've been the one, had fate and my path been different. Shaking off the unsettling thoughts, I concentrate on what we have to get done today.

Setting the unit down, I look at Eric and we grin as he offers me a high-five. Eric is Lottie's younger brother and a great kid who faces each day like it's a challenge to be overcome. "Good job, buddy."

My phone rings in my pocket and I sigh. There's never a dull moment when you run a club like ours. I wouldn't change it though. It's what keeps me moving forward. The screen shows an unknown number and I hesitate to answer it, but with my mother's health declining, I know I can't. "Hello?"

"Is this Mr. Harrison Brooks?"

"Speaking." I turn toward the window, a frown forming on my brow.

"This is Janice from Riverdale General Hospital."

My spine stiffens and every neuron in my brain starts firing questions, but I keep it to one single query. "Is it my mother?"

"Um, no. I don't believe she's your mother. We had a Nora Richards brought in earlier. She'd been hit by a car."

My gut clenches, hearing that name and the memories it evokes as an onslaught of emotions hit me all at once. Fear, regret, and guilt, all fighting for space but the biggest is confusion. "Is she alright?"

"She's in an induced coma right now and the doctors are looking into her other injuries."

"Oh God, that's awful." An instant wave of worry washes over me at the words. I can't imagine the vibrant, vital woman I knew so sick, nor do I wish to. "I don't mean to be obtuse but why are you calling me? Shouldn't you be calling her next of kin?"

"You're down as her next of kin and more importantly, you're down as your son's next of kin."

Air whooshes out of my lungs and everything around me seems to fade away as if I'm in a tunnel. The world narrows to just the last few words she spoke to me, my mind fighting them with every atom of my being. "My what?" I rasp sharply as I reach for the wall to steady myself.

"Your son is with us. He's unhurt but we can't keep him here. If you don't come and collect him, we'll have to call social services and have a placement found for him."

"No, don't do that. I'm on my way."

I have no clue what she's talking about or if this is even true, but I know that if by some miracle this child is my son, he's not going into fucking care.

"Good, we'll see you shortly."

I hang up and find Eric waving a hand in front of my face. My hand is in mid-air, my phone still in it and I quickly shove it into my pocket.

"Are you okay, Harry?"

Not many people are permitted to call me that, but he's one. The other two are my mother and the woman lying in a hospital bed. My thoughts swarm like bees, stopping me from grasping onto just one, each stinging more than the one before.

I need to leave, a sense of urgency, heavily dosed with panic claims me. A feeling of being out of control makes my stomach churn and I hate it. I'm always in control of my life. I quit letting it control me when I was sixteen years old and I'm not about to let it turn the tables now.

Striding toward Linc's voice, I find him and Violet laughing as they talk and make plans for their future.

Linc looks at me and instantly knows something is wrong. We've been friends a long time and he can read me as well as I can him. It's why I knew about Violet before the others had figured it out.

He lifts Violet from his lap with a tap to her ass, which would normally have been an invitation for me to give him shit about them not being able to keep their hands off each other, but my brain is too consumed with thoughts of Norrie and my son.

God, do I really have a son or is this all a lie?

"What's going on?"

"I have to go."

"Okay."

I swallow, the words stuck in my throat like a ball of fur, choking me. "I have a son."

Linc's eyes go wide, and he moves closer to grip my arm. "What?"

"I just got a call. Apparently, a woman named Norrie Richards was brought in after a serious accident and she has me down as the guardian of her son. Who's also listed as my son."

"Jesus. Is she gonna make it?"

"I don't have a clue. But I have to go because if I don't, they'll put him with a foster family."

Linc looks at me warily and I understand his hesitation. With wealth comes a bullseye the size of Texas and it attracts a lot of people willing to do anything to get their hands on a share of that wealth, and they don't care who they hurt or the lies they tell to do it.

"Do you know this woman?"

I feel haunted as the days and nights we spent together rush back to the forefront of my mind from where I'd banished them. Memories of an idyllic time, filled with love and laughter that was just not meant to be. "Yes."

"And is it possible she's telling the truth?"

"Yes."

"Then go, and take Beck with you. He'll be able to help you with all the medical jargon."

I nod and feel as if some of the fog is lifting as someone else takes control of the situation until I can take the reins back. "Yeah, good idea."

We walk out and Linc waves Beck over.

"Why? You slackers having a mother's meeting?"

Linc glares at Beck who seems to grasp my mental state and turns his teasing to a concerned stare. "What's going on?"

"I just got a call that a woman I hooked up with last year is in the hospital in a coma after a serious accident."

"Okay, you want me to get an update on her condition for you?"

"Yes, but that's not all. Apparently, my son was with her, and they need me to get him."

Beck takes a step back, his brows winging up. "You have a fucking son and you didn't tell your best friends?"

Linc shoves him. "He didn't know himself until five minutes ago, asshole."

"Oh, shit."

"Yeah. Oh, shit."

"Okay, so we should get going. I'll come with you and see if I can slice through any red tape."

"Thank you."

"What are you boys all looking so serious about?"

Linc's mom, Heather, wraps an arm around her son and the other around me and I take the comfort she's unwittingly offering. Heather is different from my mother in so many ways. They've both been through hell, Heather more recently. But unlike my mom, who let it define her life, Heather came out fighting.

Linc explains the situation to her as Beck grabs his car keys.

"I'm coming with you."

"You don't have to do that, Heather."

"Nonsense. If you're going to be taking a baby home, you'll need help."

Jesus, I hadn't even considered that. I don't have a clue how to look after an infant and if my math serves me correctly, which it always does, then he's only around three months old.

"Okay, thank you."

As I sit in the car, beside Beck, I tune out the sound of them talking quietly and focus on gaining control back. The first thing I need to do is call a lawyer, the second is to get a paternity test. The hospital comes into view and I breathe through the boulder on my chest and exit the car. Beck has parked in the doctor's spot closest to the entrance. I race ahead knowing Beck and Heather are right behind me. I reach the desk and face the woman with curly gray hair and half spectacles.

"Yes?"

"I'm here for my son. He was brought in with his mother." God, it's hard to think about the girl with the biggest dimples and the sweetest smile as a mother.

"Name?"

I give her the name and I'm directed to the second floor where I go through the same rigmarole.

Impatience and worry makes me snap. "Hurry up."

The woman grits her jaw but nods her head, not giving me the fight I'm looking for. I'm being an asshole but this whole situation is out of control and I hate it. Control is what keeps my life stable. The slightest distraction or move off course means all hell can break lose. Case in point. I took a vacation and look where I am now. In a hospital waiting to meet the son I never knew existed. A son she hid from me until she couldn't.

Beck taps my arm. "Let me go speak to the doctor and see if I can find out what is going on."

I give him what I hope is a confident smile. "Thanks. That would be good."

Wandering down the corridor, I pull my anger around me like a cloak, pushing against the fear. Heather is behind me, and I just need a few moments alone to pull myself together.

"Heather, would you mind grabbing us a couple of coffees?" I move to hand her some money, but she pushes it away.

"Of course, honey. Whatever you need, I'm here for it."

"Thank you."

She offers me a soft smile and a look only a mother can give and moves toward the bank of elevators. I lean against a wall with a window behind me, noticing that this is the neurology ICU, and my mind spins with what that could mean. The smell of antiseptic clogs my throat, making me feel nauseous. I hate hospitals, having spent too much time in them growing up, although none were like this. Psychiatric hospitals are different again but the feeling is the same. The scent, the sounds, all of it makes me feel ill.

The door beside me opens and I glance at the foot of a bed being wheeled out. Nurses and doctors surround the person in the bed, and I sit up from where I'm slouched when I spot a familiar tattoo of a butterfly on a delicate wrist.

"Norrie?" I move toward the bed as it's wheeled past me, shock punching the air from my chest at the sight before me. "Excuse me, is that Nora Richards?"

I try and push past the nurses, but they're moving quickly.

"I'm sorry, sir, we can't give out patient information."

"I'm her next of kin." I hear the coldness in my voice and apparently so does the doctor with them.

He stops as he nods for them to continue, but my eyes are glued to the figure in the bed. She has bandages covering most of her head. A cast is on her left arm and a white sheet covers any other injuries but it's her face and the breathing tube that takes my breath away. She looks broken and frail and nothing like the vibrant woman I spent a week in bed with last spring. I don't know what's wrong with her, but they'll fix her. If I have to threaten every person in this hospital with ruin I'll do it, but they'll bring back the woman I knew from that broken state.

"Mr....?"

The doctor tries to catch my eye and I pull my attention away as she rounds the corner out of sight. Gritting my jaw, I lift my eyes and see him straighten as if sensing the change in me.

"Mr. Brooks. Tell me what's wrong with her."

Beck comes up beside me and as I glance at him, I see the recognition on the doctor's face.

"Dr. Goldsmith, why are you here?"

"I believe Mr. Brooks was asking about his girlfriend."

I startle at the sound of her as my girlfriend, not because I hate it but because I'd been so close to asking her for that before I'd come to my senses and realized that we'd never work, no matter how strong our connection had been. So, I'd walked away and lived with regret over it ever since.

"Talk to me. What's wrong with her?"

"I'm Dr. George, the neurointensivist looking after Miss Richards. She has a broken arm, two broken ribs, and a bleed on her liver."

I suck in a breath at the list, but I sense he's holding back, and I'm right.

"They aren't the worst of her injuries though. She also has a moderate contrecoup TBI so we're giving her anti-seizure medication and pain relief."

I clench my fists in frustration and fear as he spews words at me. "What the fuck does all that mean?"

"What was her GCS?"

Beck has gone into doctor mode and perhaps it's best if he asks the questions and gets the answers I need, because right now I'm seconds away from tearing this place apart.

"It was eleven at the scene but quickly dropped to an eight when she was brought in."

"So, a secondary injury?"

"Yes. An MRI showed a small bleed and some swelling."

"Are you fitting an ICP monitor?"

"Yes, that's being done now."

"What's the plan?"

"Watch and wait."

I'm following about half of the conversation and plan to interrogate Beck the second I can. "When can we see her?"

"Give us an hour to get her settled and then I'll have a nurse come and find you. As you know, Doctor Goldsmith, this is a minute-by-minute situation, but we'll keep you updated on everything that's happening."

"See that you do."

Dr. George turns to move away but I stop him. "Where is my son?" God, I still can't believe I have a son. Or maybe I don't. Perhaps she lied to me, and all of this is an attempt at a money grab. My brain rejects the thought, but I'd be a fool not to consider it and I'm not a fool.

"I'm sorry, your son is under the care of the pediatric team. I'll have someone take you down to see him."

"Was he injured?"

"No, it seems when the car hit Miss Richards, she'd taken evasive action and put herself between the vehicle and the stroller, therefore saving him from any major injury."

Something about that sentence makes my stomach cramp, that she'd done that for him. I don't even know his name yet relief floods me, quickly followed by rage.

"What about the driver? Were they injured? Are the police charging them?"

Dr. George rolls his lips. "The driver died. He had a heart attack at the wheel."

I'm not sure how to feel about that, regret or anger that there's nobody to blame for this nightmare. "Thank you."

I turn to Beck, dismissing Dr. George. Beck is watching me carefully, waiting for an emotional reaction I won't show him. "Give it to me in layman's terms."

"Let's sit." He guides me to the chairs by the window and I sit as Heather rushes back toward us with a tray of coffee.

"Any update?"

"We just spoke to the doctor and Beck is going to break it down for me." I take the coffee and sip the bitter brew to try and calm the emotions swirling through me like a vortex.

"So, at the scene, she was most likely conscious and talking, that's why her GCS or Glasgow coma score was high. But a contrecoup injury is when the brain is shaken, like ice in a cocktail shaker. It hits the side of the skull, which is rigid and can cause a secondary injury and that's what's happened here."

"What about the seizure drugs? Did she have a seizure?"

"I'd need to see her chart but most likely it's a precaution, patients are more likely to seize after a traumatic brain injury."

"And the bleed, what will they do for that?"

"The best course of action for a brain injury is as minimal as we can be. We don't want to go poking around in there if we don't have to, so watch and wait is a good plan. They're fitting her with an ICP which is a small catheter into her brain to measure the pressure. It means they can act quickly if her brain continues to swell."

"Is that likely?"

Beck shrugs, blowing out a breath. "Brain injuries are notorious for being unpredictable. They'll monitor her closely and I'll call a few friends who are specialists and see if we can have the best flown in, but Dr. George is doing everything he should be right now."

"What about the liver bleed?"

"Again, they'll monitor it, but most likely it will heal on its own. I won't lie though, she has a long recovery ahead of her."

"Tell me straight, Beck, would you leave her here or have her moved someplace better?"

"If it were me, I'd have her moved to West Mercy where they have a specialist unit but let me speak to some people and make some calls."

"Thank you and tell them I don't care about the cost. If what he said is true, Norrie saved my son's life and that earns her the best care money can buy."

"Mr. Brooks?"

I glance across at a man wearing scrubs covered in dinosaurs, and tattoos covering both his forearms, as he speaks to me.

"I'm Dr. McCaffery." He shakes my hand as I stand.

"Are you the one caring for my son?"

"Yes, Isaac is perfectly fine. We've run every test possible, and he's completely healthy. He's currently wrapping my nurses around his tiny fingers."

Isaac. She named him Isaac.

Suddenly hearing his name, it all feels real and a sense of urgency bites at my heels. I need to see my son. "Can I see him?"

"Yes, of course. Follow me and I'll take you to him."

We follow as Beck and Dr. McCaffery talk and I feel Heather squeeze my arm in reassurance.

"It will be okay."

"I hope so."

"It will. Trust me, a mother knows these things."

We reach the peds ward and see a gaggle of nurses fussing over one in the middle who's holding a baby.

My son.

That's the second I fall head over heels in love.

A feeling so big, as if my body can't contain it, fills my chest. I put my arms out and he's handed over to me and the bundle of squirming energy in my arms steals my heart. He looks up at me with big dark eyes and I see his mother, but I also see myself in his tiny perfect face.

I'd always thought the love at first sight rhetoric was a cliché but I know now it's true because in that moment I know that I'd die for this tiny human. I'd fight to the death to keep him safe. A love like nothing I've ever felt before blooms and settles and I know I'll never let him out of my life. I'll be the father he deserves, the man he can look up to.

"Hey, Isaac, I'm your daddy."

2: Harrison

"Now that the paperwork is done you can take Isaac home."

I've barely let my son out of my sight since we walked onto this ward, but now the young nurse is handing him over to me, I feel terror. He's tucked up in a car seat, his eyes closed, his long lashes lie against his cheeks, and his mouth is pouted as he sleeps.

How can I look after a baby? I have no experience with children, let alone a helpless baby and now I'm about to take on sole responsibility for his every need.

"Harrison?"

I glance at Heather, who's been a rock, and she smiles encouragingly.

"You can do this."

I swallow the emotion in my throat wishing again that my own mother was more like Heather. Instantly shame washes over me. My mother is sick, she can't help that. I love her and owe her so much but even now as a grown adult, I still miss being able to go to her and have her support.

"What if I hurt him?" My fear spills out and I want to drag it back. Exposing my weakness to anyone isn't my style. I'm the one in control. I run the club with absolute preciseness and never show my ugly side to the world. I'm seen as the nice one, the boss they all respect and that's how I like it.

Her hand lands on my arm as I glance back at my son, who rests so peacefully, completely unaware of the turmoil his presence has thrown my life into.

"You won't hurt him, Harrison."

I lift my chin and pull my confidence around me like a shroud. "Of course. I'll be fine." I pick up the carrier, amazed at how little this life-changing bundle weighs. His doctor informs me he was born premature so is four months old, not three. A million questions run through my mind and the only person who can really answer them is floors above fighting for her life.

"I want to see Norrie before we leave." I've been consumed with Isaac since I arrived, and it apparently took longer to stabilize her than they anticipated so this will be the first chance I get. In reality, I'd rather walk away and not look back. I have so many emotions running through me regarding Norrie. Worry that she might die and my son is left motherless, concern that she might not recover fully and be the hot mess that I fell for so hard, and underpinning all that is a black fury that she kept my child from me. It's that anger I hold on to. I feed it every time worry tries to take over.

Beck frowns at my words from his position on my other side. These two people have been my rocks today and I won't forget it.

"They won't let you take a baby into the ICU."

I turn and glare at Beck. "I don't give a fuck what they will and won't allow. I'm taking my son to see his mother before we leave."

Beck throws up his hands, knowing he can't reason with me when I use this tone because he's the same.

"Fine, I'll make it happen."

I nod as he walks away, knowing that this is about to cost me a hefty sum, but it's something I feel in my gut is the right thing to do. I thank the staff who've been wonderful with Isaac and shown me the ropes the last few hours while we crossed the *T*s and dotted the *I*s.

"You can go home if you want, Heather. I've taken up enough of your time today."

"You saved me from the risk of walking in on my son mauling his fiancée every five minutes."

An unexpected laugh bursts from me at her statement. "Young love."

"It makes my heart happy to know how in love they are, but a mother has no wish to see it every five minutes."

"I'm sure. I'm just relieved my surprise was a son. I can't imagine the extra drama a girl would bring to my life or the potential jail time keeping her away from men like me."

"Well, I don't know about that. Two boys have certainly given me enough gray hairs over the years, but what I do know is that you're going to be a wonderful father to this little boy."

Her words stabilize the rocky foundations of my newfound parenthood and I glance at Isaac as the doors slide open letting us out on the Neuro floor. "I hope so."

"I know so." She pats my arm as she's done many times today as if sensing I need the contact and reassurance without voicing it. I exude confidence to the outside, but she sees through me. "Now, why don't I go to your place and make sure everything is set up and ready?"

I'm dreading the moment my front door closes and I'm left alone with my son for the night. "Would you mind?"

"I wouldn't offer if I minded, Harrison."

"Then thank you. That would be wonderful."

I hand my spare key over and watch her walk away before she turns. "I almost forgot, Audrey checked on your mom today and she's fine."

Jesus, in all of this I forgot about my mother. What kind of shit son does that? How was I ever going to explain this to her, and would it change her in any way? I don't know why I feel any flicker of hope. At this point, her illness is so embedded in her behavior that I'm not sure she'll ever go outside again and she doesn't seem to want to get better, so it's a moot point.

"Thank Audrey for me."

Heather waves and is gone.

"You ready?"

I turn to look at Beck who has come up behind me, and my son stirs in his carrier. A mewing sound that makes me freeze in utter panic.

Beck takes the carrier and holds it up for his inspection. "He's cute."

"What is that noise he's making and why does he keep squirming like that?"

"He's a baby, they make weird noises, and he probably has wind. Relax, Harrison, he's fine."

"Easy for you to say. You're not about to have your entire life turned upside down by one."

Beck pins me with a steady look. "It's not too late, Harrison. You can have someone come pick him up right now and walk away. You have no proof at this point he's even yours."

Fury and denial slam into me so hard that it takes everything in me not to haul back and punch my friend for even suggesting it. Only my son in his hands stops me, but I let him know my feelings with my tone. "If you ever suggest that again, I'll fuck you up." I watch Beck's eyes widen in shock. I'm the least violent of the lot of us, and that includes Audrey.

"I was only saying."

"Well don't." I take my son back from him, feeling suddenly protective.

"Noted."

Beck had been a Godsend today and I feel bad for being an asshole, but I'd reacted before I could consider anything else, and I don't regret it. "Can I see Norrie?"

"Yes, and I promised the board a new MRI machine for the peds ward."

"Fine, thank you."

Beck nods and steps away and the door to the ICU looms in front of me.

Norrie is behind that door. I haven't seen her since she'd been rushed past me earlier today. Beck has made arrangements for her to be moved tomorrow morning to West Mercy where he's head of Cardio. I can't deny it makes me feel calmer knowing he'll be there to keep an eye on her, even if he isn't going to be in charge of her care. I trust Beck wholeheartedly despite our cross words a moment ago.

He places a hand on my shoulder as I step forward. "She's going to be covered in wires and machines. I won't lie, Harrison, it's not going to look pretty and can be overwhelming, so be prepared."

I nod once, letting him know I understand what he's saying and step through the door. A nurse stands beside the bed, taking her vitals but all I can see is the woman in front of me. She looks so small, so still, and it's such a contradiction to the woman who knocked me on my ass last year with her bubbly exuberance. Norrie is tiny, petite at only five feet two inches but she had curves. Now she looks almost emaciated, and I wonder if she's been eating properly. I remember thinking she was a hot mess, and I was right. She rushed around doing ten things at once, a complete whirlwind of energy and joy and now she's silent and pale.

I set the carrier on the chair so she can see him if she wakes, which is silly because she's unconscious. Her arm is in a cast and lying at her side, so I take the other hand lightly in mine and feel the cool silky skin I had missed so much beneath my fingers. I brush my thumb over her knuckles wanting to kiss her cheek and place my head on her chest to reassure myself she's alive, but I don't. That isn't who I am to her anymore. We're strangers with only that one week of bliss between us and that doesn't mean I know her, and she's proven I can't trust her.

I move to step back and let her fingers fall from my grasp.

"You can talk to her. We'll give you a few minutes." Beck and the nurse walk back behind the glass screen where they can see and hear every machine but still giving me the illusion of privacy.

"What did you do, Norrie? Why did you keep him from me?" I see the bruises on her face, the grazes marring her perfect skin and rage blooms in my blood. I feel helpless because there's nobody to blame, nobody to focus this anger on except her. I have a thousand questions running through me and I can't answer a single one because she holds them all in her beautiful, treacherous head.

Isaac stirs, opening his eyes with a cry, and I go to him, moving on instinct as I release the fastenings and lift him to cradle him against my chest as I was shown. I bounce lightly, murmuring close to his cheek and he settles as I rub his back. Again, I'm slammed with that feeling of love so strong it almost takes my legs from me. I'm not a cold person by nature, but life has made me a very cautious one.

I do not love easily but when I do, I love with my whole heart, but nothing I've ever felt compares to this.

Hot on the heels of this emotion is anger that the woman with all the answers kept him from me. If I'd known, I would've been there for him from day one. I would've seen his every milestone. I could've helped and perhaps prevented this situation we find ourselves in today. Yet I'm a virtual stranger to him and while I had the paternity test done while we were here, I already know in my heart that Isaac is mine. Isaac is a name she knew meant something to me. I told her as she lay in my arms of my love for math, how it's a way for me to make the world make sense.

Sir Isaac Newton was my hero and she remembered or maybe I'm looking for things that don't exist. Perhaps she purely liked the name. I don't know anymore.

What I do know is that I won't be kept from him again. He's my son and despite this not being something I would've chosen, I won't turn my back on him. She'll heal and I'll help her get back to health and then she'll do the right thing and marry me and give my son the family he deserves because if she doesn't, I'll take him.

I know Norrie, she'll fight me. It was one of the things I admired the most about her in the short time I knew her. She's as stubborn as she is beautiful, but she's also sweet and kind and my brain is warring with the thought that she's done this to me. Perhaps it was all an illusion and I didn't know her at all.

Maybe the son I hold in my arms wasn't an accident at all and she planned this. Either way, she'll find I'm not the man to cross when it comes to this. I might want her body like the devil, I may have even considered sharing a life with her for a brief moment, but I'll fight her to the ends of the earth for custody of my son, and unlike her, I have the funds and fortitude to do it.

3: Norrie

"Nora, can you hear me?"

I lift my hand to swipe at the sound that's irritating me next to my ear. My head hurts and I feel like I've been hit by a bus. A flash of light and screeching rings in my ears and a sense of panic grips me by the chest. I feel like I'm missing something, forgetting something vital to me.

Isaac!

My eyes don't want to open, but I fight through the fog. I need to see my son. Where is my son? I'm screaming internally but the people who are murmuring urgently beside me can't seem to hear me.

"Her heart rate is spiking, BP climbing."

"We need to sedate her."

Why can't they hear me? My brain starts to fog, and I fight whatever they've given me. I need to get to my son. Blackness edges my brain and I slide into nothingness.

A beep beep beep wakes me, and I wonder if I changed my alarm and forgot about it. I lift my hand to try and reach to quieten it. My hand finds air and I frown, trying to open my eyes. I blink and close them quickly as the bright, harsh light blinds me. Confusion swamps me, so I try and force my mind to remember what happened. My body aches like I've been slammed into a wall by an NFL player.

I try to grasp a memory, to remember what I'd been doing. I was walking, I'd been to visit my brother Xander and was heading back home.

Isaac!

Oh my God, how could I forget my precious baby? My chest feels like it's being crushed by the weight of the panic I'm feeling. The beeping beside me increases as I blink my eyes again, battling to clear the fog in my head.

"Try and relax, Nora."

My eyes shoot to a man in a white coat who stands over me with a calm, kind expression on his face as he watches me closely. A thousand questions crawl like bugs through my brain and I can't seem to grasp onto any one in particular. They're like wisps of smoke I can't grab hold of.

"I'm Dr. Farrugia. Do you know where you are?"

Tears sting my eyes, and I can't answer his question, I only focus on one thing. "Isaac." I hardly recognize my own voice as it rasps from my dry lips.

Dr. Farrugia holds a straw to my lips, and I sip the cool water like I've spent the last year in the desert. Too soon he takes it away and I sag back against the pillows.

"Your son is perfectly fine and with his father."

I close my eyes, feeling as if I might cry with relief. All that matters is he's safe. "Thank you."

He smiles kindly as I open my eyes again. "Do you remember what happened?"

I frown as I search my memories and come up blank. I shake my head slowly in frustration and fear, every movement seems like it's covered in thick syrup, and it's dragging the strength from me.

What the hell happened to me?

"That's okay, confusion is perfectly natural. You're at West Mercy hospital. You suffered a nasty trauma and were badly hurt when a car hit you."

"I was run over?"

"Yes."

"Why can't I remember?" My voice is stronger now, but my energy is fading already.

"You suffered a brain bleed."

"I did?"

"Yes, among other things." He motions toward my arm, and I follow his eyes seeing the cast.

"What else?"

"Why don't we let you rest, and we can talk more later. Mr. Brooks will be by later with Isaac."

"He will?"

Dr. Farrugia smiles, and it's a wonder they allow him in a hospital with sick people when he looks like that. I bet the nurses love him with his dark hair and piercing blue eyes.

"He's been in every day since you arrived, bringing your son to see you."

"Every day?"

"Yes."

"How long have I been here?"

"Three weeks."

I feel my eyes bug out. "Three weeks?"

I sit up to try and swing my legs out of the bed and dizziness assails me, the tubes in my arms and on my face making it worse. A firm hand on my shoulder pushes me back gently.

"I need to leave. My son needs me."

"Your son is being well cared for."

I sag helplessly against the pillows, having no fight in my weak body. He doesn't understand. I haven't been away from Isaac since he was born. "Is it really three weeks?"

"Yes, but I have a feeling you'll be leaving us very soon if this conversation is anything to go by." He glances at the iPad in his hands. "Your vitals look good, and we'll run some tests later after we get some food into you and see how you're doing. I'm sure Dr. Goldsmith will also be by once I let him know you're awake. He's taken quite the interest in you since you arrived."

Why did that name seem so familiar to me? I search for the answer, but it only makes my head hurt, the dull throb now a more prominent pounding.

Dr. Farrugia must notice. "Are you in any pain?"

"A little. My head hurts and my body aches like I have the flu, especially my middle and side."

"I'm not surprised and being in one position for so long won't have helped. We'll get you some pain relief sorted out."

"I don't want to go back to sleep."

I just wanted my son, and I can't see him if I'm out for the count.

"We'll give you something that shouldn't cause drowsiness, but I must warn you, your body still has a lot of healing to do, so rest is imperative."

I don't respond, because while I know he's right, I also know I have a business to run and a child to care for on my own. Although Harrison is in the picture now and I have that conversation to face, there's no guarantee he'll want to continue being in Isaac's life. He didn't ask for a child, and he certainly made it clear while we were together that he didn't want one.

"I can see we'll have a battle with you, but for now I'll leave you with Nurse Nelson." Dr. Farrugia leaves with a wave.

The next few hours, I face the indignity of a bed bath, I eat a clear, almost flavorless liquid they try to tell me is chicken broth and now I'm exhausted again but I won't sleep. I need to see my son more than I need anything else.

"Look who's here."

Nurse Nelson is a woman of forty with two grown teenage boys. She's been caring for me all morning. I follow her gaze to the door and my heart feels like it's going to stop.

Harrison Brooks, the man who barreled into my life, and who showed me pleasure like no other man ever had, is standing in the doorway with our son strapped to his chest. For a second our eyes lock, and the air stills around us. I see a wash of emotions flit across his face and know they mirror my own.

Relief.

Compassion.

Desire.

Love.

Wariness.

But he shuts them down so fast I'm left feeling at a loss, disorientated, like my world is tilting on its axis as he ends with a cool angry glare that traps me in fear.

He's furious.

I don't blame him. He probably thinks I trapped him. I'll make it clear I want nothing from him financially, but I can't quash the silly hope that he'll want to be in our son's life.

"Harrison."

It's superficial, but I always dreamed that if we ever met again, I'd look a million dollars. I'd show him what he missed when he walked away from me. Instead, I'm skin and bone and covered in bandages, with a chunk of my hair shaved away. These circumstances leave me exposed and vulnerable as I face a man who's looking at me like we're strangers. It's almost hard to remember that we parted on good terms because the void between us seems insurmountable. I have no outward shield against what I know is coming. I wanted him to see me as he remembered me, full of life and health, not like this, broken and weak, but beggars can't be choosers.

"You're awake."

He prowls toward me, his big hand on Isaac's back, pinning me with his hard gray gaze and not for the first time I wish I could read his mind. Harrison was open with me when we were together, but I always knew he was holding something back, but never felt like I had the right to his secrets. I still don't, but in this moment, I'd give anything to know what is behind those gorgeous cool eyes.

His scent surrounds me, woodsy and clean almost taking my breath and leaving a pit in my stomach as memories of our time together rush at me. I try to focus on the moment, but he overwhelms me. He did from the very first moment we met.

"Isaac?" I reach for my son, my eyes tearing and panic rising in my chest, making it hard to breathe.

He steps back slightly out of reach. His expression flickers and I try desperately to read it, but it's gone before I can.

"He's sleeping. The nanny says it's important not to break his routine."

I shake my head feeling as if I'm losing control of everything in my life. A nanny doesn't know what is best for my son. I'm his mother. I almost died bringing him into this world and I'd do it a thousand times to hold him just once. My breath seems stuck in my chest as my heart begins to pound. The monitor behind me beeps wildly and Nurse Nelson puts a gentle hand on my shoulder.

"Just breathe, Nora."

I focus on her voice, knowing exactly what this is and how to deal with it.

"That's it. Slow in and out, in and out."

I do as she asks, closing my eyes and concentrating on her soft, calm words as I control my breathing.

A firm hand lands on my foot over the sheet and I glance down to see Harrison's big hand rubbing my foot as he watches me intently. It's soothing, his touch anchors me, gives me a sense of safety, that I miss.

"You're doing great, Norrie."

God, that name.

He was the only person except for my father who called me that and it takes me to a time in my life when everything was simple and uncomplicated. Long days and longer nights filled with sensual promise and laughter. Just him and me and the sky above us as we talked about everything and nothing.

"Good girl."

I blink at his praise, the words having the same effect on me as they always had. I brighten, wanting his praise as I work even harder to gain it over his censure. The beeping stops and I can catch my breath again.

"What happened?"

Harrison is glaring at the nurse who smiles back at him, clearly used to dealing with bossy, arrogant visitors. His hand remains on my foot in a dominant gesture as his thumb rubs firm circles against my ankle.

"She had a panic attack. It's not unusual for that to happen after a traumatic injury. Everything is overwhelming and the body reacts to it."

"Will it happen again?"

Nurse Nelson pats my arm, giving me her attention, even though Harrison is asking the questions.

"It might happen again. You've been through a huge trauma and you won't bounce back overnight but you will eventually. Now, I have a report to write up, so I'll leave you two to visit." She turns her eyes on Harrison looking at him over her glasses like he's a naughty schoolboy and I resist the urge to giggle, knowing he won't appreciate it and not having the energy anyway. "No upsetting her and don't tire her out."

He nods once to show he understands before she leaves.

Harrison pulls up a chair and sits beside me and the silence feels loaded. There are so many questions between us but the one I needed answered first is easy.

"Is Isaac okay?"

Harrison's lips twitch in a simile of a smile as he looks down at the soft, downy head of our son. "He's perfect."

His adoration is evident, and he does nothing to hide it from me. A sense of relief so strong I can barely withstand it, lifts from my chest. "I agree."

We share a smile, his eyes filling with warmth before he cuts his eyes away, denying me his warmth. When he looks back all softness is gone, replaced by a distance that has never separated us before.

"It's been a pretty steep learning curve, especially considering he doesn't know me but we have a routine now, and he doesn't hate me which is a start."

There it is, the bitterness I was expecting, and I flinch at his tone.

He hates me, I can hear it in every word he utters no matter what they are.

I force a smile, not giving him an inkling that his words wound me. This last year has forced me to become a fighter and I won't break now, no matter how weak I feel. I hear the love evident in his voice for our son and it brings me such a huge measure of peace, but also guilt and anger.

"Were you ever going to tell me?"

I glance at Isaac, wanting to reach for him again but knowing he's safe and warm where he is. God knows I spent enough time snuggled to that same broad chest. I can hardly blame my son for finding comfort there. "I can explain."

Harrison leans back in his chair, his body language changing, tensing. Suddenly he looks like a different man, not one who gave me hours of pleasure. This man is a stranger I don't know, and I have to find a way to navigate a way forward for us that won't harm Isaac. I fold the sheet covering me around my fingers, needing an outlet for this nervous energy.

"And you will, but not right now. Right now, I need you to get well so we can plan our wedding."

My jaw falls open and I blink wondering if I'm having some kind of episode brought on by my injuries, which had been explained in great detail to me earlier. I'm so lucky to be alive. I've been given a second chance at life, but I never imagined it would be like this. "I'm sorry, what?"

Harrison leans forward, a sexy smirk gracing his handsome face, the light stubble on his square jaw making him look menacing and sexy all at the same time.

"Our wedding, Norrie."

A shake my head and wince at the pain. "We're not getting married, Harrison."

He lifts his hand and I flinch slightly, but he gently strokes my cheek, the sensation intimate and innocent and I close my eyes soaking it in, trying to absorb everything he's saying. His lips find mine and he kisses me slowly, his tongue barely flicking out to touch my lips as we move in sync like one being. He pulls back slowly, letting his lips linger for just a second before resting his forehead against mine so gently. Harrison is completely aware of my injuries and the bandage I wear, his fingers sliding around to grip the back of my neck with such gentleness. His actions are such a contradiction to how angry he looked just a few moments ago that I don't know how to react.

"Open your eyes, Norrie."

I do as he asks, gasping at what I see. His eyes are dilated as I stare at him, seeing the heat between us as if the last year apart never happened. It was like this from the first moment, a desire so strong that it burned all around us until everything was ash and only we were left.

For the first time since I awoke to this nightmare, I feel hope in my chest that maybe things will be okay.

That we can make something out of the mess we've caused. If not building a life together then building a family for our son. His next words shake my mind and body to their foundations because they're delivered in such a gentle firm tone, so at odds with the way he arranges the twenty-six letters of the alphabet to destroy me.

"Norrie, you're going to marry me because if you don't, I'm going to take Isaac from you and you'll never see him again."

4: Norrie

His words break me in a way I wonder if I'll ever recover from them, causing pain so deep it overshadows every other feeling in my body.

Harrison pulls away, standing to pace to the window as if he can't bear to look at me a second longer, as if I disgust him and it hurts even more.

"What?"

"You heard me, Norrie."

"You can't be serious."

"I'm deadly serious. You *will* marry me, or I'll fight you for custody of Isaac." He pins me with a fierce look that's so foreign coming from him, that I shudder before he turns away again. "And I'll win."

I have no doubt in my mind he means every word. "Why would you do that? You don't want children."

He swings his head to glare at me, his chin lifted in a stubborn autocratic way that makes me want to punch him. My head screams in pain and I shake it to try and clear it, ignoring the pain that makes me nauseous.

"I never planned to have them but now that I do, do you really think I'll be a side character in my son's life?"

"I'd never do that to you. We can work something out so you can see him all the time."

"You'll excuse me if I don't believe you. You did, after all, lie about his existence for months."

"I can explain."

"Not interested."

"Harry, please."

His glacial gaze pins me to the bed and I feel at a massive disadvantage. "Harrison. My name isn't Harry." Disdain drips from every word.

"Fine. Harrison. Don't be unreasonable."

His arms fold over our son's back, his suit jacket pulling tight over his arms. Arms that held me tight, that cradled me close, and made me feel like the sexist woman in the world.

"Is it unreasonable to think you might tell me I had a son?"

I grit my teeth and then try to relax. He's bound to be upset. "No, of course not, but marriage is huge and unnecessary."

"On the contrary, it's a contract at its core."

"No, Harrison, it's so much more than that. It's love and devotion. It's a partnership and a thousand moments all wrapped up in love."

I see him roll his eyes and can't help the defeat that rolls through me.

"You tell yourself whatever you need to, to get through this but it's happening."

"And what I want doesn't matter?"

My eyes land on his hand resting over Isaac's back, the contrast is so stark. Here we are, having a conversation that's littered with hostility and blame, and he's so gentle with our son. "What I want stopped being important the second I found out about him."

I want to hate him, to lash out and scream but I can't. What he's suggesting is ludicrous, but I can't deny even to myself that I hadn't dreamed of it happening one day. I just imagined it very differently. That he'd realize how perfect we are together and what we could offer our son, a family of his own. Not this bitter demand fueled by anger and resentment.

"How would it even work? I have a business to run, and I assume you won't be leaving your job."

"We can deal with the details later, but I see no reason why you can't get a manager to run Pine Grove Lodge. It's managed perfectly up until now."

My chest feels tight, and exhaustion is heavy on my limbs and mind. Harrison knows what that place means to me, how much of myself I put into it and he's treating it like it's nothing. I want to hate him for it, to ask him where the man I fell for has gone but I don't have it in me.

"Fine. Whatever you want, Harrison."

He nods as if it was always a foregone conclusion and comes to stand beside me. His brows lower as he looks at me. "You look terrible."

I snort without humor. "Thanks. Just what every girl wants to hear after that romantic proposal."

His fingers thread through mine as he sits, and I glance up from heavy eyelids to look at him and feel the urge to weep.

"I'll look after you, Norrie, after both of you. I may not be the man that you want but I can be the man you need, and I promise you this. Not a day will go by when Isaac doubts how much I love him. Surely that's what we both want?"

"It is."

A snuffling sound makes us both look down and I feel tenderness pull at me as my arms ache to hold him. Harrison must read my mind because he gently unhooks the carrier and lifts our son into the crook of his arm.

"Are you up for a cuddle?"

Tears fall freely as I nod and reach my good arm out. Harrison places Isaac in between us but doesn't let go, holding us both steady. I'm surprised by how much my son has changed in just three weeks, his cheeks look fuller, his body longer.

"Hey, baby boy, did you miss me?"

I let him grasp my finger and pull it to his mouth.

"He does that a lot. My friend Heather says he might be teething."

I hate that I'm finding this out second hand, that I missed it and I feel a tiny remnant of guilt and empathy for the man whose body is pressed up to mine as we hold our son.

"That's gotta be rough."

"Honestly, it's been a rollercoaster but the good kind. We kind of figured it out now and have a routine."

His words make me want to weep, I feel like such an outsider. "He's grown so much."

"He's on the seventy-fifth percentile."

A warmth invades my body at his words and the proud tone of them.

"He was so small when he was born. Only four pounds, one ounce."

"He caught up quick."

"He did. He's a fighter."

"You will tell me about it when you're feeling better."

It's a demand, not a question, and a reminder that this isn't the same man who arrived on my doorstep a year ago seeking a rest from the stress of life. This is the man that trades millions in stocks for fun and runs a secret sex club.

"Yes, I'll tell you whatever you want to know."

I look at Harrison and a hundred unsaid words flow between us, and I think perhaps I can do this. I can marry him for my son's sake and maybe even my own. Because no matter how much I deny it, I still want him and the dream of us to be real. I see something of the man I met when he looks at Isaac, even if the man who looks at me is a different, colder version.

"Good. I'm glad you're being sensible."

He lifts Isaac up and moves off the bed as he kisses his head. "I need to get him home and to bed. Audrey is coming by later and I want him settled before she does."

My mellow mood vanishes like smoke on the wind at his words. "Audrey?"

"Yes, you remember I told you about her?"

"Yes, I guess." Jealousy slams against me and I hate the way it makes me feel. I have no right and yet isn't he about to be my husband?

"The doctor said you might be confused and disorientated for a while."

"Yeah, I guess that's it."

I can hardly tell him the truth, that I know he and Audrey were together, are together? I don't have a clue what they are now, and I hate that I'm so in the dark about what is happening in my own life.

"You should get some rest."

I don't want to rest but right now my body doesn't care and already I can feel my energy leaving me.

I nod as he moves close and dips his head. He gently cups my cheek and leans in to kiss the corner of my mouth. It's innocent and almost sweet but my breath hitches just the same and tears sting the back of my nose. Despair and loneliness wash over me at the tender gesture, but I know to him it's nothing more than him being kind in the face of the corner he backed me into.

"I will."

"Good girl."

God, his pleased tone, the way he makes me feel like I won the lotto by making him happy is still there. It makes me love him and hate him, that he can bring me to my knees with a few softly spoken words in his deep voice.

I close my eyes and feign sleepiness, but I feel him watching me for a few minutes before I actually do drift off and the process of healing my broken body continues. My emotions, however, might take a little longer.

5: Harrison

Norrie has barely looked at me since I made my intentions clear. I feel her eyes on me, the burn of her gaze hot on my skin. I itch to touch her again, to take back the harsh way I'd treated her, and just remember the moment we shared as we held our son between us for the first time. Parents with one goal, to make his life the best it can be, but I can't. She lied to me and I have no intention of letting her back into my heart or trusting her again. My bed, however, will be a different thing.

Just that one kiss and I knew the desire was still throbbing between us. I want the woman who promised to become my wife with a desperation I detest. She makes me weak, my need for her is distracting, and I find myself thinking of her when I shouldn't. The fact that she'd conceded so easily to my demands, her head falling and taking those brown eyes I love from me, makes my stomach clench uncomfortably every time I think about it.

I see how hard she's working to get better. The sweat running down her body as she walks to the bathroom unaided, just to prove she can, makes me respect her. I feel myself softening to her plight, but I won't show her that, I can't give her even an inch, not yet.

I still won't let her explain her actions. As far as I can see they'll be excuses and nothing she says will change how I proceed. Yet, I hate the way she bends to my will, even as I force her to do so. The woman I met a year ago would never have done that. She was energy and joy and had enough attitude to drive me crazy. This Norrie is quieter, meeker, her zest for life is dimmed and I find myself missing that part of her nature.

At least Isaac makes her smile. The way she lights up when I bring him in to see her would warm the coldest heart. The first time she held him the day I proposed will live with me until the day I die. Total and utter devotion poured from every pore of her body as she lavished kisses on his face. Drinking him in, running her hands over his tiny body, checking he was safe. Nothing else mattered to her at that moment. She'd have agreed to marry the devil himself for her child and in that we're agreed. In some ways, maybe that's what we're both doing. Agreeing to a loveless marriage for a child we adore.

No matter how angry I'd been with her about keeping him a secret, I can't dismiss the love she has for Isaac. Like mine has done in the last three weeks, her heart beats for him. She's the mother I always imagined she'd be, I'd just never imagined our story would go this way.

"Are you ready to go home?"

Her smile, which had been aimed at our babbling son, freezes on her face. "Do I have a choice?"

"Not if you want to keep your son in your life."

Her eyes move to mine then and all the heat and desire she's shown me so openly in the past is gone, replaced with disdain which makes me uncomfortable. I shove it away and ignore the niggling in my gut that says this is wrong. I never pretended I was good. I've done things at the club that most would find abhorrent, including getting my hands dirty on occasion to keep the people I'm responsible for safe. This thing with Norrie is the least of those crimes.

"I hate you for this."

I shrug, pretending her words don't carve a hole in my chest. "You won't be the first woman to say that to me."

She mutters something under her breath that I don't catch, and I almost like that her damnable spirit is starting to glimmer again. It will make this marriage more fun for both of us. I move forward and lift Isaac into my arms, ready to fasten him into his car seat for the ride home. "What was that?"

Her fight is still there, buried but it still simmers. I can see it in her mutinous expression and the way she tries to censor herself.

"I said I probably won't be the last either."

Bending over her, I let my lips skim her ear and feel her shiver. I don't hide my grin as I press my lips to her soft neck. "You will be the last, Norrie. No other woman will ever get close enough to hate me ever again, because you're mine and I'm yours. Until death do us part."

"You make a good case for a jump off a bridge."

A laugh erupts from my chest, and I can't resist the urge to plant a kiss on those pouty upturned lips. "I've missed you, Norrie."

"Yeah, well, I haven't missed you."

The prim way she turns away makes me want to prove to her how easily she lies to herself but now isn't the time. "Come on, let's get you home. The physio will be waiting, and I want to get you settled first."

"This isn't necessary."

"Stop arguing with me." I secretly like the way she argues because it shows some of her fight is returning, even if it isn't the way I want.

Norrie stands, taking my arm grudgingly as I help her into a wheelchair. She has a slight weakness in her left leg which is from her brain injury. It's a blow to her. Norrie is viciously independent and hates asking for help. I'm just relieved she got away with only a weak leg. I shudder every time I think about how this could've played out. I could be burying my son's mother instead of marrying her. I'd have her hate me a thousand lifetimes over than watch him lose her.

"I'm just saying."

I stoop to her level and kiss her hard, stopping her tirade in a second. She stills, not expecting it, almost fighting me and I continue my assault on her mouth until she softens against me and kisses me back.

I pull away and look into the eyes I could drown in and smirk. "That's better."

"You can't kiss me every time we disagree, Harrison."

"I can and I will."

"I have my own mind."

"Oh, I'm aware."

"You need to stop this."

"What? Kissing my wife?"

"I'm not your wife."

"Yet."

"You're ridiculous. We don't need to get married. We can co-parent."

Anger churns in my belly at her words. I want to lash out and hurl harsh, hate-filled words at her, but I don't want my son growing up with parents at war with one another, so I do the only thing I can. I kiss her again.

Gripping the back of her neck in my hand, I bring her closer, so our bodies are touching and kiss her until we're breathless.

"I won't co-parent. You'll marry me or face the consequences."

"So, I don't have a voice at all?"

"You have a voice, Norrie, but you need to understand that I don't lose a fight, and this is the biggest one of my life thanks to you keeping me away from my son. You did this, not me."

Her sigh feels like it's forced from her soul. "Will you ever let me explain?"

I pull away quickly, shutting down her request silently as I move behind her, avoiding her deep brown eyes and the dimples which have become my weakness. They're something my son shares with his mother. We wait for Beck to arrive in awkward silence. He'll push the wheelchair while I carry my son to the car. I can't look at her when she's sweetly asking for me to let her lie to me.

"I don't want to hear what you have to say. Nothing could excuse what you did." Bitterness eats at me causing my gut to burn.

"Strongly disagree."

"Anyone would think you wanted me to kiss you with the amount of sass coming from that sweet mouth."

She crosses her arms and frowns. "Absolutely not, you repulse me."

I bend close, taking in her sweet vanilla and cinnamon scent mixed with the antiseptic smell of the hospital. "How easily lies slip from your lips, Norrie. If you don't want my mouth on you, perhaps you should start agreeing with me, because that's exactly what I'm going to do."

Beck arrives with a smile, his eyes skimming over Norrie and then me before he chuckles.

"Trouble in paradise?"

"Shut the fuck up, Beck," I spit out, not in the mood for his shit today.

"Your friend is ridiculous. You should probably check him for a tumor or something, he's acting like a lunatic."

Beck pushes me out of the way with a laugh and squeezes Norrie's shoulder, making me tense. A growl of warning escapes my throat and the jerk just smiles wider.

"Get your hands off my wife."

Beck holds his hands up in surrender. "Just being friendly."

"Well do it without touching what's mine."

"For the record, she isn't your wife yet."

Norrie turns in her chair to grin at the smug bastard and jealousy rides me hard. "That's what I said."

Beck laughs. "Don't mind him, he has a stick up his ass. I offered to get it surgically removed but I think he likes it."

I roll my eyes at the pair of them and pick up Isaac, who's sleeping soundly in his seat. I walk away to the sound of them laughing and secretly wish I was the one making her laugh with such joy.

I hate that they've grown so close these last few weeks when I'm still on the outside looking in at them. It's a feeling I should be used to by now. I've always played this role, from being the child stuck between parents that barely noticed him, to a son whose only purpose was to care for a woman who barely noticed he existed until he was useful.

Norrie had charmed Beck within minutes of meeting him, and he her. If I was the type to act on my jealousy, which I absolutely am not, I would've slammed that mother fucker's pretty face into a wall, but I hold back because I'm not jealous. I'm merely protecting what is mine. I know deep down Beck would never lay a finger on Norrie. He's a player, but he's loyal to the bone. He helps us into the car and then promises to call me later and check in on things. He has a big surgery this afternoon so know it will be a late call, not that it matters. I sleep very little these days, too many thoughts spinning through my mind to relax.

The ride home is quiet, but I can feel the tension radiating off Norrie the closer we get. I don't mind silence, never feeling the need to break it, but I have the overwhelming desire to ease her worry. I tell myself it's for her health. Beck has warned me that she needs calm to continue her healing and I'd promised she'd get that.

"Audrey says Pine Grove is running smoothly and your temporary manager has everything in hand."

"That's kind of her."

Her face brightens slightly at the news, a smile curling on the corner of her lips, but it doesn't meet her eyes. I smile, wanting a little of her sunshine on me, and ignore the sadness in her eyes. She'll come to accept her fate and move on. She just needs time.

"We also tried to get a hold of your brother, but no luck yet."

Norrie shakes her head. "You won't. He's working away and is unreachable when he's in the zone."

Irrational anger seeps into my blood and I clench the steering wheel tighter, my knuckles going white. "So even in an emergency he can't be contacted?"

"He likes to live in the moment."

That she defends such selfish disregard for others makes me furious. "And what about you?"

Norrie cocks her head, her dimples appearing and making my dick hard. She's so damn beautiful, innocent, and captivating in a way that's so rare and what's worse is she seems to have no clue the effect she has on others. I've relived every moment of the week we spent together, fucking my hand to the images of her eyes almost black as she stared at me with uncontained need.

"What about me?"

"Who was there for you?"

She looks blank as if she's searching for the answer and I wonder if it's from the injury and the small gaps in her memory or if she'd just never considered it before.

"I have friends."

I don't know why I'm pushing this, or what point I'm trying to make, but I can't let it go. "I don't mean people you have fun with or your employees, I mean people you can call in the middle of the night when you need them."

"I don't need anyone."

"How can you say that? What if something had happened to you and Isaac was left alone?" I know my tone is harsh, but I can't seem to help myself.

I see her skin pale, her cheeks losing any color they might have gained since we left the hospital.

"That's why you were down as my next of kin and emergency contact."

"So, I wasn't good enough to know about him before but I'm okay in an emergency, is that it?"

"No, you're putting words in my mouth."

I turn my car into the spot outside my brownstone on the upper east side and kill the engine. I angle my body to her, draping my hand over the steering wheel so I can see her face and she flinches at my hard glare. "You should have told me."

Her head drops and guilt immediately assails me when I hear her sniff. I reach for her and tilt her chin up as she tries to fight me. With a gentle grip, I hold her chin and force her eyes to mine. Tears well like diamonds in the chocolate brown orbs and I feel like utter shit for pushing her as I have. My anger seeps away and I haul her across the console onto my lap.

Stroking a piece of her golden blonde hair away from her face, I study the beauty in my arms. "Don't cry."

Her tears are my kryptonite and I fight the urge to promise her it will be okay. I know if I do, I'll crumble and release her from our deal. I can't be that man. I have to be in control, to make things right so I can be in my son's life every single day, not on weekends. I'm not my father. I'll never abandon my child as he had. "Let's just forget I said anything, okay?"

I force a smile I don't feel, and Norrie nods. I go to drop my hand, but she holds my wrist in her light grip, anchoring me to her.

"Harry, I need you to know I'm sorry. I know you don't want to hear why, and I won't make you but I'm sorry you missed out."

Her words slay me, and I feel the truth in them to my core. I can't speak so I just nod. Her body, so soft and pliable, makes me harden against her sweet ass and I groan as desire pulses through me. My cock recognizes her sweet heat so close and she inhales sharply when I move to ease my desire to pump my hips against her. My hand feathers over her hair, fingers skimming the shaved patch where the ICP monitor was fixed, before I grip the side of her neck, feeling the pulse pound in time with her heart against my chest. I skim a thumb over her full bottom lip, pulling down as her eyes fall closed. I want to devour her, to consume her like she does me. I want to fuck her fast and hard, hear the sound she makes when she's filled with me, see the way her eyes dilate as she comes down my cock, but I also want to spread her out and kiss every delicious inch of her until she's begging for relief.

This is what's real between us. Everything else might be a lie, but this she can't hide from me. She wants me as badly as I want her, and she'll get what she wants as soon as the doctor gives her the go-ahead.

A loud horn breaks the moment and I release her, quickly depositing her back in her seat.

The next few minutes are spent getting her and my son out of the car. As I maneuver to the base of my steps, I wish I had called ahead. As if hearing my silent plea my front door opens, and Ryker and Audrey step out.

"You're home already."

Audrey stares at Norrie for a second, tilting her head as if she's going to speak before seeming to reconsider and smiling instead. Ryker gives her his most charming grin and then winks.

I glare at my friend, he and fucking Beck will be the death of me. "Hey, cut that shit out and help."

Ryker moves first, taking Isaac from me and moving ahead as he babbles nonsense at my son. Isaac giggles back and the sound is the best fucking thing I've ever heard. Audrey holds the door and grabs the bags. I turn and swing Norrie into my arms bridal style, making her gasp. She weighs nothing but the feel of her in my arms gives me pleasure, especially when she holds on tight. Her arms clamp around my neck as she rests her cheek against my chest and I want to stay like that forever. All too soon we're at the top of my front stoop, and I slowly lower her, holding on to her as she gets her legs under her. I don't let go, easing my arm around her back and keeping her close beside me.

I'm watching her as she takes in my home, seeing it through her eyes.

"Wow."

Norrie stops dead in her tracks, her eyes moving about my home. I'd had the property renovated from top to bottom and as I look at it now, I again feel pride in what I've achieved. All the old architecture is restored and refinished, the arches, the fireplaces, the paneling.

I'd gone with black paintwork, and off-white or exposed brick for the walls in some parts. The floors are all refinished hardwood in a dark stain with soft tactile fabrics in dark greens and blues for the soft furnishings.

"You like it?"

"Like it? I love it. Harry, this place is spectacular."

My chest almost puffs out with pride at her delight, and I even find myself liking the way she calls me Harry when her guard is down.

"You like this, you should see the kitchen."

"Show me."

I lead her toward the kitchen where the entire back wall is glass and windows with thick black frames open to a small yard with a deck. I can already imagine Isaac playing out there and have plans in my head for a playset and swing.

I never imagined myself with children, always content with what I had. Having a father who walked out on you and your mother was scarring. Especially when that mother always needed so much of my care and as a result, there was never the desire for kids of my own. Yet now I can't imagine my life without him. I glance at Norrie and frown slightly. I can't imagine my life without her either now, and that terrifies me.

I grit my jaw, hardening my heart. Our conversation in the car unsettles me. I hate that she has nobody to rely on, but it also makes me unbelievably angry with her for putting her and my son in that position.

"This is beautiful, Harrison."

I snap out of my momentary musing and focus on the woman beside me, easing my arm away from her seductive lure. I don't know what it is about Norrie but from day one I've swung between the dark desire to fuck and claim her, to mark her as mine, to the sweet need to adore and protect her.

Her effortless sensual side is something I don't think she even realizes she has. The way she moves, smiles, dips her head, are all natural to her and they make my blood heat with need for her. She's like a seductive drug, swimming through my system. Even now as she fusses over how much she loves my kitchen, I want to spread her on the nearest surface and fuck her until all she can think of is the way I make her feel. I want to punish her and make her beg. What kind of man am I that I'm watching her barely able to stand mere minutes after being released from the hospital after an injury that nearly ended her life, and all I want to do is slide my cock into her tight cunt?

She tilts her head to give me a tentative smile, the dimples in her cheeks making my dick ache. That's the draw of Norrie, she's this enigma that has two opposing sides.

She has a sweetness that I'm not used to seeing, especially around the club. She'd rather move a spider to the yard than kill it, even though she's terrified of them. She wouldn't hurt a fly, yet she hurt me more than I ever thought possible with her cruelty in keeping Isaac from me. Whatever her reasons are, they're not enough, and I need to guard against her. She blinds me with her beauty and guile, but she's shown me a glimpse of the harm she can cause. I'd be a fool to ignore that, and I'm nobody's fool.

"Let me show you to your room."

Norrie nods looking unsure, and like a bastard, I smile, happy to have her as off balance as I feel.

I let her take my arm as I lead her to the stairs.

"Can you manage, or would you like me to carry you?"

A slight blush tinges her cheeks and neck at my question, and I know she's remembering how she let me carry her in my arms as we walked to her room back at the lodge. I could never resist the feel of her against me and she loved it just as much. Her jaw flexes and I see a determined glint come to her eye that makes me want to smile.

Norrie is stubborn, and despite her sweetness has a magnificent temper, which I love to witness.

"I can do it on my own, thank you very much."

Ryker comes thundering down the stairs like a baby elephant interrupting our little stand-off.

"I put her bags in her room and Isaac is in his room with Claire."

"Claire? Who's Claire?"

"The nanny I told you about."

Norrie turns and begins to head upstairs, her progress swift for a woman who's been through what she has and still has some steep obstacles to face.

"Slow down, Norrie. It's not a race."

"Oh, bite me, Harrison. I want to see my son."

I move close behind her, ready to scoop her up should she fall, and her spine straightens as my breath feathers over her neck. "Where would you like me to bite you, angel?"

Her pulse flutters in her neck and I slide my hand around her front, palming the flat of her concave belly, and pulling her flush against me. I wait silently for her to speak, giving her time to find her words.

"I'm sorry to disappoint you, Harrison, but I don't fuck bossy, demanding assholes."

I love it when she cusses, when she stands up to me, pushing back and showing her claws. "Keep talking, Norrie. You know it makes my cock hard when you cuss. Maybe later you can use your claws on me too."

I move back before she can respond and give her a gentle nudge up the stairs. "Let's go."

"Bossy."

I grin and glance down to see Audrey watching me with a knowing tilt to her lips and my smile fades.

The second floor has three large bedrooms and a large bathroom, although two bedrooms have ensuites, so the bathroom is mainly for the third bedroom. The first bedroom is mine, the one next to it is Isaac's nursery and the opposite one is where Norrie will sleep until we're married. Unless of course I can persuade her to share my bed beforehand. My choice would be her in my bed, but I won't force her against her will.

"Where is Isaac?"

I lead her to the room where Claire is changing his diaper. I study Norrie for her reaction, hoping she likes the space I've made for our son. I had a designer decorate it in pale green with an animal theme the first week he was here, but she can change it if she wishes.

Instead of pleasure, I see anger flush her cheeks as she pushes away from me and moves toward, Isaac.

"I can do that." She nudges Claire out of the way with a cool look and then turns her sunbeam bright smile on our son, who giggles. "Hey, baby, what ya doin'? You wanna let it all hang out and kick your legs for a bit?"

Claire looks at me, unsure of what to do. She's tall, blonde, and beautiful. Despite the flirty looks she gives me and the clear invitation to fuck her, I find myself uninterested in what she's offering.

"You can head home for the night, Claire. I can take it from here."

"Are you sure, Mr. Brooks? I'd be happy to stay and assist you in any way I can."

Anger knots the back of my throat at her blatant come-on in front of the woman she knows I'm to marry.

"He said we have it, Claire, and could you kindly refrain from using that giggly tone around me, it makes my teeth ache."

I roll my lips in an effort to stop the chuckle building in my chest. Norrie might not see it, but she's marking her territory and I like it. She might say she doesn't want to marry me, that she hates me for threatening her, but there's a part of her that wants me, and it fills me with hope.

"I.... I don't."

"See you in the morning, Claire."

Claire tips her head and rushes from the room and down the stairs. I raise my brows at Norrie who's now diapering our son, after letting him kick his legs naked for a few minutes. A risky business with a boy child who can pee straight up. I found that out the hard way. His giggles are worth the risk though.

"That was mean."

Norrie flashes me a glare. "She was rude behaving as she did."

"You were jealous."

"I wasn't. I don't care who you sleep with, but she won't disrespect me."

"You tell yourself whatever you need to sleep at night, Norrie, but we both know what that was."

"I hate you."

"So you said."

Her words slide off me like Teflon because her actions are so much louder. I shove my hands in my pockets to keep from reaching for her as she cradles Isaac to her shoulder, breathing in his sweet scent and I know that look on her face. It's complete and utter contentment and love. I know because I feel it too when I hold her in my arms.

"Where is my bed?"

I frown as I watch her look around the room. "In your room."

"But I sleep in the same room as my son. He sleeps beside me, he always has."

I shake my head, moving to take him from her when I see her wobble, but she pulls away and I end up guiding her to a rocking chair I'd brought in for the middle of the night feedings.

Seeing her sit there with Isaac cradled close is a vision that will stay with me for life. She's the dream I never knew I needed, and it terrifies me because I can't be what she needs or deserves. "Isaac sleeps in here and is perfectly fine."

"What about if he needs me in the night?"

"Then the monitor will hear him, and you have a camera beside your bed so you can check on him."

"I don't like this."

I crouch beside the chair, and she keeps her eyes on mine. "You need rest to heal, Norrie. You won't get that sleeping with him. I'm happy to do the night routine so you can rest."

"It feels wrong. I've always done everything for him."

My jaw clenches and I bite back the retort on the edge of my tongue, reminding her whose fault that is. I want this marriage to work and sniping at her every two minutes won't make that any easier. "I know, but now it's time to let me help. I'm here for you and Isaac and truthfully, I've come to enjoy our midnight man chats."

Her lips quirk. "Midnight man chats?"

"Yes, you know, where I offer him all of my fatherly tips about life and such."

Her grin splits her face and lights her eyes with unabashed joy, and it makes my chest tighten. "Well, I wouldn't want to get in the way of such important bonding time."

I pat her knee, reveling in the feel of her soft skin. "Thank you." I stand, ready to head back down to the kitchen so I can get dinner sorted and speak with Ryker and Audrey. "Will you be okay for a few minutes while I see Ryker and Audrey out and order dinner?"

"Yes, of course."

I nod and move toward the door, looking back to see her watching me.

"Thank you, Harrison."

My brows drop. "What for?"

"Everything, but mostly for biting your tongue just then, and not reminding me why I was alone with Isaac. I know that can't have been easy for you."

"It wasn't."

We share a smile that feels like the first sign of peace between us and relief floods me, even as I remind myself not to let my guard down. I could too easily fall back under her spell, and I know how that story always ends.

6: Norrie

I sigh as the front door closes and I hear a car start. I move to the window of my room which overlooks the street and watch as he's driven away, the back of the Mercedes the car service uses disappearing. It would be nice to have this time alone with Isaac, but he's already downstairs with Claire the nanny. I hate that she's here at all, and after yesterday I know it will be awkward.

With a sigh, I head down, slowly navigating the steps on my bum like I promised Harrison I would. It was the only way I could convince him to go into work for a few hours and I desperately need space from him. Yesterday was a lot, both physically and mentally, and my emotions feel like they've been through the wringer. He blows hot and cold, going from being an overbearing jerk to total sweetness as he explained his middle-of-the-night bonding with our son.

The sound of crying makes me hasten my step and I walk into the kitchen to see my son sitting in his highchair, crying like his heart is breaking. Claire has her back to me as she talks on the phone with someone about last night's party.

Incredulity and anger have me rushing toward Isaac as fast as my bum leg will let me. I lift him quickly and soothe his cries just as Claire notices me and ends her call. I glare at her over his head as I soothe and rock him back and forth. Kissing his head, I stroke the soft, dark hair so like his father's.

"You shouldn't coddle him."

Claire is the epitome of a mean girl; beautiful, slim, confident, and not afraid to use her sexuality to get what she wants in life. I've dealt with my fair share over the years. Especially since my brother made it in his chosen career.

Heat rushes up my spine and if I was a cartoon character, steam would be shooting from my ears. I straighten my spine as the blonde bombshell looks me over from head to toe with a sniff of her delicate little nose.

"How dare you neglect my son while you yammer with your friends and then have the God damn nerve to tell me how to care for him." Claire rolls her eyes as if I'm boring her and it flips a switch in my brain. "That's it. Get out. You're fired."

Claire snaps straight, indignation in every muscle. "You can't fire me. I work for Mr. Brooks."

"Watch me. You get out of this house right now or I'm going to throw you out and don't let the limp fool you."

Something in my words must register that I mean every word because Claire tosses her mane of hair and grabs her designer bag from the counter.

"Whatever. I don't need this."

I hold Isaac close as he tugs on my hair and hear the door slam shut moments later.

Closing my eyes, I kiss my son's head as he coos up at me, babbling nonsense that makes my heart soar. Everything is right with the world for a few minutes until I realize I'm now all alone. A wave of familiar loneliness assails me and my lip wobbles as tears burn the back of my eyes. The doctor told me it was possible my emotions would be all over the place and gave me the name of a therapist to talk to if I need it. I didn't think this was caused by the accident though, this was a long-running battle of my own doing. "Just you and me, baby boy."

I spend the morning fighting tears as I try and care for Isaac, who's grown so much in the five weeks I spent in the hospital. I missed the first time he rolled from his back to his tummy. A small milestone but one I should have been there for and that feeling only fills me with more guilt for what Harrison missed out on.

Around eleven I'm about to put Isaac down for his nap when the doorbell rings. I freeze, not sure what to do. Harrison told me this was my home, but it doesn't feel like it. I'm a stranger here and have no business answering the door, especially as I know it isn't for me.

The bell rings again and I know I don't have a choice. I rush to the door. "I'm coming, hold your horses." I open the door with a smile, and it freezes on my face.

"Hi, Nora. Do you remember me?"

Audrey, the woman I'm sure Harrison is, or at least was, in a relationship with, is standing on my doorstep with two other women.

"Uh, yes. Sure." Audrey is beautiful, she could be in a perfume advert she's so classically stunning and chic. "Audrey, right?"

"Yes. Can we come in?"

"Harrison isn't here."

I don't want to let these women in, I have no energy for another mean-girl scene right now. Although I haven't gotten mean girl vibes from her over the last two minutes.

"I know. We came to see you."

Well damn. "Okay, come on in then."

I open the door wider, resigning myself to the situation, and wait for them to pass. All three are beautiful, even though two are dressed down compared to Audrey. "I was just about to put Isaac down for a nap."

Audrey looks around as she dumps her bag on the couch and shrugs out of her coat. "Where's the nanny?"

I roll my lips before I straighten my shoulders and lift my head. I have nothing to be ashamed of. Isaac is my son. "I fired her."

Audrey's mouth drops and she turns to the dark-haired woman who grins and shrugs.

"Damn, girl, that was fast. Good for you."

"Really?" I cross my arms as I sink into the plush blue couch and tap Isaac's bouncer with my toe as I see his eyes droop.

"Yes, that she-devil was way too hungry, but how have you managed this morning on your own? Harrison won't like it."

"Harrison isn't the boss of me. I've managed fine on my own without him before and a little injury won't get in my way."

Audrey steps closer and sits beside me and I can't help but compare us. She's like a glam Hollywood-era goddess, and I'm in loose sweats and a tee with a stain on the front. We're worlds apart in every way and I can see why Harrison likes her. I like her.

Her arm comes around me and she smiles. "I like you."

I frown, perplexed by her behavior toward me. I'm not sure I'd be so forgiving if I was in her situation. "I like you too."

"Good. Now, what can we do to help? We're here to make things easier for you and because I'm pathologically nosey."

I glance at the other two women who are smiling.

"I'm Violet. I'm engaged to Lincoln, and this is Amelia, a friend of Beck's." The dark-haired woman leans forward, offering her hand with a warm smile.

The woman beside her, who has gorgeous auburn hair and freckles across her nose, waves. "Hey, sorry to barge in like this."

"It's nice to meet you all."

"So why don't I make us a light lunch and Violet can put Isaac down for his nap? If that's okay with you, that is."

"Sure, I guess." I wave my hand, not really sure what's happening as Audrey takes over as if it's the most natural thing in the world.

Violet laughs. "Excuse her. She works with men all day and forgets sometimes that women don't take orders as well as them and that her charm won't work on us."

"No, it's fine. I just hate being like this. I'm very self-reliant usually."

Audrey places a hand over mine and smiles. "I know that. I can see how hard you work by how successful your business is and how happy your staff are but let us help. We care about Harrison, and you're part of his life now."

"Oh my God, I haven't thanked you. Pine Grove Lodge means everything to me."

"I can tell and it's running like a finely tuned machine."

"Thank you for overseeing it."

"I haven't done a lot. Your staff are excellent, but it was my pleasure. It's a wonderful place, you have there."

"It is. My grandmother left it to me when she died and I kind of threw myself into it."

"You have an aptitude for it."

I look at Audrey, this powerful woman, and can't help but like her. "Thank you, that means a lot coming from you."

"I can't believe you did all that and took care of a baby."

"It wasn't always easy, but I love them both so that made it easier and I have a good team behind me."

"Talking of the little guy, he looks like he's almost out for the count."

Violet grins and I pull my gaze back to my son and away from the woman who I sense knows more than she's letting on. My head is beginning to ache and I already feel exhausted even though it's barely lunchtime.

"Do you want me to set Isaac up a crib down here so you can manage easier? I know getting upstairs is tricky. We could set up a travel crib in Harrison's study so you don't have to navigate the stairs every time?"

I look at Amelia who suggested it and nod. "That would be wonderful, but I'm not sure what Harrison would think. This is his home, and I don't want to intrude."

"It's your home too now, right?"

Violet is lifting Isaac from his chair and cooing at him as he babbles back. "Shall I put him down in his crib?"

"Thank you, that's very kind."

Audrey has already moved into the kitchen; I can hear her moving around as if the space is familiar to her and I suppose it is if they were lovers. As Violet and Amelia disappear to do whatever it is they said, I know I need to speak with Audrey and apologize. But how does one say sorry for stealing her man when she never wanted this in the first place? I'm still hoping Harrison will come to his senses and agree to co-parent. Yet another side of me has bought into the dream of being his wife, although I'd never imagined it going down quite like this in my wildest dreams.

Audrey has shed her gray jacket showcasing toned, tan arms and a gorgeous figure that doesn't have a wobbly middle or a stretchmark in sight. It would be easier if I could hate her, but she's lovely.

I twist my fingers around themselves as nerves assail me. "Hey, can we talk for a second?"

"Sure, what's up? Is Harrison being a bossy jerk again? I can kick his ass for you if you want."

Laughter bubbles up my throat. "No, he's fine. I just want to apologize."

Audrey's head pops up from the sandwich she's making. "Apologize! For what?"

God, why is she being so nice? "I know you were together before and I hate that I'm coming between that. It was never my intention. I didn't know he had a girlfriend at the time, and I certainly didn't plan to get pregnant." I throw up my hands as I pace. "I was on the pill, and we used protection. I don't know how it happened and then it did. I was going to tell him but I got sick and life went to shit and now here I am ruining everything for you."

I suck in a breath, fully aware I just word vomited all over her. Audrey places the knife she was using to cut tomatoes on the chopping board and wipes her hands on the dish towel.

"Nora, I don't know what you think you know, but Harrison and I have never been a couple. He and I are friends and have been for a long time. Not to be nasty but the thought of Harrison and I like that makes me queasy."

"But I saw you."

Audrey purses her lips and comes around the counter to stand in front of me, taking my hands, she towers over my much smaller frame.

"Nora, I remember seeing you the night I went with Harrison to the

Kennedy Foundation Ball. We were leaving this house and you were across the street."

I nod, unable to stop the pain that the memory evokes. I'd spent so long getting up the courage and after a very rough start to my pregnancy, it had taken me months to get to that point.

"You were laughing and holding his arm and you looked so perfect together and he looked so happy. I didn't have the heart to come between you."

"Oh, honey, we've been friends a long time. I'm a tactile person, a hugger and it drives my friends crazy, and I'd been teasing him about something. It was never anything more. I wish I could go back and point you out to him, but you were gone before I realized that the moment was important."

Tears clog my throat and grief pools in my belly like a stone. All those lost months over a misunderstanding. "I robbed him."

Slim arms come around me and Audrey hugs me tight. "Don't do that to yourself, Nora. You didn't rob him. It was circumstance, and he's not innocent."

A sob escapes as guilt washes over me. "He hates me."

Audrey laughs. "I can assure you he does not. He's marrying you, isn't he?"

I sniff and wipe my tears on my sleeve. "That's because he wants Isaac. He doesn't want me. Whatever we shared is gone and I killed it."

"I wouldn't be so sure. Harrison loves his son, any fool can see that, but I don't for one second think he'd marry you if he didn't care for you too."

"You think?"

"I do. Just give him some time to get his head around things and go easy on yourself. You didn't murder anyone."

"I guess."

Audrey goes back to the counter and continues making lunch. "Did you tell him your pregnancy was rough?"

"No, he doesn't want to hear my excuses." I make quotation marks with my fingers.

She shakes her head, pursing her lips in displeasure. "Men are stupid as fuck sometimes."

A laugh breaks free from my throat and I smile, a feeling of friendship blooming in my chest. "They are, that's true. My brother is the same. Stubborn to a fault but also charming."

"I swear if I didn't love cock so much I'd be a lesbian."

I blush at her words and hear movement behind me. I turn and see a red-faced and angry Harrison behind me.

"Harrison, you're home!"

He dumps his laptop bag on the counter and pins me with a glare as he prowls toward me. The look on his face is intense and angry and I take an involuntary step back and bump into the counter.

"Audrey, get out."

"Harrison, go easy on her."

His eyes never leave mine, but his voice drops an octave. "I said get out."

Audrey huffs but shows no fear as she slams the knife on the counter and moves around us. She pauses to kiss my cheek. "I'll call you later."

I appreciate her kindness and murmur a thanks, all the time wondering what the hell has gotten into Harrison.

The front door softly closes as the three women leave with just a wave to me. The silence is oppressive, the air is heavy with tension but his heady scent envelopes me and I'm glad to have the island at my back, keeping my weak knees from spilling me to the floor.

His eyes flash to my lips as I nibble on the bottom one in a display of nerves. I'm nervous, not frightened exactly, but he has my emotions so tangled I don't know which way is up, especially after the conversation with Audrey.

"You sacked the nanny."

Despite my hammering heart, I lift my chin in defiance. "I did."

"Why?"

"Do I need a reason?" I don't know why I'm taunting him.

He draws in a breath through his nose, his eyes closing before he lifts his head to glare at me his jaw tight. "Don't test me, Norrie. You won't like the reaction you get."

"You don't scare me, Harrison."

His hand lifts quickly and he holds my chin in his fingers. "What did I say about disagreeing with me?"

Desire makes my belly flop, and my breasts feel heavy as the air stills. Desire thickens every breath I take until I'm dizzy with it.

"Answer me."

His voice is low, and I lean into him, wanting to soak in this feeling only he gives me. Safety and danger all at once. A heady combination that I seem to have no defense against. "That you'd kiss me every time I disagree."

His head moves closer, and I shiver slightly as his breath feathers my jaw, his nose sliding along my ear. "Good girl, that's right."

His teeth graze my neck and I whimper.

"Is that what you want, Norrie? My mouth on you."

Every fiber in my being wants to scream 'yes' but I hold onto the last shred of dignity I have left as I exhale. "No."

His chuckle is warm as he lifts his head and I see his heavy gaze holds a thousand decadent promises. "Liar, but I'll let you have that for now."

He steps back letting me go and I shudder, closing my eyes, trying to grasp some kind of control.

"You put yourself in danger today, Nora. Don't do it again."

"I was fine."

Harrison regards me from across the kitchen. "What if you'd gotten dizzy? What if your leg gave while you had Isaac in your arms?"

"It didn't happen." Swift disappointment that his worry is only for our son is followed by shame that I want him worried about me. Isaac is all that matters and perhaps he's right. "You're right. I'm sorry. I just couldn't stand her letting him cry while she was on the phone with her friends making plans."

He spins to look at me, his body going still at my words. "She did what?"

I cock my head, trying not to react to the cold anger in his question. "I guess she never told you that."

"She never told me anything, the agency called me. I have no interaction with that woman beyond her care for my son."

"Well, either way, I don't regret firing her and for the record, I don't coddle our son."

He moves closer and places his palms on either side of mine on the counter, trapping my body with his. A pulse flutters in my neck and it takes every ounce of control I have to keep from leaning into him.

"I know that. Did she infer you did?"

He's studying me, waiting for my answer. "She said it outright."

Harrison frowns, a dark look easing over his features again as he moves closer into my personal space, invading my senses. He grips my arms and I lift my hands to his chest to steady myself. He's hard beneath his white shirt, all sinew and muscle and I know every inch of his cut body from memory.

My fingers flex and I want to run my hands over him and relearn every inch, but I drop my hands to my sides, fighting my reaction. His hands move over my arms until he links our fingers and brings them back to his chest.

I can feel his heart steady and strong beneath our clasped hands and it settles me.

"She was wrong. No matter the differences between us there's one thing I'd never doubt and that's what kind of mother you are. You're a wonderful mother, Norrie, of that I have no question. Don't ever let anyone tell you differently."

"Thank you."

I'm not sure he could've given me a compliment that means more to me, and it softens my heart to this man as he shows me a glimpse of the person I shared the best week of my life with.

"Good. Now, why don't I finish lunch, and then you can take a nap."

"Don't you have work?"

"I'll be working from home for a bit."

"Because of me?"

"I can't think of another reason."

"I'm sorry I'm being a nuisance."

"You are not a nuisance. You're my family and it's my job to take care of you and that's what I'll do. But you have to let me, Norrie, and not fight me at every turn."

I let the warm feeling slide through me at his words, but the next sentence shatters the momentary fantasy of a happy ever after.

"After all, we both know the consequences if we can't make this work and I know you don't want to lose your son."

7: Harrison

I STEP INSIDE MY MOTHER'S HOME AND INSTANTLY MY STOMACH KNOTS with tension. It's the same feeling I get every time I come here, and I wish for just one time it would be different. That I could visit with her and not have this ball of dread sitting on my chest. "Mom, I brought your prescription."

"In the kitchen."

Her voice is light and airy, and I think today must be a good day. I stride toward the sound of her voice, which takes about two seconds in this tiny apartment. I've offered countless times to move her into a better, bigger place but she won't hear about it. This is her safe place and I must live with that, even if I don't like it. Closing my eyes, I take a breath and step into the room.

Her kitchen is warm and bright with flashes of yellow in the décor to lift the white of the walls. Sitting at the white oak kitchen table is my mom. A smile is on her face as she turns to me, an expression filled with such love that I feel guilt for all of the horrible conflicting thoughts I have swimming in my head.

I bend to kiss her cheek, her long gray hair catching on my scruff. "Hey, Mom, how are you doing today?"

I sit at the table placing her prescription for anxiety meds on the side beside the huge pile of magazines she's collecting. She suffers from agoraphobia among other things and has for the last twelve years. She never leaves the house and is reliant on me completely for food and her health. Everything she needs, I find a way to provide. The only people she sees apart from me are Audrey and Beck, who checks her health once a year for me and she allows that grudgingly.

It's the reason I never wanted a family. I was never sure I had the mental bandwidth to spread myself so thin. Now, I wouldn't change my situation, at least not the part where I'm a father. My position with Norrie is too complicated for me to unwind or confront right now.

"I'm okay. I have a new magazine coming tomorrow so that's exciting and my knee is playing up a bit. Other than that, I'm fine."

My brow creases as I look at her. She's slightly overweight due to a lack of exercise and a love of baking but her mind is clear today. It breaks my heart that she's this way but no matter how hard I've tried to help her, I can't fix her. She's like a bird trapped in a cage and all the money I have won't help her because she has no wish to be helped, and I'm not enough to make her change. "Do you want Beck to come and look at it?"

She flexes her leg out as she looks down at the black, velour-clad leg and shakes her head. "No."

"Are you sure?"

She bangs her hand on the table as she responds sharply. "Yes. Stop fussing, Harrison."

I bite my tongue to stop from spitting out the retort that I wouldn't have to if she'd just be the parent for once, but I know I can't because this isn't her fault. I hate that I'm reduced to this every time I visit, and it always follows the same format. It's why I've put off this news so long but it's past time she learned about her grandson.

"I have some news." Now is the time to tell her about Isaac and Norrie, and nerves and anxiety at her reaction dot my temple with sweat.

"Oh?"

I take her hands in mine, wanting her to see how happy I am, how much this means to me, and smile. "I have a son."

Her whole body freezes, tension radiating through her as she pulls her hands away and I fight the urge not to react with the hurt I feel.

"What are you talking about?"

"I met someone last year. I found out recently that she got pregnant and I have a son."

My mother stands and starts to pace, agitation clear as she wrings her hands over and over. I stay silent waiting for her to speak and hating that I'd let myself hope for a different reaction from her.

"What does that mean for me? Will I see you still? Who will do my shopping and get my things?"

My teeth almost crack with the pressure I put on them as I try and stay calm and not let the hurt take over. I should be used to this by now. My entire adult life, every success has been punctuated with how it will affect her. "Nothing will change for you, Mom."

She throws her hands up as she continues to pace her small kitchen. Anxiety is like poison, tainting everything in her life. I hate that for her, but what I can't get to grips with is the fact that she won't make any effort to help herself.

"Of course it will. A child is a lot of work, and I won't let you be like your father and abandon your son."

Her eyes find mine and I know she sees my father when she looks at me. I have nothing of my mother in me apart from intellect. "I have no intention of abandoning Isaac or Norrie."

"Isaac? That's his name?"

I nod, a feeling of overwhelming pride coming over me. "Yes, would you like to see a picture of your grandson?"

Tears brighten her blue eyes as she nods. I take out my phone and swipe through the hundreds of pictures I already have of Isaac and turn the phone toward her.

Her hands shake as she takes it. "Oh, Harrison, he's gorgeous?"

"He is, and so clever and strong."

"How old is he?"

"Nearly five months."

She sits back down slowly as I scroll through, showing her a few more, ending with one of me holding Isaac next to Norrie that I'd taken when she got home from the hospital.

"He looks exactly like you at the same age, and you were such a smart baby too. I remember you acing all your check-ups like they were a competition even then."

"I did? You never told me that."

She frowns at me as if she's seeing me clearly for the first time. "Didn't I? I must have forgotten, but yes you did, and you were such a happy baby. Unless you were hungry, and then all hell broke loose."

I laugh and try and stay in the moment that's so precious and rare between us these days. "I'm still like that."

"Does he sleep well?"

"Pretty good, although he's teething so that's not fun for anyone. Poor guy, his cheeks are all red and he's a drool machine."

"Try a frozen washcloth. Just wet it and freeze it for half an hour and let him gum on it."

I never imagined I'd be having this moment of bonding with my mom, where she was giving me advice. For the first time in twelve years, I'm the child again and it feels good.

"I'll try that. Any other wonder tips you can give me?"

For a few minutes, she shares her tried and tested tips and her face is lit up much like I imagine mine is right now. And even though a few of them I won't be trying, like the brandy on the gums for starters, I soak up the moment.

"Why didn't you tell me about him before?"

That should be easy to answer but I can't without hurting her feelings, so I keep it vague. "It's complicated, but I didn't know about him until recently and his mother was hit by a car."

"Oh no, is she okay now?"

"She will be."

"Why didn't she tell you?"

I shake my head and shrug. "I'm not sure."

"I'm sure she had her reasons."

"Perhaps, but I don't care to listen to them."

"So will you see him regularly?"

"We're getting married, so yes, every day."

Her face goes still and she pales. "Married? I can't come to a wedding. All those people looking at me and the dangers around every corner."

I sigh, the moment between us lost as she reverts to the panic of what things mean for her. "We haven't set a date yet, Mom, but maybe you could try and come? It will be small, only a few friends and family."

She shakes her head, the gray of her hair aging her past her fifty-five years and it saddens me how much she misses out on. Once again I'm struck by the losses we both suffer from this awful illness, and I know it's an illness. She isn't this way because she wants to be, but that doesn't stop me from getting angry about her lack of desire to get better.

"I can't. I can't, Harrison."

I move to wrap my arm around her. "It's okay, Mom, you don't have to come. Perhaps we can set up a video call so you can speak to Norrie and see Isaac?"

"Yes, yes, okay. That would be alright."

I press my lips to her head and tightness makes it hard to breathe. I love my mother with everything I am and would do anything for her, but now I'm a father I see things slightly differently. I fail to see a single thing in this world that would make me miss his wedding. "I have to go."

"Okay. *Jeopardy* is on soon, so that's good."

She looks up at me with wide eyes and I see the loneliness there that she can't hide.

If wishes were horses, beggars would ride. A saying my grandfather always used before he died when I was ten.

I leave my mom's home with mixed emotions, happy that we got a few minutes of normality where I could spend some time as her son, and defeated because even my son isn't enough to force her from her comfort zone.

I'm meant to be heading back to the club, but I have this overwhelming urge to see Norrie and Isaac. The last two weeks since she fired Claire have been better than I expected. We've found a rhythm that works, and an unspoken truce has been called. I get up to Isaac in the night and do the mornings, and she handles the daytime. It's easier for her now my study has been turned into a day nursery for Isaac. I work in my bedroom which isn't ideal, but it won't be forever.

Norrie is determined to get back to how she was. Every day I see how hard she works at her physio routine, and little by little she's getting there. She's still underweight, and I don't know the cause of why she lost it all, but I won't ask. I've taken to ordering her favorite pastry, bear claws, to be brought in around eleven am in the hope it will help her get her curves back.

A tentative peace reigns in my home and yet I wish she'd fight back a little, even if it's to give me an excuse to kiss her again. We haven't talked about how our marriage will be but I want it to be as real as it can be. I know I owe her a say in that, even if fear makes me demand her compliance.

Opening the front door, I take a step and stop dead as the smell of burned sugar invades my nose. She's been baking again, and my guess is it went the same way as the others. Norrie is a great cook from what I remember but baking isn't her forte at all and I won't embarrass her by mentioning it. Thankfully my housekeeper does the shopping and cleaning twice a week, and I pay her to leave meals in the freezer we can just defrost and eat, at least until Norrie is up to cooking again. It's something she enjoys, and that was our compromise when we discussed the everyday arrangements. Mrs. Meredith would cook and shop until she was up to the task.

"Norrie!"

I dump my briefcase on the green velvet lounger in the hallway and head toward the living room. She's sitting on a mat on the floor with our son, who's kicking his legs and reaching for the toy that's hanging from an arch above his head. She's stretching her legs and my eyes move over her body as if I have no control over them.

The yoga pants hide nothing, and the top has risen so I can see a sliver of creamy flesh on her abdomen. My dick perks up at the sight and I battle to drag my eyes away from her delicious body as I crouch down to tickle Isaac's tummy. He babbles and I grin, the space in my heart seeming to expand every day with the love I feel for him.

I glance at Norrie, and she's watching us with a smile that's pure serenity on her face. Not for the first time I have the urge to ask her why she kept me out for the first few months and only let me in when she had to. Pride stops me every single time, but the anger I had at the beginning is starting to fade and I don't know if that's a good thing. The wall I erected to keep her out is much harder to maintain now, and I don't like it.

Norrie is a danger to my heart because she almost made me believe in a happy-ever-after and then she showed me how wrong I was. I'm good for fun but not for the long haul, and that's why I won't back down on this marriage or the empty threat to take Isaac from her. It hadn't started empty. But after seeing what a wonderful mother she was, I'd never deny my son that, not when I know how precious it is, but she doesn't need to know that.

"Hey."

"Hi."

"You're home early? Is everything okay?"

I bite my lip and nod, my voice coming out gravelly. "Yes, fine. Do you want to go for a walk? It's nice out." I hadn't planned on asking her that, but now I have, I know it will be a good time to discuss how we move forward in a physical way. Keeping my hands off her was easy when it was for her health but now she's been cleared by her doctor for more strenuous activity, and I checked with Beck that meant sex, I find myself eager to touch her every time she's close.

Norrie cocks her head and looks at me with a question in her eyes. This is the first time I've proposed we do anything together except eat dinner or take care of Isaac, and I know I've caught her off guard.

"Sure, sounds fun."

Only Norrie would find the fun in a simple walk along the street to the local park.

"Well, I can't promise fun but I can promise fresh air and maybe an ice cream."

She stands and I put my hand out to help her, surprised when she takes it with a smile.

"Sounds like fun to me. Do I need to change first?"

I let my eyes trail over her and see only perfection in the way she looks. Her hair is loose around her shoulders, her face scrubbed clean, and a smile that would send nations to war. I don't say any of that. "You're fine."

"Cool, do you want to grab the stroller or do you want to carry Isaac like a kangaroo?"

"I'll carry him."

"I'm starting to think I should have called him Joey."

"I'm very glad you didn't."

I pause and she picks up on it, as she often does. "Ask, Harrison."

"Why did you call him Isaac?"

She catches my gaze and gives me a soft look which makes my chest feel tight.

"I know you don't want to hear this, but I had every intention of telling you about him and I wanted him to have something that was linked to you. I know Isaac Newton was your hero and it's a good name. Did you know it means 'one who laughs'?"

"I did know that, yes."

Norrie rolls her eyes. "Of course you did. I forget how big that brain of yours is sometimes."

I'm used to being desired for how I look or for what I have or can give, but she's probably the only woman I've ever met who has voiced how attractive she thinks it is that I'm clever. "Thank you."

Her smile is wide when I thank her for naming our son something that means something to me. "My pleasure, Harrison."

8: Harrison

I reach for her hand as a cyclist flies past us on the sidewalk, pulling her close as she jumps in fright. I'm deciding whether to chase the idiot down when I remember I have Isaac strapped to my chest. Giving someone a beating would be rather difficult with a child attached.

"Are you okay?"

"Yeah, I'm fine. He just made me jump, that's all."

"Damn maniac should be on the road, not the damn pavement." I hold tight to her, not wanting to let go of her small soft hand in mine or the sense of contentment I have simply strolling with my son and the woman who has me wrapped up in knots. "Do you remember the accident?"

She's silent for a while as the late spring sun warms our skin and I think perhaps she won't answer my insensitive question. "I'm sorry, I shouldn't have asked."

"No, it's fine. I remember bits of it like it was in slow motion, but other parts feel so fast I can't grasp the memory fully. Like a movie in fast forward, it's just flashes."

"I'm sorry. I wish I could've stopped you from having to go through that."

Norrie shrugs and squeezes my hand to comfort me, her thumb rubbing circles over my skin. God, this woman, and her compassion and strength slays me. She makes it impossible for me to hate her when it's the only thing keeping me safe from her ripping my heart to shreds. When you've been hurt and rejected by the people meant to love you unconditionally, you get an instinct and mine is screaming that if I let her she could really break me. Which is why I can't give in to how she makes me feel.

"It is what it is. I can't change it and in the end, everyone is fine except the driver, poor guy. Imagine going to your grave with that as your last memory. Anyway, I can't let it stop me from living my life, I refuse to be that person." I think about what she said as we walk into the park, the trees blossoming into their glory, and I marvel at her resilience. I wonder what else it is about this woman that I don't know. I know the hot mess that made me lose my mind the week we spent together. The woman who was fun and full of joy, but there's more to her than I ever dreamed, and I want it all, I just need to figure out a way to make her give it to me without losing myself.

We walk on in companionable silence toward the park, letting the late afternoon warmth kiss our skin. I'd changed out of my suit and put on jeans and a navy shirt, which is currently getting covered in drool from my son, making me smile when I glance down at him.

"How was your visit with your mom?"

I fight the sigh, remembering I mentioned it last night at dinner and wondering why I had. "Wonderful, horrible, frustrating."

"Talk to me."

I hesitate, not used to sharing my thoughts with others and especially someone who I don't trust fully. Norrie stops walking and I turn to face her.

"Harrison, I get why you want this marriage, that you want a family for Isaac, and I've agreed but I won't go through life like a side character. If we're going to do this, we need to be friends at least and friends lean on each other."

"Are we friends, Norrie?"

"I want us to be. I don't want Isaac to think his parents hate each other. I want him to grow up surrounded by love and even if we don't love each other that way, we should try and be friends."

I hate how much her saying she doesn't love me hurts when I already know what we are and aren't to each other.

"I want that too."

I continue walking and she falls into step beside me, the weakness in her leg almost gone now. Realistically I could go back to working at the club but I like being around them. Hearing them chatter and the smell of whatever disaster she's made in my kitchen. It's nice to have my house feel like a home, to have that warmth when I walk in the door and not the oppressive silence. Against my better judgment, I decide to meet her halfway.

"My mother was surprised, then she went into a full-on panic about how Isaac being here would affect her life. Then she was perfect for just a few short minutes and she was my mom again." Even I can hear the wistful tone in my voice, and I clear my throat to get rid of it before I continue. "She gave me advice on teething, and we talked about my childhood. Then she was gone and her panic about the wedding overtook her joy."

"That must be hard for you being the parent to your parent."

I nod. "It is, and frustrating. I love her but I get so angry sometimes and then I feel like shit for that. It's an endless loop."

"I can understand that you want your mother, and that's not the relationship you have with her now. Is that why you didn't want kids?"

"Mostly. I feel like I have one already. Plus my life is hardly ideal for a family." I look down at Isaac who's fallen asleep and a rush of love for him fills my chest. "I'm glad I had the choice taken out of my hands. I can't imagine my life without him now."

"Me either."

We stop at the ice cream vendor, and I order us both a vanilla cone, making sure to add extra chocolate sauce to hers. We sit at a bench, watching families picnic and dogs run around without a care, and I wish I could've had that carefree life. A simple family dynamic that I always dreamed of, but my life isn't bad. I need to appreciate what I do have. "We sure did make an awesome child."

"We did. What about now? Do you want more kids, Harrison?"

Her words stir something in me, a need I didn't know I had. Her pink tongue flicks out as she takes a swipe of vanilla cone and I almost groan as blood heads south.

"I haven't thought about it." I can feel my heart beating faster and the air is suddenly too warm. The need to steer the conversation to something simpler is strong.

"I always wanted a few maybe two or three."

An image of three children running around who look like Norrie and me, skims through my mind and it makes my heart hammer almost painfully in my chest, but not all of it is fear. Some of it is excitement and anticipation of what that might be like and the road to getting there.

"And now?"

I see the blush steal over her cheeks and know where her mind has gone.

"I don't know. We haven't talked about the details of what happens after we say I do."

I wrap my arm around her possessively, skimming my fingers over the jut of her hip. Soft flesh molds to me and I breathe in the scent of her, so seductive and sweet at the same time. I bend my head and nuzzle her neck. Since the first moment we met, our connection has been like wildfire, instant heat that burns out of control, and time and circumstance haven't changed that in the slightest. I still want her as much now as I did then, and from the way her nipples press against me I know that she feels it too.

"We haven't talked about this but let me make it clear for you so we have no misunderstandings. I have no intention of spending my life celibate and I don't cheat on people, especially not my wife."

"Oh?" Her single words is more like a puff of breath against the skin of my neck.

I smirk, feeling back in control again. "Oh?"

"What do you want me to say?"

"How about you tell me that you want me in your bed, that you think about my hands and mouth on you day and night. That you pretend your fingers are mine every time you touch yourself."

Her breathing hitches and I feel her pulse jump against my lips.

"Do you do that?"

My eyes fall closed as she volleys my question, and I can't believe I lived without this for an entire year. I want this woman so badly it's a constant ache and that's what I tell her, giving her the only thing I can. "All the time. I think about your mouth on my cock, what it feels like to be inside you. How you taste on my tongue when you come. The sounds you make when I'm so deep inside you that you can't feel where I end and you begin."

I bite slightly on her neck, sucking the skin lightly. "I think about how I want to put my baby in your belly again. How I want to stuff you so full of my come it would be impossible for you not to get knocked up. How I want to watch you grow heavy with a brother or sister for Isaac, how I want to hold your hand as we share this miracle together."

A loud horn snaps me from my words. I hadn't even known I felt that way myself until the words were out but it's the truth. I want more children and I want them with her. The only thing she can't have is my love. I can't trust her with that, but my son deserves a sibling and fucking her won't be a hardship, far from it in fact.

"Do you really want that?"

I look at her flushed face and then reach to cup her cheeks. I kiss her softly, letting my tongue explore her mouth as she opens for me. I pull away before it can go too far, aware of who sleeps between us unaware of the emotional storm brewing above his tiny head.

"Yes. I want all that, but I won't lie to you, Norrie. I can't give you my love. What we have has to be enough for you. It's all I can offer, but we can make a good life together." I've put her in an untenable situation. I won't love her but I want to fuck her and fill her with my babies or I threaten to take away the one we already have. If a bigger bastard was ever born, I don't know him.

I see her eyelids fall closed and wonder if I've just fucked up and panic seizes me.

"I don't know if I can agree to that. At least not yet. I need to be able to trust you, Harrison. Can you see the irony of having a second child with the man threatening me into marriage with custody of the first?"

"Don't you think Isaac deserves a brother or sister?"

Norrie pulls away with a frown and I feel her loss but let her have this space, knowing I just hit her with a lot to process.

"Of course, I do but this isn't a normal situation. Usually, men don't blackmail the woman they're marrying. If it were up to me, I'd meet a man who can't live without me, who makes me feel like I'm his world. We'd fall in love and get married and then we'd give Isaac a sibling one day."

Anger at the thought of any other man touching her makes me want to punch something, hard. To rearrange this imaginary asshole's face. "Not happening, unless you want blood on your hands."

Norrie rolls her eyes, not scared of me in the slightest even if I do mean every word. "So you've said. But you can't just demand another child of me either, Harrison. I'm giving up enough already."

"Fine," I grunt knowing she's right but hating that I can't just bend her to my will, but that's Norrie's draw. She keeps me on my toes. She's not what I'm used to. She won't bow and scrape to me like other women will.

"Dial it down and give me some time to get my bearings and we'll talk after the wedding. I didn't exactly have a fun pregnancy and I'm not sure I relish the idea again so soon."

I feel angry that she'd had a rough pregnancy and I wasn't there for her, but she has nobody to blame but herself. "Fine." I know my voice is harsher now and almost wince.

"I'm not saying no, Harrison, just not yet. I need time to adjust to my new future."

I know Norrie, she believes in love and romance, but she's walking away from it. I should be happy, but I can't help feeling like I'm cheating her out of a chance to find what I can't give her and it doesn't sit well with me.

I stand abruptly. "We should go, it's getting late."

The walk home is quiet, punctuated by the sounds of Isaac, who's awake and babbling as he tries to shove his fingers in my mouth.

We arrive home and I unclip my son and hand him to his mother with a kiss on his chubby cheek.

"Thanks for today, Harrison, and for being honest with me. I'll think about what you said."

I shove my hands in my pants to keep from reaching for her and demanding she does as I say. I could break her, and I never want to do that. I'm not like Lincoln or Beck. I can't be cruel and cold like they can. God knows I wish I could sometimes, it would be so much easier.

"Sure." I go to move away from the pull of her company and then stop. "I almost forgot, I'm going to set up a call with my mom so she can meet you and Isaac."

"That sounds good. Just let me know when. Are you in for dinner tonight?"

I shake my head. I need to get away from her and clear my thoughts. "No. I'm going to shower then head to the club."

I see her features pinch and pale, but she nods. "I'll see you tomorrow then."

Norrie knows exactly the type of club I run. She's never mentioned it but I wonder now if she's curious or if what I detect on her beautiful face is jealousy. I never had her pegged for the jealous type, but I like that shade of green on her.

"Goodnight, Norrie."

I walk away knowing my evening is going to be filled with paperwork, but she doesn't know that and it brings a smile to my face.

9: Norrie

"So how are the plans for the wedding coming along?"

Lottie gives me a warm smile as I sigh and tip another batch of ruined cookies into the trash. I'm trying to be the mom mine was and failing miserably. "Fine, I guess. I haven't really done a lot yet."

Audrey pushes a glass of wine toward me, and I abandon the cookie idea and sit up on the stool at the island. Audrey and Lottie have become a permanent fixture in my life these last few weeks, and honestly, I don't know what I would've done without them. They're the girl squad I always wanted and never had.

"Norrie, what the hell? You get married in a month!"

Audrey looks appalled and I almost laugh at the expression on her face. We had finally set a date for June, and it's rushing toward me as I bury my head in the sand.

"Chill, Audrey, not everyone is a control freak like you."

Audrey raises her eyebrows at Lottie. "Don't even get me started on you."

I see Lottie shrug at Audrey's threat, knowing full well that there's only love behind it. These two women have been by my side every day as I grow stronger and learn my new life. It's been a few weeks since Harrison hit me with the revelation he wants more kids and I've barely seen him since. Every night he goes to the club, and I'm left alone with nothing but my thoughts for company.

But Lottie texts every day and Audrey has bustled into my life in a way I'd never expected, enforcing girls' night be a thing once a week.

"I just don't have much to do. Harrison wants a small wedding with just close friends and family."

"And what do you want?" Lottie asks softly.

"It doesn't matter what I want. This isn't real. None of it's real."

Audrey raises a brow. "I wouldn't be so sure."

I take a large sip of the wine and swallow before asking, "What do you mean?"

"Some of it's real. You have a child together, you live together. He cares about you."

"Yes, all that might be true, but it isn't what I dreamed of growing up."

Audrey cocks her head and flicks her dark hair off her shoulder. "You dreamed of getting married?"

"Yes, of course. Didn't you?"

"I guess, but my dream was always to run the Kennedy empire. Marriage and babies were more of a given slotted into that at some point in time."

"What about you, Lottie?"

Lottie chews on an olive as she seems to give it some thought. "I did when Linc and I were together. I wanted a big lavish affair in a church and flowers everywhere, but after we split, I didn't really think about it again."

"Yeah, well, get thinking because as soon as I've wrangled this one, you're next." Audrey points at Lottie who pokes her tongue out.

"Me? I don't need wrangling."

Audrey stands and goes to her bag where she pulls out her laptop. "We're sorting this out right now."

I move to check the lasagna I made and pull it from the oven. I can't bake for shit, but I can cook like a goddess, even if I do say so myself, and it's nice to take that part of my life back from Mrs. Meredith. As lovely as she is, I prefer to cook for my family. Although the kitchen always looks like it's been hit by a tornado after I finish. Tidiness isn't natural to me, although I'm better than I was. I plate up three portions, making sure to leave some for Harrison, and push it in front of Lottie and Audrey, hoping to distract her from her current mission.

The truth is the wedding makes me feel sad. All my life I've been a dreamer. I dreamed about my birth parents and what they were like. I dreamed of the man I'd marry, and I had an entire Pinterest board full of my dream wedding ideas. Over time it became less and less important as other things became my focus.

My adoptive parents dying and my grandmother leaving me the lodge gave me something else to focus my energy on and I loved it. The business thrived under my hand, but my personal life disappeared until Harrison woke me up and gave me a glimpse of a life surrounded by passion. Then it was snatched away.

"Okay, so tell me about your dream wedding, Norrie."

I throw up my hand, fork in the air as Audrey pins me with a look I know is meant to frighten me. I'll admit at first she scared the heck out of me, but now I know it's all for show. She's the sweetest person you could meet and fiercely loyal. "Fine, I have a board I can show you but it's a waste of time."

"You have a board? Oh, I love this." Lottie scoots closer as Audrey turns the laptop so I can log into my account.

"Here."

I turn the screen to them, and Lottie begins scrolling through the hundreds of pins I've saved over the years.

"Oh, that dress would look beautiful on you."

I peer over Audrey's shoulder and see the dress I dreamed of wearing. It's floaty and romantic with lots of layered tulle and satin, and nothing like the off-the-rack dress I picked for my upcoming nuptials.

"Yeah, it's gorgeous. Why haven't you picked something like it? Your dress is totally different."

I'd shown Audrey the dress I'd picked from a magazine and ordered online. Harrison had given me a credit card and made me promise that all wedding expenses went on it.

"I know. It just feels wrong to wear that for a courthouse wedding."

"I suppose. So where would your dream wedding be?"

I smile, knowing instantly. "Pine Grove Lodge. I always wanted to get married with the mountains behind me in the gazebo by the lake. A lot of wildflowers, Champagne, finger food, kids running around, people laughing and wanting to share in the joy and love between me and my new husband."

"That sounds beautiful."

I feel the pang of sadness in my chest that I'll never get that but push it away feeling silly, knowing I'm giving my son his father. Nothing is more important than that, especially not a silly dream.

I hear the front door open and quickly shut the laptop as I see Harrison walk into the room. His eyes come to me, and I see a question in them at my suspicious behavior.

"Ladies."

"Hey."

Lottie and Audrey greet him as he moves toward me, touching his lips to my forehead. It's how he's taken to greeting me and I can't say I don't love it because I do. There's something sensual and loving about that simple press of the lips that makes me feel safe.

"You're home early."

"Yeah. I left Ryker in charge."

I nod, sensing Audrey and Lottie watching our interaction. "Do you want me to fix you a plate?"

He shakes his head, stepping back as he slips his jacket off and I get a waft of his intoxicating scent, something unique that's just him. The muscles in his shoulders move under his shirt and I feel my clit throb with need, remembering exactly how it feels to be at the mercy of all that flesh.

"I can do it. You enjoy your night."

"We were just leaving."

I glance at Lottie, who's standing to grab her bag and nudging Audrey in the ribs. "You were?"

"Yeah, I forgot I have a thing I need to do for Eric for school, and Audrey is my lift."

I roll my lips at the blatant lie and how obvious Lottie is in it.

"But…"

Lottie glares at Audrey. "Audrey, we need to go."

Lottie shakes her head at me and Harrison, who's standing with his hands in his pockets watching the show with amusement barely hidden on his face.

"Oh, yes. You have that thing."

We watch them gather their bags and I walk them to the door.

"Good luck with your thing, you little liar." I laugh as I kiss Lottie goodnight on the cheek.

"What? Did you not see the way he was looking at you? I don't want to be around when that inferno lights."

My heart feels like it stutters in my chest at her words, but I remain silent, not sure how I'm meant to respond to that. I do feel like something is brewing between me and Harrison but I can't deny it frightens me as much as it excites me because he confuses me. He's sweet and protective, in some ways showing me how much of a good man he is but then he reminds me in subtle ways what we really are to one another.

He's gone from the kitchen, the food missing when I return, and I feel disappointment heavy on my shoulders. I begin the clean-up, the metaphor of wiping the surfaces clean not lost on me as I wish I could do the same. Go back and do some things differently, then maybe this story would be different.

I miss Xander and have the overwhelming urge to talk to my brother. I hurry through my tasks before heading up the stairs to my room. I stop outside his room, knowing he's just the other side, so near and yet a million miles away from me. I check on Isaac and he's sleeping soundly, his little fist in his mouth. I tuck the blanket around him and stroke his downy head.

I thought I knew love when my parents adopted me after my own were killed in a fire, but nothing prepares you for the all-consuming love you have as a parent.

I close the door and head for my room, hoping my brother is back in the land of the living. I've no idea what time zone he's in but I've learned he'll either answer or not. Xander is ten years older than me but ever since the day his dad brought home a waif of a child who'd lost her parents in a fire he'd put out, we've had this bond.

He was my protector, my friend, and someone I could always turn to. That is until he left for a life of fame and fortune. We're still close but not as much as we were. He still doesn't know about the accident or that I'm marrying Isaac's father. I just can't find it in me to tell him, knowing how he'll react. He'll want to meet Harrison, and those two are both bossy alpha males that will butt heads for control.

Maybe after the wedding when things have settled, and he isn't in the middle of filming. I dial and wait, wondering if I'll get his voicemail.

"How's my favorite sister?"

A grin creases my face at the sound of his voice. "I'm your only sister."

"And you'd still be my favorite."

"Okay, you can turn it off now, Xand. I'm not one of your fan girls."

"I would if I could, sis."

"Sure. So, tell me where you are right now?"

It's a game we play when he's shooting on location and I live vicariously through him.

"Right now we're in Italy, near Lake Como."

"Oh, wow, I'm so jealous."

"It's beautiful for sure but not all fun. We're filming a scene where I end up in the lake and it's ball-shriveling freezing."

"Eugh, thanks for the visual."

His laugh is deep and comforting and like a piece of home to me.

"You're welcome. Tell me how my gorgeous nephew is."

"Great. He's teething but he babbles like mad now and he's growing like a weed."

"Aww, I need pics, Nor. You haven't sent me any in ages."

Guilt washes over me and I know he'll be furious when he finds out that I hid my accident from him, but that's a worry for another day. "Yeah, I know. I'll send a load over when we get off the phone."

"Good. Now how is the lodge? Still boring as hell?"

"Xander."

My brother never wanted the lodge. He hated the slower pace of life and said it felt stifling. Whereas I felt like I was born to run the place. I miss it even now and wonder if there's a way I can get that part of my life back in some way.

"The lodge is fine, and it's not boring, it's traditional."

"Same thing, but I know you love it so I'll shut up." I hear someone shout in the background and a muffled sound.

"I have to go. We're doing an early morning shoot."

"Okay, be safe. I love you."

"Love you too, baby girl."

I hang up and spam him with pictures of Isaac, a smile on my face. Slipping on my shortie pajamas, I brush my teeth and climb into bed. I open the book Lottie gave me and find my place where the hero is about to sweep the heroine off her feet in an attempt to get her back. I snuggle down, just getting to the good bit when I hear a sound on the monitor. Isaac is unsettled and I'm about to go to him when I see a shadow on the camera.

Harrison strides to the crib and gently lifts our son in his arms. The screen isn't clear because of the dark but I see he's only wearing boxers and I fight my reaction to the sight of his strong body. I see him walk to the changing table and place Isaac on his back, bending to whisper something I don't catch. I feel slightly guilty as I turn the sound louder so I can listen in on this private time between them.

"There, isn't that better? All clean and dry."

My stomach flips at the tone he's using, so tender and full of love. I've never doubted his love for Isaac but seeing this private interaction reminds me of why I'm sacrificing a chance at love for the guarantee of parental love for my son. Whatever Harrison feels for me is, and always will be, secondary to how he loves his son.

"You want to know a secret, Isaac?"

I wait on bated breath for him to divulge this secret, even knowing what I'm doing is wrong.

"You won't know this yet, but you're the luckiest kid alive. Your mommy loves you so much she's willing to marry your grumpy dad, who she hates, just to make you happy."

My chest feels like it's too small for my heart and unbidden tears prick my eyes as he continues.

"I can't promise you everything will be perfect in your life, son, but I can promise that I'll always protect you and your mom, and I'll never let anyone hurt either of you as long as I live."

I want to turn it off, suddenly swamped with emotion at his words. Harrison believes he can't love me, but he doesn't realize that he just showed me more emotion and heart than any boyfriend I ever had before he crashed into my life.

I see him place Isaac back in his crib, tucking the blanket around him, and kissing his head before he leaves the room. I hold my breath as I hear him pause outside my room. I don't know what I want, whether it's for him to come in and show me what I know is between us or whether I need this time to process. He takes the choice away when he walks on and I hear his door close.

The book forgotten, I turn off the light and try to sleep. I find my mind gets tired easily and while I'm almost better, I'm not back to what I was before the accident. My memories of it are still elusive but I get flashes when I least expect them.

I slip into a slumber filled with memories of my childhood at the lodge, my parents, my adopted parents, Xander, and then I'm on the street. I know I'm dreaming but as I smile down at Isaac in the stroller, I see a car barreling toward me. Harrison is behind the wheel, and he's coming straight at us as if he can't see us.

A scream locks in my throat and then I'm being lifted and cradled against a hard chest.

"Norrie, it's me. You're safe, I have you."

A sob escapes me, and I tunnel closer to Harrison's bare chest as if I'm trying to get inside his skin. My heart is racing fast and I can't stop the tears or the abject terror that the dream brought from singeing my skin.

Harrison lifts me and I hold on tight, my fingers digging into his shoulders as he carries me to his room.

"Where are we going?"

He doesn't answer me until he puts me in the warm space in his bed where his body had been just moments before.

"You sleep here now, Norrie. I won't have you suffering alone when I can hold you through it."

I go to speak but then the bed dips and he climbs in beside me, pulling me into his arms and giving me the first sense of true peace I've felt since the car almost took my life. He moves me so my head is on his chest and the feel of warm hard muscle drives any thought of the dream away. Harrison threads his hand through mine and lays it over his heart next to my head that's nestled against his shoulder.

"Harrison?"

He grunts a reply.

"Thank you."

He grumbles something I don't quite catch, and I wonder if he regrets his decision to bring me here, but then he does something wonderful and unexpected, which makes it impossible for me to keep him from shredding what is left of the wall around my heart. He begins to sing my favorite song—"What a Difference a Day Makes" by Dinah Washington.

His voice is low and deep as he tries to keep from waking our son next door.

It's a song that has meant so much to me over the years because my life never seems to change gradually. All the big things that shape my world happen like an explosion. My parents dying as they did, going to live with the fireman that saved me, meeting Harrison, having Isaac, and even the accident. Or maybe especially the accident.

I feel the hot tears fall from my eyes running over the bridge of my nose to settle against his skin and wish I could stop them, but he's unleashed a torrent and I don't know how to stop the flow.

"Don't cry, Norrie. I won't let anything bad happen to you."

His promise only makes me cry harder and he holds me close to him, his lips against my hair and I wish with all my heart he could love me like I love him. But he can't or won't, and I have to accept that and take what he's offering and that's a good life.

Perhaps part of Harrison is enough. He's a good man despite what he might think or how he acts sometimes. He tried to tell me that he was no good. That I should run but he never showed me a single thing to make me turn from him, and he still isn't.

I wish I could tell him the only thing that could hurt me is the one thing he can't protect me from but I don't. I let the tears fall, safe in the knowledge that no harm will come to me or Isaac this night.

Tomorrow is another thing, because as the song says, what a difference twenty-four little hours can make.

10: Harrison

I wake to the feel of soft flesh pressed against my hard cock. My hand has somehow traveled up under her top as we sleep, and I have a palm full of plump breast. My hips rock forward of their own accord seeking out her heat and I almost groan when Norrie arches her spine to meet me, a moan stirring from her throat.

I still, knowing in my subconscious that she's asleep and can't be held responsible for her actions. Her body is made for sin. She's petite but her curves would tempt a saint to commit to the devil and I'm no saint.

Her hips rock again, and I feel my cock slide against her core. Knowing there are only two thin layers of fabric between me and what I want is torture but I can't seem to pull away. I feel the second she wakes, her body going still, her breath rushing out of her in a rush.

I wait for her to scramble away from me, but she doesn't. She takes the hand on her breast and covers it with her own, pressing and flexing as she shows me what she wants.

I close my eyes, pressing my lips to her bare shoulder, the smooth flesh warm and silky. "Are you sure, Norrie?"

"Yes."

I rub her nipple between my fingers, loving the sound of her whimper as she pushes into my hand. I snake my hand down her front, over her ribs, feeling the tiny goosebumps feather over her skin. Easing my hand inside her shorts, I find her small triangle of hair and feel the anticipation of touching her again.

She's wet when I slide my fingers through her, soaked with desire as I stroke through, coating my fingers with her before I circle the bundle of nerves that drives her wild. A breathy moan erupts from her and I feel her hand grip my forearm as I tease her.

"More."

Rolling her, I pull my hand away just as she's about to fall over the edge. Her eyes meet mine and I see frustration flash there as she lets out a little growl that makes my cock weep.

"Patience, Norrie." I lean down to kiss her, and she turns her head away. I growl as I grip her chin in my hand and force her to look at me. "Don't turn away from me, ever."

"I have morning breath."

"I don't give a fuck."

I kiss her hungrily letting my anger show, dominating her until she goes soft and pliant beneath me, and I lift my head. "You want my hands or my mouth?"

"Both."

I smirk at her answer. "I forgot what a greedy girl you are." I kiss my way over her neck as I position myself between her spread thighs. She tastes familiar and exotic all at once and I have to reach into my shorts and grip my cock to keep from coming all over her creamy thighs.

She watches me, her eyes hooded with desire. Here she is, my good girl and I see her watching me for guidance.

"You're so beautiful."

A blush steals over her cheeks as I reach for the hem of her top and move to lift it. Her hand lands on mine, stopping me and my eyes flash to her big brown ones.

"I'm not the same."

My brow furrows in question. "What do you mean?"

"My body is changed. I have marks now that are ugly."

Fury winds through me at her words. I have the overwhelming urge to tear down the social media culture that would make a woman think she's ugly because she's not fitting into a structure of what they consider normal.

I tug her hand away and hold her eyes as I lift her top over her head and expose the perfect tits I've dreamed of. "You are changed." I see shame color her cheeks before I continue. "You were beautiful before, now you're a fucking goddess." I take her hand and wrap her fingers around my dick, which is harder than it's ever been before. Her hand barely touches me before I rock into her palm. "Feel what you do to me. You're beautiful, Norrie."

I dip my head and suckle her breast into my mouth as she continues to stroke me steadily. I flick her nipple with my tongue, and she bucks against me, making her lose her grip on my cock. "Fucking perfect."

I kiss my way to the edge of her shorts before I tug them down to her mid-thigh. Her belly is soft, the skin covered in fine lines that are fading to silver at the edges. My son lay there, grew there while she kept him safe, and let nature ruin her body in her mind but to me, she's never been more beautiful.

I kiss each line as her fingers thread through my own, her grip tightening when I flick her clit with my tongue. My scalp stings and I growl against her skin, nipping her thigh with my teeth. "Open your legs wider. I want to see you."

She's still hesitant so I pull away and stand from the bed. Norrie looks lost lying in the middle with her sleep clothes all askew. I bend and take her in my arms before scooping her up as she gasps and holds tight to my shoulders, her fingernails scoring against my skin.

I stride to the walk-in dressing room, up to the full-length mirror, and set her down.

"What are you doing, Harry?"

"Showing you."

I strip her shorts down her legs abruptly and she looks away from the mirror as I stand behind her and shuck my shorts. We stand together. She's so much smaller in front of me in the mirror, both of us naked but only one of us vulnerable, and despite what she thinks it shouldn't be her.

"Look at yourself."

"Why?"

"Because I need you to see what I see when I look at you." I run my finger over her chin and tip her head back so I can take her lips. She responds instantly, opening for me, trusting me, and I pour every ounce of emotion I can't speak into the kiss I give her.

I pull away and her eyes are languid with desire. "Look."

I turn her face to the glass and run my forefinger over her collarbone and down her chest. The tip catches on her tight nipple and she hisses, her eyes falling shut.

"Eyes open."

She instantly opens her eyes, meeting mine in the reflection.

"Look how you respond to me. Your nipple is tight, aching for more." I cup her heavy breast in my palm. "This body nurtured a life, Norrie."

I smooth my hands down her belly, still flat, and trace the marks where her skin stretched. "This body grew a person. How can anyone hate something that did that?"

"But the women you see at work…."

"Are nothing to me. When I look at you, I see the most beautiful, strong woman and it gets me so fucking hard."

I thread my fingers through the tiny thatch of hair at her core and rub her clit in slow circles. Her eyes are on my hand in the mirror and she looks like a fucking vision. If I do nothing else for her I'm going to make her see how fucking stunning she is, and will always be, to me.

Her head hits my shoulder as she begins to rock against my hand, her desire leaking down her thighs as I push two fingers inside her tight heat. I close my eyes in pleasure, imagining how she feels with her cunt gripping my cock.

"Ride my hand, sweetheart."

I band my arm around her waist, holding her up as her legs begin to shake. She grips my forearm as my name falls from her lips and her pussy squeezes me so tight it's a wonder my fingers don't break and I fucking love it.

"Harrison."

Her cheeks are flushed pink, her hair a mess around her shoulders and I want nothing more than to fuck her until neither of us can think straight. But this is about her, not me, and I'm not done yet.

"Don't move."

I move around her so my back is to the mirror and drop to my knees. She looks down at me, but I still feel like the power is mine, even as I kneel at her feet. She looks at me with eyes almost black with desire as I grip her hips and kiss the lines that cover her lower abdomen.

I grip my cock, stroking from root to tip, my body so turned on by her that it feels like bolts of electricity are running through my skin.

"Open your legs wider, let me see that pretty cunt."

She does as I ask, and I smile, rewarding her with a swipe of my tongue over her engorged clit. She tastes fucking amazing, and I can't believe I lived without this for so long. "Utter perfection."

I tease her, sucking and nibbling on her clit and alternating that with long licks of her sweet pussy. Her hand lands on my head, her fingers threading through my hair and I almost purr like a fucking cat, so fucking whipped by this woman in this second. She owns me. She must never know it but I'd do anything for her.

I grip her ass with both hands as I flick my tongue in a rhythm that makes her cry out and buck into my mouth, her fingers tightening on my hair until it's almost painful. I slide a finger through the cheeks of her ass and feel her press back against me as I skim her ass. She used to love me fucking her ass, so open and excited to try new things, and I can't wait to take her there again, to own every part of her. Now I have forever to introduce her to the pleasure I can give her in every way and indulge in every fantasy.

I move my hand and plunge two fingers into her dripping cunt as her nails scrape my scalp. I drop my other hand and stroke my cock, gripping hard to try and control the pleasure I'm getting from eating her pussy.

Crooking my fingers, I massage that place inside her and she lets out a sound between a whimper and moan, pleasure and pain.

I lift my head and look at her, knowing she can see the wetness of her desire coating my face. "I want you to come all over my face, sweetheart."

I don't wait for an answer. I dip my head and feed like a starving man, flicking, teasing, and fucking her until she releases a long plaintive cry and her knees buckle. I hold on to her as she comes, her pleasure sweet on my tongue, and I coax her down to the floor and kiss her sweet mouth. As she kisses me back like I'm the oxygen she needs to survive, I know I'll never get enough of her.

"That was…. nice."

"Nice?" I laugh as I drag her to me, making her straddle my lap and kiss her again.

"Well, you know, more than nice."

"No, I don't. Tell me, what other adjectives are there?" I'm teasing her and it feels easy like it had before at the lodge.

"Amazing, heavenly, otherworldly."

"Better, but I was thinking earth-shattering and life-changing to start with."

Her smile is sweet but the look in her eye is devilish as her hand grips my cock and I hiss at the contact. "I'm saving those for next time."

Her hand strokes me and I close my eyes. "You need to stop or I'm going to come." She feels too good, and we haven't got time for me to fuck her how I want to, and I don't want to rush the first time between us since we're back together.

"I don't want to stop."

As I lean my back against the glass, Norrie scoots back, her embarrassment and shyness gone. She sits between my legs, and I reach out to thumb her nipple, unable to keep my hands off her perfect body.

"What are you doing?"

She dips her head and I feel her tongue along the underside of my cock, and it takes everything in me not to thrust up into her hot mouth.

"What does it look like I'm doing?"

I huff out a small laugh. "It looks like you're trying to kill me."

"Not kill you, Harrison. Just torture you a little."

"This was meant to be about you."

"This is for me."

I see the heady passion in her eyes as she looks at me, her hand still stroking my cock. This gives her power and that's something I know she's had precious little of these last few years, even before we met.

"Open your mouth, sweetheart, I want to fuck that sweet mouth."

Her smile makes my dick twitch against my belly as I stand and move to her. I take her hair in my hand and wrap the silky strands around my fist as she groans and licks her lip.

"Such a dirty little cock sucker."

Her nipples strain against my thighs as I feed my cock into her waiting mouth. Warm wet heat engulfs me, and we both groan in pleasure. I grip her lightly as I rock in slowly, letting her tongue smooth under my crown and I know it won't take long for me to come down her beautiful throat.

"So, fucking good."

Her cheeks hollow as my pace increases and I know she's getting as much out of this as me, or maybe not as much but she's getting off on this. "Look at me, Norrie."

Her head tips back and her eyes find mine. They're wet with tears and heavy with desire as I fuck her mouth, my dick hitting the soft palate of her throat. I moan, feeling my balls tighten and my spine tingle. She's looking at me with so much hunger and trust, a perfect mix of sweet and dirty, a deadly combination and I can't hold back.

I thrust forward and spill my come into her mouth with a roar of pleasure so strong I have to reach out and grab the wall to stop my legs from going underneath me. I pull out and watch her as she swallows down every drop of my come before wiping her hand across her mouth. I reach down and help her to her feet, bringing her close to my body and cupping her cheeks in my hands.

"Are you okay? Did I hurt you?"

Suddenly the realization that I just fucked her face hard when she's barely recovered from a brain injury slams into me and feel like a piece of shit.

"No, you didn't hurt me. I wanted that. I liked it."

I kiss her gently, my mind getting the memo too late that she's still fragile and it's like she reads my mind.

"I'm not broken, Harrison, and I don't want you treating me like I am. If I don't want something, I'll be sure to tell you."

"Good girl."

Her body seems to preen as she slides her arms around my neck and kisses me again.

"Thank you."

My brow furrows. "What for?"

"Making me feel beautiful."

"Sweetheart, I have two things to say about that. One, you're beautiful and sexy as fuck, and two, it was definitely my pleasure."

A loud cry comes through the monitor and we laugh, knowing the bubble is well and truly burst for the day.

"Go shower. I got this."

"You sure?"

"Yes, you smell like sex. If you don't shower it off, I'll never be able to leave for work, because I'll want to stay home and fuck you and I want to finish early so we can go shopping."

"Shopping?"

I point to her hand. "Ring shopping."

It's past time I got her an engagement ring and made it official. I hadn't wanted to before because I was giving her time to come around to it without being too overbearing, or at least any more overbearing.

"Do I need one?"

I move into her and grip her hips, my dick growing hard between us again at the feel of her soft skin. "Yes. I want this to be real."

She smiles and my heart seems to miss a beat in my chest at the sight.

"So do I."

"Good, now go before I change my mind and fuck you instead."

"Well, we can't have that, can we?"

Her question makes me laugh and I swat her ass to get her moving. "Go."

I watch her retreat, her ass swaying temptingly as I go to pull on shorts so I can feed my son his breakfast.

I can't wait to get home, because now I've had her again I need more, and I haven't even left yet.

11: Norrie

Lottie had arrived ten minutes ago to look after Isaac while we went shopping for an engagement ring. It felt surreal even saying it. I was engaged to Harrison Brooks. Genius, billionaire, father of my child, and I was beginning to realize the man who could break my heart if I let him.

His mixture of sweet, bossy, grumpy, sex god was my kryptonite, but I'd be a fool not to heed his warnings of not loving me. I've lost nearly every person I've loved in my life except for Isaac and Xander, and I'm wary about putting myself in that position again, especially knowing how he feels.

Yes, the sex is amazing. Yes, he's a wonderful father. Yes, he cares for me, but that's Harrison. He takes care of people. He makes sure everyone is okay, but he doesn't let people in and that's something I need to keep reminding myself.

Harrison walks through the front door as I'm pulling on my sandals. He looks at me and my skin prickles with awareness at the hunger in his eyes as he strides across the space separating us. He grips my arms and kisses me lightly on the mouth, pulling back as I lean into him.

He smirks as if he can read my mind. "Ready to go?"

"Almost, I just need to grab my bag and say goodbye to Isaac."

He takes my hand and tugs me toward the living room where Lottie has Isaac on her knee, chatting away to him like they're old friends. She looks up and sees us, her eyes moving to our joined hands. A knowing smile plays on her lips and I can almost read her thoughts and know there'll be a text thread in our group chat when I get home.

I snatch my bag off the couch and lean down to kiss Isaac's head. "Be a good boy for aunty Lottie."

"He'll be an angel, won't you, son?"

Harrison kisses him and then we're out the door, Harrison holding the car door for me as I get in the back seat. Nerves flutter softly in my belly as the car drives us into Manhattan. Harrison seems to sense it and reaches for my hand, uncurling my fingers from the death grip I have on my bag.

"Relax."

"Easy for you to say, you're used to all this."

He cocks his head as if he's thinking about what I said. "All what?"

"Money, people bowing and scraping to you."

"I am now, but at first, I found it strange. I didn't grow up rich. I was dirt poor most of my life. Only in the past ten years have I had any kind of wealth."

His words bring me up short and I realize how little I actually know about the man I'm about to marry. I sigh and look out of the window. "I guess I assumed."

"What is it?"

His hand grips my knee, and I can feel his thumb making small circles on my bare thigh. I'd worn the nicest dress I owned, which is a cream silk skater style with a vee neck and no sleeves. My sandals are pale gold and strappy and more suited to a night out, but they're all I have. Harrison has tried to get me to spend his money on clothes, but it doesn't feel right. I'm not a kept woman. I pull my weight.

"I need to get the rest of my stuff shipped up from the lodge."

"We could go up this weekend and spend a few days there. You can pack what you want and ship the rest."

My eyes move over his handsome face, and I see nothing but genuine willingness. "Really?" I try and curb my excitement at the thought of going home, but he sees through me.

"Yes of course."

I lean across the car and cup his face, kissing him in gratitude. "Thank you."

He smiles against my mouth. "My pleasure."

I feel lighter as we arrive at the jeweler on 5th Avenue and let him take my hand and guide me out of the car that has stopped at the curb outside a well-known and high-end store. When I say well known, I mean by name because I sure as hell have never set foot in here. We reach the door, and it opens with a flourish as a man in a sleek black suit ushers us inside past the security guard.

"Mr. Brooks, what a pleasure to see you."

Harrison winks at me and I feel my tummy flutter. "Mr. Drake, we spoke on the phone." He turns to me and pulls me close to his side, his arm winding around my back. "This is my stunning fiancée, Nora Richards."

Mr. Drake thrusts his hand at me. "It's a pleasure to meet you, Miss Richards."

"Oh, please call me Nora."

He nods, his lips pursed. "Nora it is. Now, I have a selection of rings picked out for you to look at but if you see anything else you like, feel free to point it out."

He leads us to the back of the store where there are two glasses of Champagne waiting for us. Harrison hands me one and I take a sip, wrinkling my nose at the bubbles. The truth is I hate the stuff, but I choke down a sip to be polite.

Harrison leans into my ear and I feel his breath tickle my neck. "Don't drink it if you don't like it, Norrie."

I smile wide. "It's fine."

Harrison turns to Mr. Drake. "Can we have some tea?"

He doesn't explain or elaborate just makes the request like it's his right. Mr. Drake nods accordingly as if it's his job to make our life easier, and I guess it is. I work in the hospitality trade and while this is slightly different, it's still all about the customer experience. The difference is the commission he'll get if we buy a ring.

"Thank you."

"Never be afraid to ask me for what you want, Norrie. If it's in my power to give it, I will."

I feel all warm inside at his words and then the tray of rings is put in front of me and I feel like I might go blind from the amount of bling. Diamonds in every size and shape are laid out before me and I track each one, feeling more and more out of my depth. These must cost more than what the lodge is worth.

"Do you see any you like, Nora?"

Mr. Drake is looking at me with hope and excitement in his eyes and I'm sure he's used to seeing brides die with excitement but that's not me. "They are all stunning." I turn to Harrison, but he's looking at me with an expression I can't decipher. "What do you like?"

"I like you."

I can't help but smile at his response, but it doesn't help me. "Thank you, but I meant the rings."

"Why don't you try a few on so you can get an idea of how each style looks on your hand?"

"Okay."

My hand shakes slightly and sweat dots my brow, even though the air conditioning is the perfect temperature.

Mr. Drake hands me a tear-drop-shaped diamond in a white gold setting, and I slide it on my finger. I thank God my nails are clean and tidy, even if they lack the polished manicure I'm sure he sees on most brides in his store.

"What do you think?"

I don't want to offend anyone, and the words get stuck in my throat as I speak. "I... um...I."

"Give us a minute."

Harrison's hand lands on my lower back and the weight of it anchors me. I'm seconds away from a panic attack and he seems to sense it.

Mr. Drake dips his head and disappears.

Harrison turns to look at me, his hands gripping my arms, his hands stroking gently up and down in a soothing motion. "Talk to me. What's wrong?"

"I don't know."

"Yes, you do. You just need to say it."

"I don't belong here."

"Why not?"

I shake my head. "Because."

"Because isn't an answer, Norrie. Why don't you think you belong here?"

"Because I don't deserve it."

"Why would you say that?"

"I'm just a kid with no parents who gets given all these things she doesn't deserve. I'm nothing."

"You are everything, you hear me. You deserve all the nicest things because you're a good person."

"So are lots of people."

He dips his head to catch my gaze. "That's true, but do you think Audrey doesn't deserve what she has, or me, or Isaac? We're all in a position of privilege."

"Yes, but that's different. You worked hard and used your brains. Audrey is a woman dominating a man's world, and Isaac is my son. Of course I think he deserves the world."

"And you survived, losing first your birth parents to a fire and then your adopted parents to a car crash. You took the business they left and turned it into something magnificent. You put yourself through college without any help, and you gave me the greatest gift a man could ask for in my son."

"I had help, with college. Xander paid for some of it."

"Xander?"

"My brother."

"Oh, the deadbeat you never hear from."

It hurts to hear him say that about Xander, but it's my own fault.

I've hidden his identity from Harrison, knowing that once they meet, I'll fade into the background. For some reason, I always want to be the star of the show around Harrison, not the little sister of the big, famous movie star. Only now he has an unfair opinion of him and I can't defend him without admitting to another lie, and we were just starting to get to a good place. I'll fix it and explain it but not now. Perhaps I can tell him and explain after the wedding.

"Norrie."

I blink out of my musings and find I'm calmer, my minor freak-out forgotten under the weight of my secrets. "I know you're right. Let's have another look."

Harrison stares at me as if trying to figure out a mathematical puzzle he can't grasp.

"I'm fine. I just got overwhelmed but I'm fine now. Call Mr. Drake back."

"Are you sure? We can forget this and go home if you want?"

"You would do that?"

Harrison nods at me. "Of course, we can look online."

My heart feels like it might burst with the emotion I feel for him. He truly sees me and likes me, warts and all. This is the man I met last year at my family home. It feels like we're finding our way back to each other, the things I hid from him and the damage I did slowly being eroded. I ignore the niggle at the back of my mind telling me I need to be honest about Xander. I want to bathe in this light for a little longer before my famous brother takes the limelight back.

"I love that you'd do that for me, but no. Let's find me a ring."

He loops his arm around my waist and pulls me close to kiss my temple and my knees go weak as I close my eyes and soak this moment in.

"Mr. Drake, we're ready."

Mr. Drake appears from the back room with a smile on his face, which I return. He wants the commission and I get that, but he seems like a nice man too.

"Is it possible to see some colored stones?"

"Yes of course and if I may, I think we have something that I think would look divine on your delicate hand."

"You may."

Mr. Drake rushes off and I smile at Harrison. I point at the rings on the black velvet tray. "Do you like any of these?"

"They're all perfectly nice."

"Yeah, that's the problem. They're nice but not amazing."

"If I recall, you used nice to describe something else this morning."

My grin widens. "I did, didn't I? Perhaps I misspoke because of a lack of oxygen in my brain."

"Is that so?"

"Uh-huh."

His head dips and his lips find my neck. "Maybe we should ban that word from your vocabulary."

"Maybe we should."

"Here we are."

Harrison lifts his head, not caring in the least that he's been caught kissing my neck. But he runs a sex club, one I haven't even seen. I'm intrigued and wonder now things are more open with us if I can persuade him to take me there one day.

"Eyes on the rings, Norrie."

I glance down and that's when I see it, the ring from my Pinterest board. "Oh my." I reach out to touch the emerald-cut pink diamond surrounded by tiny white diamonds in a geometric design.

"It's beautiful isn't it?"

Mr. Drake hands it to Harrison who slides the ring on my finger. It fits like it was made for me and I can't help the tears that sting my eyes, blurring the beauty of the ring on my hand.

"What do you think, sweetheart? Do you like it?"

I nod as I cover my mouth with my fingers to keep the sob from breaking free. Harrison wipes my tears with his thumbs, and I choke out a laugh, embarrassed at my over-the-top reaction.

"Now that's the reaction we wanted."

"It's perfect."

"We'll take it."

"No, Harrison, this ring must cost a fortune."

He angles me to look at him. "I don't give a fuck how much it costs, that reaction right there is worth every penny."

"I don't know what to say."

He stuns me with his next move as he drops to his knee and takes my hand.

"Nora Richards, will you marry me?"

I nod, this moment feeling so surreal like it's happening to another person. "Yes."

Harrison kisses me and I know I shouldn't hold on to the hope blooming in my chest. That I should rein in my excitement because this isn't real. But it feels real, so I ignore the warning in my head and let my heart rule instead.

"Let me just ring this up for you."

Mr. Drake rushes off to put the sale through and I look down at my hand again where the diamond sparkles.

"You should see the look on your face."

I shake my head. "You have no idea what this means to me."

"I think I might."

"No, honestly, since I was a girl I dreamed of getting married. This ring is almost a perfect match to the one I always imagined wearing one day."

"Then I'm glad I could make at least one of your dreams come true."

I grasp his face and pull him close, feeling the bristle of stubble under my fingers. "I'm going to rock your world later."

"You rocked my world this morning, sweetheart, and you don't need to do anything to pay me back. This is my way of saying thank you for saying yes. I know it's not something you wanted, and you're doing it for Isaac, and even though I can't love you, I want you to know I care and I want this to work."

His words sting, almost popping the bubble of joy but I push it away. He doesn't love me but maybe that's for the best. Love has never turned out well for me anyway.

"Even so, thank you."

"You're welcome."

We head home in companionable silence, my eyes sliding to the ring on my finger and the promise it represents. I may not be worthy of a man like Harrison Brooks, but my son is and that's what matters.

"I'll walk you in."

I start at his voice. "Are you going out?"

"I have to head into the club, something came up."

"Oh, okay." I hate the disappointment I feel at his announcement or the kernel of doubt that eases beneath my skin.

"I won't be long."

"It's fine. You have to work right, and God knows I've taken up enough of your time this last month or so."

Harrison frowns. "That doesn't matter to me."

"Well, it should. You need to work, and I need to bathe Isaac and make some calls about the wedding stuff."

"Are you sure you're okay?"

I smile brightly. "Of course."

"I want you in my bed tonight."

"Oh."

"Oh?"

"What do you want me to say?"

"That you'll be in there when I get home."

I'm not sure I can stomach being in his bed when he gets back and risk smelling other women on him. "I need to go."

"Norrie?"

"Fine. Now I need to go, my feet hurt from standing." I rush up the steps and head inside closing the door. I hear the car pull away and close my eyes. *Way to go, Nora, he just did the sweetest thing and you reacted like a freaking maniac because you're jealous.*

"Hey, how did it go?"

I lift my head and see Lottie watching me with Isaac in her arms. "Great. It went great."

I kick off my shoes and walk toward her with my arms out,

wanting my son in my arms. She hands him over and follows me into the living area.

"So did you get a ring?"

"Yes." I flash my hand at her, and she grabs it gushing about how beautiful it is and how perfect it is for me and then I burst into tears.

12: Harrison

I HEAR THEIR VOICES AS THEY WALK DOWN THE HALLWAY AND WISH I had an office I could lock so I could have some peace. Today had been fucking confusing and I wasn't sure how to feel about it.

"Here he is, the daddy."

I roll my eyes at Ryker. "Don't call me that."

He laughs as he sinks down into the chair opposite me. "What? It's true."

"Yes, but the way you say it makes it sound degenerate."

Beck laughs as he heads for the cabinet where we keep our liquor. "He has a point, Ryk."

"Whatever. So how is the delectable Nora?"

I growl at his use of the word delectable and her in the same sentence and know I walked right into his trap. "Norrie is fine. We went ring shopping today."

"And why is that making you frown so hard?" Beck leans against the cabinet, his arms crossed, waiting for my answer.

"I don't know. It was all fine and then she started acting weird."

"Weird how?"

I toss the pen I was doodling with on my desk and sigh. "Are we really doing this, gossiping like a fucking knitting circle?"

"Ooh, gossip."

I groan as Audrey walks in wearing leather pants and a red bodice. She's clearly been using the third floor tonight and I'm not in the mood for her brand of bullshit.

"Nothing."

"Lies. Harrison took Nora ring shopping and then she acted weird."

"What did you do?"

I find myself on the wrong end of her accusatory glare and throw up my hands. "Nothing."

"You must have done something."

Her hands fly to her hips, and she looks ready to go to war for Norrie. I love that for my girl, I just hate that it's aimed at me. "Not necessarily. Head injuries can cause erratic mood swings."

Beck moves to sit on the couch and Audrey sits beside him, taking his drink and knocking back half of it.

"It didn't seem like it was a mood swing, but I guess it could be."

"Exactly. You don't really know this girl apart from one week in her bed which is six days too many if you ask me."

I give Ryker a cold glare. "I didn't."

It doesn't deter him at all.

"All I'm saying is you don't know much about her. She has no social to speak of, no family apart from a brother who you've never met, and you're about to hitch your life to hers."

"Ryker is right. What do you know about her?"

Beck is watching me carefully. He likes Norrie and he knows perhaps more about her medical history than I do because of his position but he'd never betray his Hippocratic oath.

"Her parents died in a fire when she was a kid. The fireman who rescued her and his wife went on to adopt her. They died when she was nineteen in a car accident. She owns Pine Lodge and has a brother who's ten years older than her and does a bit of acting. They're apparently close, but she doesn't see him a lot."

My chest aches at the thought of all the losses she's had to endure in her short life. That she can still smile and be such a warm, giving person is a miracle really.

"Shit. Poor, Norrie. She never told me any of this." Audrey takes a sip of her drink, and I can see she's as affected by this as I am.

"She's very private."

"She could still be a raving lunatic for all you know, especially after what she's been through."

Anger makes my fist tighten. "She's not a lunatic and watch your mouth when speaking about her or I'm going to ram my fist down your throat."

"Oh, God. He's going all Linc on us."

"Did I hear my name?" Linc strides through the door and takes the seat beside Ryker.

"I was just saying Harry is being all sensitive and precious about Nora like you were with Lottie."

"I'm nothing like that," I vehemently deny.

"Hey, I wasn't sensitive."

We all look at Linc who has the audacity to look offended.

"You were a dick."

Linc glares at his cousin who just laughs. "So, what did you do?"

I frown at Linc. "Why does everyone think it was me?"

"Because we're emotionally stunted pricks, and she's little Miss Sunshine. Also, Lottie told me she burst into tears when she got back from ring shopping so...." He shrugs his shoulders and pretends to balance something in his hands, but he's smirking, the jerk.

I sit forward sharply suddenly interested in what he has to say. "What the hell? What did she say?"

Linc shrugs and stands to get himself a drink.

"Pour me one of those." I think I might need it.

He hands me the whiskey and I knock it back in one gulp, the burn coating my chest in heat.

"So, tell us what Lottie said."

"Not much, just that Nora was upset and burst into tears. Apparently, she thinks you're fucking anything in a skirt here at the club."

I shoot to my feet and pace the space in front of my desk. "What? Why would she think that?"

"Do you plan to be faithful?"

I give Ryker a cool glare. "Of course I do."

"Have you told her that?"

I run my thumb over my bottom lip as I think back over our past conversations. Have I told her that? "Do I need to? I proposed and she said yes. Surely it's a given?"

Audrey slaps her forehead with her hand. "Why are men so stupid?"

"Is that rhetorical? Because I can probably find you a scientific paper you can read on it," Beck offers with a smirk.

"Yeah, no thanks. I don't need a paper. I have enough evidence in this room."

"I find that offensive," Linc states.

Beck twirls his glass with his fingers. "She's probably right though."

"Can we please stay on topic? You assholes are meant to be my friends."

"Okay, we're listening. It's Project Help Harry Out of the Doghouse."

I rub the back of my neck. "Does she really believe I'd come to work and fuck the staff or the clientele?"

"Does she know about the club?"

I pause because I know Beck won't like the answer. I broke the rules by telling her without an NDA and if this was anyone else, I'd be the one going ballistic.

"You told her."

"I didn't mean to."

"Jesus Christ, Harrison."

"I know, I should have made her sign something, but she won't say anything. She'd never do anything to harm our son."

"And is he your son? Have you confirmed that?"

I glance at the drawer where the unopened envelope sits with the results. They came weeks ago but I haven't opened them. In my heart I know he's mine, and while that envelope is closed, I don't have to face the pain if he turns out not to be my son. "I have the results."

"And?" Ryker rolls his hand like I'm a child he's forcing a confession out of.

I move behind my desk, putting it between me and the others like a barrier that will save me from their ridicule. "I haven't opened them."

"Why not?"

It's Audrey who asks and somehow, she does it in a way that doesn't make me feel like an idiot. I shrug as if I don't know but the truth is, it's fear that the child I've grown to love will turn out to be another man's and I'm not sure I could take that.

"Want me to open them?"

Beck steps up to the desk and I nod. I open the locked drawer and pull out the innocuous white envelope and hand it to him. I can feel my heart beating so fast it's almost out of my chest as he tears it open.

Silence is heavy in the room, and it feels like the air is stuck in my chest but I give no outward sign that I'm terrified. I see his eyes scan the document his face a complete mask and I wonder if this is what he's like with his patients.

"Well?"

He lowers the paper and looks at me before a smile breaks out on his face. "Congratulations, Harrison, you're the proud father of Isaac Richards, soon to be Brooks."

Relief makes my shoulders sag and the air whooshes from my lungs on a laugh. "Really?"

He hands me the paper and there it is in black and white. Isaac is my son, and it feels amazing. I never wanted this or asked for it but I'll be forever grateful that Norrie gave me parenthood.

"This calls for a celebration."

Linc is on his feet, popping the cork on a bottle of Champagne we keep in the fridge. Ryker is grabbing glasses and Audrey comes over and hugs me.

"Congrats, Harrison. I can already see what an amazing father you are, and Isaac is lucky to have you."

"Thank you."

Ryker hands out the glasses and Beck raises his glass. "To Harrison and his super swimmers."

"To Harrison."

We clink our glasses and take a sip of the bubbles and it reminds me of Norrie earlier, and I have the overwhelming need to see her and share this moment with her. I take another sip and push the feeling away. It's this exact thing that I can't afford to let into my life. When you yearn for something you can't control, it has the ability to hurt you, so I don't let myself. I can't stop the pang of regret that my life is this way.

I hoist my glass and look around the room at the people who gave me a family when I felt like I had none. "To friendship."

"Friendship."

They all toast and I laugh as Ryker throws his arm around my shoulder. "Now what are we going to do about your little situation with, Norrie?"

"I'll talk to her and find out why she's upset."

"You need to tell her you're not fucking other women, dumbass."

I turn to Audrey who's relaxing on the couch, her feet on the table. I think we're the only ones she allows to see this side of her. To the outside world, she's the picture-perfect vision of a woman of power and control, to us she's still the tag-along cousin who acted as the best wingman in history.

"I can't believe she'd think I would after I proposed marriage. I'm a lot of things, but I'm not a cheat."

Audrey rolls her eyes. "We know that, but does she? Ryker might be a doofus but he has a point. You two don't know each other very well, and this isn't a love marriage. She might think you won't be faithful because of that."

I instantly reject the notion of me with another woman, and the thought of another man touching what is mine makes white-hot anger burn in my gut. "I disagree. It's a real marriage and there's love, just not romantic love. I love my son."

"It's not the same, sweetie, and Norrie is a romantic. I'm totally breaking the girl code right now, but do you know she's had a Pinterest board about her perfect wedding since she was fifteen? Every single detail is pinned there, from the flowers to the dress, the ring, and the venue. All of it. This is a big deal to her."

I hate that I didn't know this, that I was in the dark about something so significant to her. I meant what I said, I want her to be happy because one day Isaac will look to us as an example and I want it to be positive for him. "Show me."

Audrey purses her lips. "I shouldn't, it's a breach of her trust."

"Please?"

I don't ask for much from my friends and because of that when I do they always step up.

"Fine. But you can't tell her, I'll do that myself."

"I won't say a word."

Audrey stands and goes to sit behind the desk as I crowd behind her, vaguely listening to the guys talk shit to each other. Usually, I'd be in the thick of it. It might sound like trash talk but it's how we are and I know they'd have my back in a heartbeat. Fuck, they've proven it over the last few weeks with every action they've taken to support me and I won't forget it.

"Here, just scroll through."

I hover my finger over the trackpad and begin scrolling through the images. Some of the things I see make me grimace, like releasing butterflies and doves but others, like the flowers and the setting, make me smile. This is Norrie to a T. The soft peachy pink colors, the lake, and especially the dress that I can already imagine her wearing as she walks toward me.

"Is this the dress she bought?"

"Not even close."

I tip my head. "Why?"

"I don't know. But if I'm guessing, which I am, then it's because she doesn't feel right having this wedding when it's clear it's only happening because she got pregnant."

"But I want her to have this."

"Then tell her that."

"What if she uses my weakness to manipulate me?"

Audrey cocks her head to the side and watches me like a bug under a microscope. "You care about her."

"Of course I care about her wellbeing, she's the mother of my son."

Audrey shakes her head. "No, you really care about her. If I'm not mistaken, you're in love with her."

"Nonsense."

"Deny it all you want but you are."

I slam the laptop lid closed and stand. "You're being annoying."

"Maybe but it's true. You love her and it scares the crap out of you."

"I'm going home to sort this mess out and clear up any silly notions she has. Then you're going to make sure she plans the wedding she wants."

Audrey grins.

"Stop that."

"Stop what?"

"That incessant smiling."

"You love her."

"I do not, and if you carry on with this ridiculousness, I'm going to call Hudson and give him a VIP membership free for a year."

Hudson was at college with us, although not one of our friend groups. Audrey and Hudson do not get on, although I find him palatable enough.

Audrey's jaw drops. "You wouldn't dare."

"Yes, I would. Now, do we have a deal?"

"Fine, but I can't wait to rub your face in it when you finally come to your senses."

I walk out the door leaving my friends to party without me. I have a fiancée to appease and then I'm going to fuck her until she never doubts my fidelity again.

13: Norrie

I stand on the landing and look between my bedroom door and his, debating what I should do. He told me he wanted me in his bed, but then the next breath he was out the door to the club. Delaying having to make a choice, I move to check on Isaac.

He's sleeping soundly, happy and peaceful, all his needs met. He's none the wiser about how much emotional turmoil is in my head and that's as it should be. I stroke his downy head and my heart fills with love as his little lips pout into a moue. My eyes catch on the ring I now wear and I don't know how to feel.

When I picked this style out years ago I had so many hopes and dreams. My life was happy, and I had a future filled with unlimited possibilities. Now it feels like my life has been planned for me and I'm merely a chess piece being moved around the board with no knowledge of the rules.

I sigh and exit the gorgeous nursery Harrison had made for Isaac. It's everything I would've chosen for him and I'm not sure I thanked him for it, but he's like a whirling dervish in my life. He scatters my thoughts and makes me forget everything or maybe that's just me. I've always been scatterbrained but now it's worse.

I find myself back on the landing debating my next move. In the end, I retreat to the room I've made my own for the last few weeks. I shower and brush my teeth before putting on my pajamas and climbing between the sheets.

I should text Lottie and apologize for earlier. I hadn't meant to burst into tears but the whole day had been so emotional, and it got the better of me. When she'd wrapped me in her arms and hugged me, the floodgates had opened. I'd admitted how much it upset me that he went to the club and spent time with those women when he was meant to be mine.

Now though in the darkness, I can admit the truth. It's not just that, it's that I know he'll never be mine. Harrison is a handsome, clever, genius and I'm just me. A small-town girl who has an empty savings account and a mediocre degree in hospitality.

Lottie seemed to think Harrison would never do that, but I know how much of a sexual person he is, and he hasn't been getting it from me. I guess I can't blame him, he never promised fidelity or asked for it. Perhaps that's my future, both of us continuing the ruse for our son while finding what pleasure we can elsewhere.

The thought leaves a bitter taste in my mouth. I'm so done with crying and being sad today, so I push the thought away, putting it in a lockbox in my brain and sealing it tight. It's something my adopted mom, Mary, taught me, and it works. Over the years I've become a genius at burying painful thoughts and emotions, although sometimes they explode in the form of a panic attack.

Closing my eyes, I let my imagination take me away to a happy place filled with snowy mountains and Christmas lights. I love winter and Christmas and can't wait to spend my first one as a mother. All the little traditions we'll forge together and as I fall asleep I'm happy again.

Turning my face, I seek out the warmth as I feel my body lifted into a pair of muscular arms. A familiar fresh scent wraps around me as if he's just showered, and even in my half-asleep state, I know it's Harrison.

"I thought I said I wanted you in my bed, sweetheart."

His chest rumbles as he speaks and I don't want to argue with him, so I snuggle closer, pressing my lips against his neck. "Sleepy."

His chuckle is sexy as hell. "Nice try, gorgeous, but we're going to talk about this in the morning, among other things."

I vaguely wonder what else he wants to talk about but then I'm in his bed and he's sliding in behind me and pulling my back to his front. His arm lies across my middle as if he's scared I'll try and escape in the middle of the night. If he only knew that I never meant to escape him, I just want him to love me, and that's the sad, pathetic truth. I want his love which is the only thing he can't give me.

Awake now, I feel every part of my body tingle with the need for him. It's like an out-of-control avalanche of desire. I press my legs together to ease the ache that's building from having him close and touching me in such an intimate setting. I wriggle, trying to get comfortable and still as I feel the hard evidence of his erection against my butt.

"Keep still, Norrie."

I draw in a breath at his words. I could do as he says, or I could turn over and take what I know he'll give me. Do I dare? Do I want to cross that final hurdle? Before I can second-guess myself, I roll over and face him. His hand rests on my hip, his eyes on me in the almost dark. From the sliver of light, I can see him watching me.

I reach up and trace my fingers over his lips. He's so beautiful it should be a crime. His body is hard in all the right places. I let my fingers move over his collarbone, tracing the planes of his chest and he hisses when my fingertips graze his nipple.

"What are you doing, Norrie?"

"Isn't that obvious?"

I dip my head and kiss his neck, as his hand flexes on my hip.

"We need to talk first."

I shake my head, I don't want to talk, I want to feel. "No. Just fuck me, Harrison."

A growl grumbles from his chest and it makes desire pool in my belly, hot and heavy. My clit pulses from just the sounds he makes, and

I know I want this. Whatever other doubts I have in this moment, I want to feel him inside me.

He rolls so he's looming over me, his legs tangled with mine, his bulging biceps on either side of my head. I should feel trapped, but Harrison has only ever made me feel safe.

"Are you sure?"

I see caution in his eyes as if he's weighing something up and I don't want him to reject me, so I lean up and kiss him. He seems unsure, as if he's holding back, but then it's like a switch is flipped and he takes over. I whimper in relief and press against him.

His tongue slides between my lips and consumes me. This is no gentle kiss; this is an assault on my senses. He overwhelms me in the best way, his taste, the soft firm lips that are now trailing over my neck.

I moan as I run my hands over his back, feeling the muscle and sinew move. His strength is evident, but he's always aware of how much bigger he is than me.

"Fuck, I've been dreaming about touching you."

He takes my hand and pulls it down his body and clamps it over his hard cock through his boxers. I squeeze and he groans. It's masculine and sexy and I want more.

"Touch me."

He doesn't make me beg, he lets go of my hand and skims it up and over my ribs, taking my flimsy pajama top with him. He's as hungry and desperate as I am, his lips finding my nipple before he can even finish removing my clothes. I love that he wants me as much as I want him. I want him wild and uncontrolled, but I still sense he's holding back.

His teeth nip at my sensitive skin. I cry out arching into him as his thumb and forefinger find my other nipple and roll the tight bud until I think I might climax just from that.

He pulls away and I moan in frustration which makes him laugh.

"Patience, sweetheart."

I stroke his cock and he drops his head with a moan as his hips rock into my hand.

"Enough."

He pulls from my grip and flips me to my front and suddenly my shorts are yanked down to my thighs as he hoists me to my knees. I'm open and vulnerable to his gaze as he smooths a hand down my spine and over my ass.

"Love this ass. Gonna fuck it, but not tonight."

My pussy tightens and pulses at his words and I feel empty and needy for him to fill me. I feel the head of his cock at my entrance as he rubs the tip teasingly along my lips.

"This what you want?"

I'm almost lightheaded with desire and the word is a breathy whimper as I reply. "Yes."

"Say it. Say you want my cock in that needy pussy."

"Yes."

His hand lands hard on my ass and the pain makes me blink before his warm hand smooths over the skin of my ass and the tingle of pain turns to pleasure. Again, he swipes his cock through my soaking pussy, teasing me.

"You like that, sweetheart? Your pussy sure does."

He knows what I like, we spent a week exploring every fantasy I had and some I hadn't known about, and this is just part of it. He likes me to beg, and I like his praise. "Yes, I love it."

"That's my good girl. Now ask me."

"I want your cock inside me."

Before I can finish the sentence, he's pushing into me and I hum with the sweet pleasure of being filled by him. He grips my hips tightly and I wish I could see how magnificent he looks like this.

"Fuck, you feel like heaven."

He leans over me and kisses my shoulder, gently. "Gonna fuck you now, Norrie, and I need you to be quiet."

I nod, willing to give him anything he wants if he'll just move. "Okay."

He feels so deep as he strokes out and slams back into me, bottoming out, his balls hitting my pussy.

"Jesus, I missed this."

His words make pleasure radiate through my entire body.

"You like me saying how much I missed you, Norrie. Your pussy just soaked my cock."

His hand tangles in my hair as he pulls me up until I'm pressed against his front. Harrison angles my neck so he can kiss me deeply, the sounds of our harsh breathing mingling with the sound of flesh slapping on flesh. It's base and animalistic, and I love it.

I wind my arm around his neck as his hand moves to cup my breast, teasing the peak as the other hand moves lower. At this angle, he's hitting my g-spot perfectly and I can feel my climax building with every stroke.

"You gonna come all over my cock, Norrie?"

I nod because his finger flicks over my clit and speech becomes impossible. Two seconds later he's swallowing my cry of pleasure and holding me so I don't collapse as my orgasm splinters inside me. My vision goes black, stars exploding behind my closed eyelids.

"Your cunt is squeezing my cock so hard, Norrie."

His words cause a second aftershock, and he chuckles and pulls out. I moan but he flips me to my back and slams back into me.

"Want to look at your gorgeous face as I fuck you."

His face is hard, the soft look in his eyes the only indication of how he feels. His cheeks are slashed high with color, his lips pursed in determination. He looks like the ultimate warrior, strong, proud, focused, and I know I'll never have this with anyone else. He plays my body like a maestro.

"You're so fucking beautiful it hurts to look at you sometimes."

"Harrison."

He doesn't let me finish what I was going to say, which is just as well because I'm incoherent. He kisses me as he chases his climax, hitching my knee high so he can get deeper. The position causes his pelvis to rub against my clit and I feel pleasure sweep through me on every upward stroke. I'm gonna come again and he can feel it as he pulls his head away and his eyes land on me.

"Come for me, sweetheart."

Moments later I'm crying out his name as he stills, his hot come spilling inside me as he roars against my neck. His weight on me is one of my favorite things but all too soon he's rolling us so I'm on top of him, our joined release sticky between us.

"You came inside me."

I should feel angry that he did that, but this is as much on me as on him. I don't believe it's up to him more than it is up to me to protect myself.

His hand slips down my belly and I can feel him slide two fingers into the mingled evidence of our desire before pushing them inside me.

"Gonna put a baby in you."

"What?"

His fingers are distracting as he continues to try and push his come back inside my body and despite my shock, I find I'm turned on by it. What the hell is wrong with me that I find him being so dominant and overbearing sexy as fuck?

He withdraws his fingers and smooths them over my belly before bringing his hand up and sucking it into his mouth. It's dirty and filthy, and I feel my body hum with pleasure as his eyes close.

"We taste fucking amazing together."

"We need to talk about this."

His eyes go flinty, but he tugs me closer. "Oh, we're gonna talk about it and the fact you think I'd fuck other women when I'm engaged to you, but not now. Now we're going to sleep because I'm in a good mood and feeling mellow and I don't want that to end just yet."

I could argue with him, but I feel the same and I have a horrible feeling I'm not going to fare well in this conversation so tomorrow is soon enough.

14: Harrison

I WAKE UP EARLY AS THE SOUND OF ISAAC BABBLING IN HIS CRIB reaches my ears. I roll gently away from the soft, spent woman in my arms, regret sweeping through me that I have to leave her in bed without making her come. She must be exhausted because she doesn't even react to the movement. I woke in the night only hours after having had her and needed her again. I woke her with my mouth and we made love, slowly this time. No words were spoken, just sensual pleasure.

I get Isaac up and go through our morning routine before I jump in the shower in the spare room. I leave Isaac in his crib playing with the mobile of colorful giraffes and lions. I need to head to work this morning and speak to Audrey about the wedding plans. Ever since last night when I'd found out how Norrie was thinking, and not from her but from my friend, I've felt the need to fix things.

As I get dressed, I hear Norrie talking to Isaac and smile to myself. Listening to them together never fails to fill me with joy. I never knew how barren my life was until they moved into it. Even her untidiness doesn't bother me, or the fact she thinks that loading a dishwasher is a case of chucking it in and hoping for the best.

I go into the nursery and see her holding Isaac, her hair wet from her shower and a wide smile on her face and feel my heart tug. She's stunning in a way that takes my breath away. She has always drawn me to her from the first time we met a year ago but now it's like I can't get enough air in my chest when she isn't around.

She occupies my thoughts even when she shouldn't. I ordered three times the amount of vodka on our order for the club the other day and all because I can't stop thinking about her.

"Hey."

I step into the room and walk over to her, my hand reaching for her hip. "Good morning." I kiss her lightly and she smiles shyly when I pull away to look at her. "Did you get enough sleep?"

"I did, although I was woken by a sex-crazed pervert in the middle of the night."

I grin at her teasing, seeing the woman I'd met, not the one who's wary around me. I lean in and kiss her neck. "Did he make you come, this sex pervert?"

"Harry!"

I chuckle as she puts her hands over Isaac's ears. "He doesn't understand, and anyway, he needs to learn these things."

"Not at five months old he doesn't."

"Fine."

I run my hand over her ass and feel my cock harden as I kiss her shoulder. Her skin is flushed, and I know she feels this pull the same as I do.

"I have to go to work for a few hours, but I'll be home around lunchtime. I need to talk to you."

Her face shuts down instantly and I feel her body tense and know I need to address this matter urgently. Isaac begins to fuss. She jiggles him and gives him her attention and I love that he's her priority.

"I'll be back by eleven."

"I have the physio coming at ten. She wants to try something different to loosen my muscles."

"Okay, do you need me to take Isaac?"

She looks outraged. "You are not taking my son to a sex club."

I laugh, realizing just how little she knows me and wanting to remedy that. "I love how protective you are, Norrie, but you can sheath your claws. I have an office uptown too. I need to speak to some people about my portfolio."

She blinks like an owl waking from a deep sleep. "Oh."

"So do you want me to take him?"

She shakes her head. "No. Amelia is having him."

"Beck's friend?"

I don't know her well, but she and Beck have been friends since kindergarten. He's been very protective of her and his time with her since she moved back from London. "I didn't know you were close."

"She, Lottie, and Audrey have kind of adopted me like a stray."

I frown not liking the way she sees herself. "You're not a stray, Norrie."

She waves her hand as if it's nothing. "I know, but you know what I mean. I don't belong but they make me feel like I do."

I cup her cheek. "We haven't got time to discuss this now, but you're not a stray and you do belong." I hate that she can't see how worthy she is and that she sees herself as a tag-along to her friendship group.

I lean and kiss her before dropping a kiss on my son's head. "I'll see you later."

"Okay. Say bye to Daddy."

She waves Isaac's little hand and I grin as I jog down the stairs. We have a lot to talk about and fix but for the first time, I feel like we're on the same page.

I SPEND THE MORNING GOING OVER MY STOCKS WITH MY MANAGER, instructing him on what to short and which ones to keep an eye on. I don't know why I have him because I always micromanage him but then I see things he doesn't. It's how my brain works. I make millions and millions without any effort because my brain is wired in a slightly different way than most. It allows me to see numbers and trends, and I can then make projections that, nine times out of ten, are right.

I glance at the clock and see it's already eleven and I want this meeting wrapped up. "So are we clear on what I want now, Mark?"

"Yes, I have all the notes and will send them over for you to review later today."

"Good." I stand, indicating it's time to go and shake his hand.

"I forgot to say congratulations. I hear you got engaged and have a new son."

I don't know how he knows this as I certainly never made any announcement but because of who I am, there's always gossip running amok so it shouldn't surprise me. "Thank you."

"Being a father is the best feeling."

I nod. "It is, yes."

I walk Mark out and we exchange a few words before I get into my car. I hit dial and call Audrey, hoping she isn't in a meeting yet. I know she has a busy schedule.

"Yes?"

"Did you do what I asked?"

We forgo formalities and get straight to the point.

"Yes, I put in a call to a designer I know and she's going to sort the dress for us, but we'll need all of Norrie's measurements."

"Well, get them."

"And how do you propose I do that without telling her why I want them, genius? I can't just rock up with a tape measure."

"I'll handle it. Just let me know which ones you need."

"I'll text you."

"Thanks."

I hang up and then call my mother. She's been putting off my attempts to set up a video call and I want to pin her down. "Mom."

"Hello, Harrison."

"Sunday. I want the call with you this Sunday."

"Oh, I don't know if I have time."

I sigh and shake my head, pinching the bridge of my nose. She has nothing but time and we both know it. "Make time or would you prefer we just come over unannounced?"

"Sunday is fine."

Her voice is brittle, and I know she won't like me forcing her but sometimes she tests my last nerve.

"Talk then. I'll send you the time that works best for Norrie and Isaac."

I'm driving down my street when I eventually hang up and I can't help the smile that spreads across my face. It was only a few weeks ago we sat in my car as I brought Norrie home for the first time. How much things have changed and yet I still haven't allowed her to explain what happened when she was pregnant to stop her from contacting me and I don't know why. Perhaps it's because it doesn't matter anymore. Or maybe it's because if she does I'll see that she's not to blame, and I'll have to take a long look in the mirror at my own actions and behaviors.

I run up the steps eager to see her and open the door. "Norrie."

I call out and head toward the basement gym where I know her PT sessions usually take place. I tug the knot on my tie to loosen it and still as I hear the sound of male laughter. My brow furrows and I listen harder, hearing a feminine groan.

What the fuck?!

I move slowly until I can see clearly and there's a strange man dressed in shorts and a t-shirt and his hands are all over my half-naked fiancée.

"What the fuck is going on?" I roar as I thunder into the room like a man possessed. Fury is rushing through me so fast my vision is red. I yank the man away from Norrie who looks shocked and guilty and stand between them. "I asked a fucking question."

Norrie sits up and pulls a towel to cover her nakedness.

"My name is Stefan. I'm the physio working with Nora today."

"The fuck you are."

He's a big guy, fit and muscular but I think I could grind him into a pulp just from my rage alone right now.

"Harrison, stop."

I turn to glare at Norrie, who looks pissed now too. "You said your physio was a woman! Was that a lie too?"

Norrie glares at me angrily. "No, it was the truth but, my usual physio is sick so they sent Stefan. This is the first time I've met him."

That should make it better but it doesn't ease the rage inside me at what I witnessed.

"You let another man put his hands on you?"

"Oh, calm down. He was giving me a sports massage to try and loosen my muscles. He's a professional."

She gets off the bed and turns around, dropping the towel and exposing her bare back so she can put on a shirt. I move to cover her from his eyes, but he's turned away.

"I don't care. Nobody touches what is mine, is that clear?"

She rounds on me fast like a lion pouncing on a gazelle and I don't like that I'm the fucking gazelle in this scenario. "You're a hypocrite. You don't want any man touching me, but you can fuck whoever you want at the club?"

Stefan points to the stairs with his thumb. "I'm gonna go."

I turn to stare at him, angrily. "Good, and don't fucking come back unless you want your jaw rewired."

"Oh my God, you're such a pig."

"You good here, Nora?"

It's like he's trying to piss me off by asking that question. As if I'd ever harm a hair on her head.

"I'm fine, Stefan. You can go."

Norrie is standing tall in only a shirt and a pair of panties, and I want to rip his eyes out for seeing her this way.

He gives me one last warning look and leaves.

"I can't believe you."

She's angry but so am I. I move closer towering over her, and she faces me down, her heated stare not wavering. "Let's get a few things straight shall we." I hold up a finger. "Number one, I have not, and will never, fuck anyone at the club not now, not then." I hold a second finger up as she plants her hands on her hips. I step forward, forcing her to step back until she's pressed against the wall. "Two. You're my fiancée, and that means the only place my lips, hands, or cock are going to be is on you or in your sweet little body. I don't cheat. When I asked you to marry me, I meant every word. I will be, and have been, faithful to you since the second I found out about Isaac."

Her eyes go wide in surprise and I like having her on the back foot. "But that isn't why I'm faithful to you, Norrie. I'm faithful because I'm a man of my word and when I proposed, I became yours." I lean in so we're nose to nose and I can see the flecks of gold in her irises. "And you're mine, and don't you fucking forget it." I indicate her half-naked state with my hand. "Nobody, not man or woman, ever gets to see you like this but me. And lastly, I want to address what you said earlier."

I see her glance at my mouth as I speak, and my dick goes hard. She's turned on. Her nipples are pressed against her shirt begging for my touch. I lift my hand to brush my thumb over her nipple through the cotton and her breath hitches.

"You fucking belong, Norrie. You're not a stray to be taken in, a homeless wanderer without a place of your own. You belong to me. You belong with me, and everything I have is yours."

I trace a hand down her belly and shove my hand inside her panties, feeling how soaked she is. "Is this for me?"

I strum her clit and she grips my shoulders as her eyes close.

"Yes."

"Take my cock out of my pants, Norrie."

She fumbles with my zipper as she does as I ask, her small hand gripping my hard-as-steel cock. I tear her panties from her body and boost her up so her legs go around me.

I thrust deep, her cry tearing from her body as I fuck her fast, my eyes never leaving hers. This isn't about romance or love. This is me marking my territory and she knows it, and if her pussy strangling my cock is any indication, she loves it as much as I do.

I cup her head as I piston into her, my pants still on as I take her hard. "Touch yourself."

I lean back so I can see her fingers on her clit and then she's crying out my name, chanting it like a prayer and I fuck her harder.

"Who do you belong to?"

"You."

"Good girl. Now you can come."

Her cunt squeezes tight and I slam my hand against the wall as I roar her name loudly, not caring who hears and spill inside her. I pump my hips, making her take every drop and then I bend my head and kiss her gently, slowly. Not a quick kiss for the sake of it, but one meant to convey how I feel, even when I don't know what that is myself. She lets me, her hand stroking my face tenderly and I know I'll need to apologize for being so rough with her.

"Are you okay? Did I hurt you?"

She shakes her head. "Not at all."

I touch my thumb to her bottom lip as I look at her and wonder how she could possibly think I'd want anyone else when I have her. "Want to grab a shower together?"

Her lips tip into a sexy smile that makes my heart turn over in my chest.

"Well, you did get me all sweaty and you do owe me a massage."

I growl as I'm reminded of what I saw when I came home. I know I probably overreacted, but I just saw red. "Don't remind me."

"Harrison, did you mean what you said about being faithful to me?"

I nod as I lift her and walk toward the stairs and head for the second floor and our bedroom. "Yes of course."

"Thank you."

I set her down on the counter and slowly strip her clothes away before removing my own. I reach in and turn the shower on as I come back to her. "Sweetheart, you don't need to thank me for that."

"I do. You've done so much for me and I've been nothing but trouble."

God, this woman slays me. "Norrie, you got hurt. It wasn't your fault."

"I know, but you could've turned your back on me and Isaac and you didn't."

"I don't know what kind of men you've been with, and quite frankly I don't want to, but let me tell you something. A man that would turn his back on his child and the mother of his child is no man at all."

"And I can attest you're one hundred percent man."

"Damn straight."

I pick her up and put her in the shower before I join her.

"Turn around."

I turn her so I can shampoo her hair. Norrie adores having her hair washed. I discovered this tidbit when we spent a week in bed last year and I like doing it for her.

"What's the matter, don't like the view?"

I pinch her ass and she squeaks making my dick twitch. "I love the fucking view from any and all angles, but my favorite is this one." I drop to my knees and proceed to show her exactly which view I mean as she holds on and whimpers my name until her knees give out.

15: Norrie

"Harrison, have you got the bottle warmer?"

"Yes, it's packed in the green bag."

"What about his lovey?"

Harrison waves the stuffed toy at me with a smirk, and I feel my stress ease a little. He moves toward me and takes me in his arms.

"You need to stop fretting and chill out. It's just a trip to the lodge. We aren't moving across the world."

I let his scent wrap around me, infusing me with calm. He's right, this is just a trip home. But it's my first time going back since the accident and with Harrison beside me. I see the light glint off the pink diamond on my finger and can't stop the little tingle of excitement that whispers through me.

Since the day Harry came home and caught me having an innocent massage, things between us have been different, but in a good way. His jealousy, though unwarranted and unfounded, showed me how much he wanted me. I know it might be very unfeminist of me to want him to be that way, but the truth is deep down I have a need to be needed, to be wanted.

"I know. I just want it to be perfect."

He dips his knees so he can catch my eyes. "And it will be. You'll be there. Isaac will be there. What else could we possibly need?"

"That's sweet."

He lifts an imperious brow at me. "I'm not sweet."

I pinch my forefinger and thumb together. "A little bit."

He growls and buries his head in my neck, biting lightly and making gooseflesh move over my skin. His tongue flicks out and laves the skin and I shiver.

"Okay, not sweet."

Harrison lifts his head, and I can see the hunger in his eyes for me.

"I want to fuck you, but we don't have time. You're going to have to make it up to me later."

"Make what up to you?"

He takes my hand and places it over the hard ridge of his cock. "Leaving me with this for the drive to the Catskills."

I squeeze lightly and he groans and rocks into my hand. That's the thing with Harrison, he makes no secret of his need for me.

"I'm sure I can think of something."

He cups my cheek and kisses me slowly, deeply, making my thoughts scatter like ash. My heart feels like it will burst out of my chest when he does this. It's not just about our passion. When he kisses me like this, it's intimacy, it's the connection and it would be so easy to let myself believe it's all real and fall head over heels for him.

On that thought, I pull away and smile up at him. "We should go."

He nods. "I'll go get Isaac and put him in the car."

"I'm just going to grab my coat."

"It's already in the car."

"Okay. Well, then I'm ready."

I've fed and changed Isaac so he should be good for the drive but if not, I have a bottle made up fresh I can give him. We're lucky though and he's perfectly content to sleep or look around.

As we near the lodge I called home for over ten years, and ran for the last five, I feel my tummy knot with nerves and excitement. Somehow this feels like my past and my future are colliding. I still haven't told Harrison who my brother is, and I'm not even sure why

I'm holding back now. Harrison isn't the type of man to be impressed by wealth or fame. Yet I'm enjoying being the focus of his attention and the idea that I might have to share it with Xander and become invisible makes me feel sad and guilty.

I love Xander and he's never done anything to make me feel like I don't count. He was always my biggest advocate, the brother everyone wishes for. But he's him, with his movie star looks and awesome personality, and I'm just me. I'm mediocre at best.

Harrison will understand, I'm sure, but I know Xander will be hurt that I haven't told him what's going on in my life. But I know what would happen if I did. He'd drop everything and come home, and I don't want that.

"You okay?"

Harrison places his hand on my thigh and squeezes gently. I glance over and see his profile as he moves his eyes back to the road. He drives like he does everything, with easy confidence. It shouldn't be hot, but it is. But everything he does has this effect on me.

"Yeah, just thinking about the wedding."

"Are you worried about anything?"

"Not really. Audrey and Lottie have been wonderful in helping out. I've hardly had to lift a finger."

"Good." He lifts my hand to his lips and kisses the tips and I know that I'm never going to be able to stop myself from falling in love with this Harrison. The bossy, overbearing asshole who threatened to take my son. I could erect walls against him, but this is the man I first met and he's devastating to my defenses.

"How is your mom feeling?"

She has a cold and had to beg off our video meeting. I know Harrison had been angry about it, but I also sensed he's hurt by her avoidance.

"Fine, I think. I haven't called her."

"Don't you think you should?"

He purses his lips before rolling his shoulders and hitting the turn signal. "Maybe, but I can't be the only one putting in the effort now. I have a family of my own and you and Isaac have to come first. If she wants to be in my life, she has to make some of the effort."

"I get that."

"Is your brother like that? He doesn't seem to make much effort."

It hurts to hear Harrison say that about Xander, but he doesn't know him and that's my fault. "Xander makes the effort. He calls regularly." I pause, not sure what or how much to say. I don't want to make this huge revelation in the car.

Harrison slides me a sharp, surprised look. "Have you heard from him recently?"

"We spoke the other night."

"And is he going to come to the wedding?"

I bite my lip and try and think of a response in which Xander doesn't come off as an uncaring asshole and I don't expose my lie to Harrison. "Um, he has to work."

"And they can't give him one day?"

I shake my head, hating myself for digging this pit for myself to fall into. "Apparently not."

"Hmm, perhaps he should get a real job, and then he could be there for his family more often."

I hear the censure in Harrison's voice and to some extent I understand it but my love for my brother is warring with my need to protect myself. "Well, not everyone can be as perfect as you, Harrison." I hear the snipe in my voice and wince, not wanting to start this weekend fighting.

"I never said I was perfect. I just think a man needs to step up."

I sigh and look at the lodge as it comes into view. Harrison parks near the front of the door and I notice how busy the car park is with a smile.

"Norrie, I don't want to fight."

I turn in my seat and look at Harrison, who's gripping the steering wheel like he's trying to choke the life out of it. I did that. I stressed him out.

"I'm sorry, I shouldn't have said that about your brother. I know you love him. God knows I can hardly lecture about family when my own mother won't even pick up the phone half the time."

I reach for his arm. "She's sick, Harrison."

"I know but having Isaac has made it harder to see her point of view in some ways."

I cock my head. "How so?"

He threads his fingers through mine, forming a connection. I realize he does that a lot, touches me when we're together. Even the simplest of touches that are in no way sexual, and my heart flips again.

"Having Isaac made me see that I'd do anything for him. I'd walk to the ends of the earth and back with no shoes, give up my fortune, and bury a body. Nothing is too much and that's how it should be. Your parents should be the people who have your back no matter what. Who put themselves second, not above their children. My mother has never done that, and neither did my deadbeat father."

"I guess that includes marrying a woman you don't love." He looks pained at my words and I wonder why I said them. I know the truth and have accepted it so why bemoan the point?

"I care about you, Norrie. I need you to know that. You've given me the biggest gift of my life and I'll always be grateful for that."

"You just don't love me."

He shakes his head. "I'm sorry."

I wipe a stray tear away and force a laugh to stop the deluge of emotion from overwhelming me and ruining our trip. "Don't be. We can't choose who we love."

"If I could I'd choose you."

"Thank you and I want you to know I'll be a good wife to you."

I mean what I say. He might not love me, but he cares, and he wants me and our sexual chemistry is off the charts. Maybe that's enough. I want to make a real go of this for Isaac and for me because I love this man. I wish I didn't but you can't decide who you fall in love with and maybe even then, I'd choose him.

"I don't doubt it."

"Ready to go inside?"

"Not yet. I have a surprise for you."

Intrigued, I study his face and see tiny little lines of tension around his eyes. "Oh? What is it?"

"I'd rather show you."

I smirk and roll my eyes. "Nice try. I fell for that last night."

He chuckles and it washes over me like warm honey. "And did you enjoy it?"

"Yes."

"Well then, how about you show a little trust in me?"

"Okay, I can do that."

Harrison gets out of the car and moves around the front to open my door. He's such a gentleman and it's the little things like this that I have no defense against. If he showered me with expensive gifts and flowers, I could keep a wall up but Harrison is sneaky. He opens doors and he makes sure the housekeeper always has ingredients for cookies in the pantry. He had my favorite clothes brought up from here and put in the walk-in closet in his room, although I think that was partly to make sure I stayed in his room. Little did he know I had no intention of moving out of his bed. I sleep easier with him beside me. He still insists on doing the night feeds with Isaac, even though the doctor has declared me almost back to normal.

Opening my door, he takes my hand and helps me down and then leans in the back to remove Isaac, who's cooing and blowing bubbles at his daddy. My son loves his daddy as much as I do and for that I'm glad.

Turning, Harrison takes my hand.

"What about the bags?"

"I'll come back for them."

"Okay."

As we walk, I imagine to an outsider we look like the perfect little family. Isaac is held safe in Harrison's arms, and I'm smiling. It makes me wish it were true, but I know it's as true as it can be. At least from my side it is, and Harrison is honest. That counts for a lot.

We step into the familiar reception area and the scents of home hit me hard. Wood smoke and the sweet scent of cakes and cookies baking in the kitchen by our wonderful chef, Yusef, who has been with me for the last few years. Even the lemon polish I use on the furniture is familiar, but the people standing waiting are not.

Shock and confusion make me still on the threshold of my family Inn.

Lottie and Linc are here with Eric, Audrey, Beck, Amelia, and Ryker. Behind him are Suzie and Kate, who have been running this place since I was hit by the car. I turn to Harrison who's watching me carefully, confusion evident on my face.

"What's going on?" Did he organize a trip for his friends too?

"Well, a little birdie told me that it was your dream to get married here. So with some help, that's what we're going to do."

"What?" My hand flutters to my face as tears burn my nose.

Harrison hands Isaac over to Lottie who gives him neck kisses. He guides me to a loveseat just inside the door and urges me to sit.

"I know how hard the last few months have been for you, Norrie, and I know some of that's my fault. When I found out this was your dream, I wanted to do something to show you that I'm not all bad."

"You're not bad at all, Harrison."

"That's kind but I know I'm not always easy either, and you could've made life a lot harder for me with Isaac than you have. Instead, you put him first and that means a lot to me."

"I'll always put him first. It's what moms do."

He shakes his head. "Not it's not and I know that first hand. So as a way of thanking you, I re-arranged the wedding based on your vision board thingy."

"But how?" I glance at Audrey who's watching. She shrugs and gives me a 'what are you gonna do' look. "So, you set all this up for me?"

"Yes, with some help. I had no idea flowers could be so difficult."

My heart feels like it might burst with love for him and these people who have done so much for me and I've done nothing to deserve it.

"I don't know what to say."

"Well, don't say anything. Just enjoy the day because tomorrow at sunset, we're getting married out the back with the lake and the mountains as our backdrop."

I launch myself at him, wrapping him in my arms and he holds me back just as tight. I want to soak in this feeling and freeze time. In this moment, life is perfect and it scares me how much power he has over me. Not just as my son's father but because I love him so damn much and he could hurt me. He could wake up in six months or a year or five or ten and decide he made a mistake and disappear from my life and I'd be alone again.

"Thank you. Nobody has ever done something like this for me."

Harrison strokes my hair. "You're welcome, sweetheart." He pulls away and wipes the tear I hadn't known had fallen. "Now you better go. Audrey is chomping at the bit to show you everything."

"What about Isaac?"

He smiles and it's like the world becomes a brighter place or maybe that's just my world.

"Me and Isaac are going to hang with Linc and Eric and the guys for a bit."

"Are you sure?"

"Yes. Go enjoy yourself and we'll meet back here for dinner around seven?"

"That sounds perfect."

I'm so overcome it's on the tip of my tongue to tell him how I feel but he won't want to hear that. I also don't want to ruin this moment when he's gone over and above to make this happen for me, so I keep my declaration to myself and push down the lump in my throat.

16: Norrie

I SIP ROSÉ AND WIGGLE MY TOES AS THE PAINT ON MY NAILS DRIES. Today has been one of the best of my life and it's in no small part to the three women sitting with me. "I can't believe you guys did this for me."

Lottie smiles though her eyes are closed as we let the late afternoon sun warm our skin through the glass of the solarium.

"Audrey did most of it."

Audrey waves it away. "It was nothing and Harrison did the hard parts."

"Really?" I'm eager to hear this story not being able to imagine Harrison organizing details like favors and the perfect cake.

"Yes, he got your measurements so I could pass them to the designer. He threatened the florist with bankruptcy if they didn't deliver the peonies you wanted. He paid the cake maker triple to make sure the cake was done, and he even worked with me to get the almond favors arranged."

"Why almond favors?"

Amelia is the quiet one of the group and I smile at her. "They represent love, fertility, health, happiness, and a long life together. That's always felt important to me."

"That's beautiful."

"I thought so."

"Why so glum?"

I shake my head trying to shake off the melancholy. "Nothing, it just feels a little silly to wish for something when it will never be real."

"Why isn't it real?" Amelia asks.

"Well, this is hardly a traditional wedding, is it? At least it's not what I imagined it would be."

"No, but Harrison has gone out of his way to make sure it's as perfect as he can make it and I think that needs to count for something."

I can hear the censure in Audrey's voice and I know she's right. Nobody is forcing me to do this, and I need to stop whining like a brat and embrace it.

I sit forward and place the glass on the metal and wood table, noticing that I almost miss my mark. I should probably slow down, but the drinks are flowing and I'm enjoying myself. My dress is everything I dreamed of and more. It fits perfectly and we all cried when I put it on, and that's because Harrison made the effort.

"You're right. He's put so much work into this and I'm going to show him how grateful I am, but I need some help." It's a split-second idea but as I speak, I know this is right.

Audrey looks delighted at my tone. "This sounds fun. Go on."

I tell them what I want to do. I know it's almost impossible but I've discovered that money can buy you almost anything and thanks to a small trust fund from my nana, I have some savings.

"I can help with that." Audrey wrinkles her nose. "Although it might involve a favor from my least favorite person."

She doesn't look happy but she knows how much this will mean to Harrison and agrees. As the afternoon progresses, calls are made and by six-forty-five, I have everything in place for my own surprise for my husband-to-be.

Dinner is a lively affair and sitting beside Harrison with his hand on my knee and seeing him among his friends I have a greater understanding of the man and the dynamic he plays. He's the fixer. The sensible one they turn to but I know from experience that among this group it's reciprocated in kind. They've been there for him, and this group is tight. They close ranks when one of them is hurting.

I also get to see other dynamics, like the love and devotion Linc shows Lottie. He watches her when she isn't looking and the love in his eyes is enough to make anyone swoon. He adores her and it's clear she feels the same.

Ryker flirts shamelessly with Amelia, but as I turn my head I catch Beck watching her with an intensity that makes my breath hitch. I wonder if she knows Beck is in love with her or if Beck himself even knows. When she disappears to the toilet, Beck follows, and nobody seems to notice but me.

"Are you having fun?" Harrison's breath tickles my ear as he leans in, his arm moving around my middle.

"It's perfect. Your friends are all wonderful people."

He looks up as Audrey throws her head back and laughs at something Ryker has said to Suzie, who's sitting on his left.

"They are. I don't know what I'd do without them."

"I think it's more a case of they wouldn't know what to do without you."

"You're beautiful, you know that?"

I glance away from his friends and find his eyes hot on me. "Are you drunk?"

He winks at me and I feel myself melt into a pool of goo at his feet. His friends had taken him out on the lake drinking, leaving Eric and Isaac with Heather, Lincoln's mother who'd been a surprise addition.

"Maybe a little but it doesn't change the facts. You're beautiful inside and out, Norrie, and way too good for me."

He brushes a strand of my hair out of my lip gloss, his eyes following the movement and my breath feels like it's stuck in my chest.

"That's not true. You're a good man, Harrison. Any woman would be lucky to have you."

"But you don't feel lucky, do you?"

He sounds sad and I hate that, but how do I answer without making things worse? I don't feel lucky because if I was lucky, he'd look at me like Linc looks at Lottie. But I'm luckier than most, and I need to be grateful.

"I'm lucky, Harrison. I wake up every day, safe and happy with the people I love who are also healthy and happy."

I know he sees through my deflection, but he doesn't say more.

"We should get to bed. We have a long day tomorrow."

I grip his chin and kiss him. "Thank you for arranging this. It means more than you could know."

"My pleasure, Norrie. There's nothing I wouldn't give you."

I keep quiet, not responding to that. "I'll have Isaac with me tonight."

He pulls away and shakes his head. "Nope, tonight my bride needs her beauty sleep."

"Dude, did you just tell your fiancée she needs her beauty sleep?" Beck shakes his head as he walks toward us.

Harrison frowns and it looks adorable, not that I'd say that to him.

"I didn't mean that."

Beck crouches between us, a beer bottle hanging from his fingers. I can see he's slightly tipsy too.

"Nora, why don't you ditch this idiot and run off with me?"

I hear Harrison growl and hide my grin. "Beck, the truth is I like my men a little smarter, and you just ain't packing enough to handle me."

Harrison laughs and shoves Beck, who almost lands on his ass.

He wobbles but catches himself and lays a hand over his heart. "You've broken my heart, Norrie. I thought we had something special."

"We do. It's called friendship and I cherish it for both me and Harrison."

"Well, that's something I guess. So, I can't persuade you to run away with me?"

"Nope."

"What about me?" Ryker appears at his shoulder, looking so handsome it's dazzling.

"Sorry, I'm a one-man woman, and neither of you are that man."

"Right, enough trying to steal my wife before I even get her down the aisle." Harrison hauls me up against his body and he stumbles, almost taking us both down and laughs. It's the best, deep, rumbly sound I've ever heard.

"Okay, my friend, kiss your fiancée goodnight, and let's get you to bed to sleep off whatever these dumbasses plied you with." Audrey glares at Linc who jumps from his seat and grabs Harrison's other arm.

We walk along the lit path to cabin six where Harrison is spending his last night as a single man. It feels fitting to have him in the place where this adventure began.

∼

I WAKE EARLY THE NEXT MORNING WITH A TEXT ON MY PHONE FROM MY brother asking where I am. I see no reason to lie and tell him I'm at home. I send him a quick selfie, glad that they only shaved a tiny portion of my head after the accident, and it's now hidden by my thick locks.

Guilt ratchets through me but I'm determined to enjoy this day and not let anything ruin it. He follows up with a selfie of him and a famous producer he's working with, and I smile. I'm so proud of him for following his dream. I text back telling him I'll call him in a few days and get a smiley face blowing a kiss in return.

It's still early but I slept for a solid eight hours and feel good. I woke with a renewed sense of determination. My adopted mom always said you get out what you put in and I'm going to give it everything I am.

Lottie and Amelia arrive with the hairdresser, but Audrey has gone to speak with Hudson about the surprise I have for Harrison. All three women will be standing beside me today. Although the wedding is small, just this group and a few people I know from the lodge, I still want them beside me. At midday I meet with Hudson, who's patient and kind, explaining everything to me in detail before he asks me to sign the forms he puts in front of me. I read through the words and feel a sense of rightness in my heart as if this is what should have happened from the start.

I sign with a flourish and Hudson witnesses it with Audrey. I see sparks fly between them, but it's shrouded in harsh barbs and quips. He's devastatingly handsome, and he and Audrey together are stunning. When I mention that, Audrey almost takes my head off so I drop it and concentrate on getting ready to become Mrs. Brooks.

My hair is curled in loose waves and pinned back from my face at the top. A comb with tiny seed pearl flowers is placed to secure the veil, which will fall to the floor. Audrey arrives as I step into the dress she'd ensured was ready on time, and by a designer that makes my head spin.

It has a v-neckline with tiny straps and a low back that reaches a wide band around my waist. The skirt is floaty, the satin and tulle hanging in asymmetric lines that swish when I move. It's romantic and beautiful and I feel like a million dollars in it.

"Harrison is going to go nuts when he sees you," Lottie exclaims as she puts a hand over her lips and blinks hard.

Audrey points at her. "Don't you dare cry, or we'll all be blubbing, and I haven't dealt with Hudson the Horrible just for you to ruin her make-up."

"I hope he likes it."

Audrey hands me my bouquet of pale pink peonies. "He's going to love it. Now let's go."

I take a calming breath and wish Xander was here. I cheated him out of walking me down the aisle and now it all seems so silly and childish of me. I glance at my phone, but Lottie and Amelia are guiding me out of the room. Isaac is with Heather, and I've seen him periodically throughout the day as has Harrison, but we haven't seen each other.

Another tradition he chose to adhere to because of me and my vision board. I wish I could say that I'm going into this with an open mind and closed heart but as I stand at the back of the deck and look out over the gazebo covered in flowers, I know that's a lie. I'm going to get my heart broken but like a runaway freight train, I can't stop it from happening.

"Ready?"

I nod at Audrey and lift my head as the music begins.

My staff are mixed in with Harrison's friends and it's a mingling of the two worlds I now straddle. Beck had offered to walk me down the aisle, but I'd thanked him and said no. If Xander can't do it, then I'll do it on my own.

Audrey, Lottie, and Amelia walk ahead of me. I feel my chest almost explode with nerves, so I lay a hand over my tummy and try and center myself. Glancing up, I see the sky exploding with color, oranges, yellows, pinks, and purples as if nature is out to celebrate this day with us.

I walk to the top of the aisle and look up and all I can see is Harrison. He's wearing a pale gray suit with a pale pink buttonhole and tie. His hair is slightly tousled like he's been running his fingers through it and I wonder if he's nervous. He smiles and turns to Beck, who whispers something I can't hear, but his eyes stay on me. I walk sure and steady until I pass Heather, who's holding Isaac. I stop and take him from her and continue down the aisle as Harrison frowns at this unexpected move.

I reach his side and he leans in to kiss my cheek as he reaches a hand out to Isaac.

"You look absolutely stunning. I have no words."

His voice sounds choked, and I smile. "Thank you. You're very handsome too."

He winks and I feel my body respond. Every atom inside me wants to throw itself at him and beg him to take me. I resist, the nerves of what I'm about to do tamping down that desire to a bearable level. I pull in a deep breath and catch Hudson's eye. He nods that everything is in place, and I relax.

"Harrison, before we begin there's something I want to say." My voice is steady even as my heart races.

He frowns and I hear the hesitant tone as he responds. "Okay."

"When I found out about Isaac, I was terrified, but I was also so happy because I knew my child had come from a place of joy. Although he was a surprise, he was very much wanted. Unfortunately, life had other plans for our reunion and things got in the way. I can't go back and change any of that, and some of it I wouldn't. I won't force an explanation on you but I wanted to do something to fix the wrong I did to you by denying you the right to be there from the very beginning."

"He was there for the very beginning if I'm not mistaken."

The people around us, some of whom are in on my secret and those who aren't, laugh at Ryker.

I turn and put my finger to my lips in mock anger at the interruption, but I smile too because this is us. We don't do things the easy way.

"Our journey hasn't been straight or fair, but I don't want to start this marriage by going into it with my son having a different name to us. So, this morning I had the papers drawn up to change Isaac's name to Isaac Brooks. He's your son and he should carry your name."

I finish my speech and hand the papers over to a stunned Harrison. He takes them on automaton, looks at them, and this is the first time I've ever seen him shocked.

"You did this for me?"

I nod, my eyes welling with tears that I blink back furiously.

Harrison steps forward and crushes his mouth to mine, his hand cupping my neck. I feel a hand slap at my face and laugh as our son tries to get in on the action.

Harrison lifts his head and I can't read the look in his eyes, but it has a depth of emotion I've never seen before and it makes my heart stutter.

He braces his forehead against mine. "Thank you."

Two simple words but they convey everything he's feeling in the way he says them. "You're welcome."

The rest of the ceremony is short and to the point. We haven't written our own vows, because how would I say them without making it clear how I felt about him? Halfway through, Isaac begins to fidget and Harrison reaches for him. We continue exchanging the rings, juggling our son who's so integral to this wedding, and it feels right that he's up here with us.

When it comes time for the kiss, Ryker takes Isaac, and Harrison cups my cheeks in both hands and kisses me long and deep and I forget everything but him. He sweeps me away until it's just us in a bubble of pleasure. Catcalls seep through the languorous fog and I smile against his lips. We break apart but Harrison holds me close, not wanting to let go and that's how we move back down the aisle to start our life together.

17: Harrison

I TWIRL NORRIE AROUND THE SMALL DANCE FLOOR IN MY ARMS, trying to absorb all the feelings she brings out in me. Wonder, joy, happiness, surprise, and something I hadn't expected; home. But Norrie *is* home to me now. For so long I've felt like I had no place of my own where I could let down my guard but, today, she gave me that.

I'm still in shock at what she did for me with Isaac's name change. It was something I was going to address with her after the wedding. The fact that she knew how much it meant to me without me telling her, and went out of her way to change it, makes my chest squeeze tight.

"You look so beautiful."

She smiles at my words and glances at the dress. "It's a beautiful dress. Thank you for arranging it for me."

"It's not the dress, it's you, Norrie."

A blush touches her cheeks and I want to strip her down right here on this dance floor and kiss every inch of her gorgeous body.

"Thank you."

I dip my head and kiss her neck, and she shivers. "How long do you think before we can leave?"

"About an hour or so. We need to mingle, and I need to throw the bouquet."

I groan and she giggles, and it makes my dick hard. "I don't think I can wait to have your taste on my tongue that long."

"It will be worth it."

"I don't doubt it."

"May I?"

I look up to see Beck standing beside me. I groan and hand my wife over to him but not before I kiss her again. I can't seem to get enough of her. I thought it would ease the desire I have for her, that it would wane, but it seems to get worse with every touch. It's like our pheromones are getting stronger with every look or something but I can't explain it, this need for her.

I stand off to the side watching her dance with Beck and laugh at something he says, throwing her head back and making him chuckle.

"You've got it bad."

I twist to see Lincoln has come up to stand beside me. He's watching Lottie dance with Eric and Audrey. I could pretend I don't know what he's talking about, but we're both intelligent men, so I don't bother. "It's not love, but I do care for her."

He turns to face me, and I look at him as he sips his drink and then smiles.

"I get it, you're in denial still. I was the same at first but let me give you some advice. Don't let pride or stubbornness come between you and a woman who would do what she did for you today. She loves you. Any idiot can see it and you love her too, so get your head out of your ass."

I understand what he's saying and how it looks but I know what love looks like. I love my friends and my mom, but this is nothing like that. This feels like an addiction and that must be lust, and lust burns out eventually. I just need to make sure Norrie and I will have friendship and respect when that happens.

"Thanks for the wisdom, Lincoln, but I've got this."

He shakes his head as if he's talking to a dumbass and shrugs.

"Have it your way, but when this implodes, which it will, you know where to find me so I can say I told you so."

"Gee, thanks, buddy."

He clamps a hand on my shoulder and squeezes. "My pleasure, friend."

He walks away to rescue Lottie from the wild dance moves Eric is showing her and I move to Norrie. The song ends and I shoulder Beck out of the way. "Give me my wife back, asshole."

"I was just trying to persuade her to run away with me again but for some reason, she likes you better."

"Of course she does. She's a smart woman."

I hook an arm around her, bringing her into my side, and instantly the knot Lincoln's words had caused to form in my stomach eases. We dance for a bit and mingle with our friends, thanking them for helping organize this day and being here to celebrate. Heather has kindly agreed to take Isaac for the night so we can have this one night in our favorite cabin alone. I'm eager to take advantage of every second we have on our own.

"You ready to throw the bouquet yet?"

"Yes."

I stand back as she drags all her female friends onto the dance floor. Ryker asks why men can't join in, so she drags them on too. Nobody says no to her, she has a sweetness that makes it so you can't turn her down.

She lines up with her back to everyone and I count her down as she swings the bouquet over her head. I watch it sail through the air and then land in the very stunned face of Beck's friend, Amelia.

She blushes and Beck gives her an angry glare before stalking off in a huff. They've been friends since they were kids but clearly, something has pissed him off. Maybe he doesn't like her current boyfriend and the thought of her getting married to him isn't palatable.

"Well, that went down well."

I glance at Norrie. Her cheeks are rosy and she looks happy. It makes me glad I did this for her. I can't give her much, but I was able to give her this. "Ready to go?"

"Yes."

I swing her into my arms, and she squeals, drawing everyone's attention to us. "Sorry, folks, but it's time for me to steal my bride away."

A raucous chorus of encouragement follows us as I carry her out of the main tent set up for the celebration and move down the lit path to cabin six. I reach the door and manage to maneuver it open with her in my arms as she giggles and kisses my neck.

We cross the threshold and the second we do, I dump her on the bed and step back, shucking my jacket. She looks like a vision surrounded by her frothy dress lying back, propped on her elbows watching me. I drop to my knees and grasp the backs of her legs, pulling her to the edge of the bed.

Bending, I lift her delicate ankle and lay kisses along her calf as I remove her shoe. I do the same with the other foot but continue up, my lips moving over the back of her knee, making her squirm. I want to take my time, but I also desperately want to fuck her in this dress. I bury my head under what feels like miles of silk and tulle, kissing her creamy thighs until I reach the garter she's still wearing. I finger it but lightly, wanting that left on for later. I have so many plans for her tonight and none of them involve sleep.

I find her pretty pussy covered in white lace and slowly pull it down her thighs before I kiss her clit and her back bows off the bed. I place my hand on her belly to hold her in place and I devour her cunt. I love the taste of her on my tongue, the way she responds to me and holds nothing back. Her desire coats her thighs and my chin as I lap at her, alternating between fucking her with my fingers and my tongue.

"Harrison, please."

"What do you need, wife?"

"I need to come."

"Then do it."

I dip my head and suckle her clit, flicking the tiny bud with my tongue, until her legs begin to shake, and her hands fist the sheets.

"Oh God. Oh God. Ooooohhhh."

Her orgasm crashes over her and she stiffens. Her body goes lax as her clit pulses against my tongue and her pussy clenches so tight it's a wonder my fingers aren't broken.

As her climax fades, I stand and wipe my chin with the back of my hand. "Stand up."

Norrie moves and I hold out my hand to help steady her as she does as I asked.

"Good girl."

I kiss her shoulder as I spin her away from me and begin undoing the zip hidden by tiny buttons on the lower part of her back.

"Step out."

She loves this dress. As much as I don't care if I throw it on the floor, I know she'd be upset if it was wrecked so I fold it over the chair and then turn to face her and find her watching me with soft eyes full of hunger. An emotion I don't know smacks me hard and I fight against it.

Then we move at the same time.

Our bodies clash as she rips at my shirt and tie, her eager hands finding my body. I shuck my pants, shoes, and socks and then I'm standing before her naked. Her hand grips my cock, and she strokes. I close my eyes and groan as pleasure rushes through me like hot lava.

"Bend over."

I turn her and she bends over the bed, her garter and the white lace demi-cup bra the only thing covering her body. She looks like sin and heaven all wrapped in one irresistible package.

I swipe a finger along the drenched lips of her pussy before pushing a finger inside her. She moans as I slowly fuck her with it before removing the digit and circling the wetness around the puckered bud of her ass.

Norrie stills for a second before she wiggles, her butt wanting more and I give it to her. Pushing my finger in slowly to the first knuckle and hearing the whimper of pleasure she gives me. She was new to anal when we met but by the end of the first week together, she loved it and we indulged several times but nothing since we got back together.

"You want me in your ass or pussy?"

I keep pumping in and out slowly and my cock is leaking pre-cum all over her sweet ass cheeks.

"Pussy first, ass later."

I smile at her answer. "That's my girl."

Keeping my finger where it is, I line my cock up with her pussy and rub my pre-cum along her entrance before I push into the hilt in one smooth stroke. She moans and her pussy clamps down hard as I feel her ripple around me.

"Are you coming already, greedy girl?"

"Oh God, that feels so good."

I swat her pale skin and she yelps until I smooth it with my palm and run my hand over her spine "Did I say you could?"

"I'm sorry, I couldn't help it. You feel too good."

I want to deny her, but she's right this feels too good. "That is going in the bank for later, Norrie, and you'll owe me."

"Okay, but can you just move, please?"

I chuckle and grip her hip with one hand as I begin to fuck her slowly, in and out in time with the finger I have in her ass. My movements speed up and I can feel the tell-tale tingle at the base of my spine, but I don't want to come looking at her back. As beautiful as the view is, I want to see her eyes.

I pull out and flip her to her back on the bed before plunging back inside her. Her hair is wild, her cheeks pink and her eyes are glassy and dilated with desire.

"Take off your bra and show me those pretty tits."

The cruder my language, the wetter she gets. As she unclips the bra and threads her arms through before throwing it to the side, the room is filled with the sound of slapping flesh.

"Fuck me, you're beautiful."

I hover over her, my forearms beside her head, and pull a beaded nipple into my mouth, suckling hard and she cries out, wrapping her legs around my hips and meeting me stroke for stroke. A frenzied feeling washes over me and I feel my control slipping from my grasp.

"Touch yourself."

I lift up so I can see her hand disappear between us, and I groan as she touches where we're joined, her fingers skimming my sensitive cock. She circles her clit. It only takes two more touches and she's coming, gripping my cock with her cunt until I think I might black out from sheer pleasure.

Then I'm coming too, my climax making my body go stiff, and I look into her eyes. A connection forms that's unlike anything I've felt before. I wonder if this is marriage and if it is, why the fuck nobody tells you how good the sex is.

I collapse onto her and roll us as our breath heaves in and out of our chests, the sweat on our skin mingling and making us slip against one another.

That was quick and raw and dirty, and I fucking loved it.

I dip my head and kiss her lips as she closes her eyes and hums with pleasure.

"That was amazing."

"It was and we're not done yet. I'm spending all night inside you one way or another."

Norrie lifts up but her hand is on my still-hard cock and her eyes go wide. "Oh, is that so?"

I nod smugly at the satisfied look in her eyes. "Yes, unless you have any objections."

She smirks and strokes my cock before pushing me to my back and climbing on my lap and hovering over my cock.

"No objections."

Then she slowly lowers herself until my cock is inside her tight, wet heat. Our joint pleasure makes a mess on my thighs, and I don't care.

I grip her hips and grin up at her. I wonder how the fuck I got so lucky as to find this amazing woman and knock her up without even knowing I wanted to. Now, though, I want that. I want to see her round with my baby, to see her body change.

"I'm gonna put a baby in you."

She laughs. "You already did that."

We haven't used any protection and I've made my intentions clear. She seems okay with it but now I want her on board. I grip her waist, my thumbs stroking her hip bones, and watch her rise and fall lazily, the pleasure building slowly, languidly between us.

"I'm serious, Norrie. I want another baby with you. I feel like I missed out on so much and I want that."

Her features freeze but then she relaxes and smiles as if she's come to a decision. "I want that for Isaac. A sibling he's close to in age, but I also want you to have that, Harrison."

I sit up and grip her chin gently making her look at me. "What about what you want?"

"I want it too."

I hear the 'but' she doesn't voice. "But?"

She tries to look away, but I won't let her. "Tell me."

Norrie tries to get off my still-hard cock, which is inside her. I let her go, knowing she needs space, but I won't allow her to hide from me. She picks up my shirt and puts it on, gathering her thoughts.

I stand and touch her shoulder before wrapping my arms around her waist from behind. "Talk to me."

"I'm scared."

I sit on the bed and pull her onto my lap, holding her close. "Tell me why?"

She angles her head and I wait patiently even though I feel anything but.

"I thought you didn't want to hear this."

My brow furrows. "You didn't tell me because you were scared?"

"No, but the reason I'm scared of pregnancy is also why I didn't tell you."

"I see. Will you tell me now?"

She shrugs. "If you want."

"I do, but how about I run us a relaxing bath and you can tell me in there where we aren't all sticky?"

"I like that idea."

I tap her butt to get her to move and lead her toward the bathroom where I draw us a bath and add the bubble bath I know she loves to help relax her. When the temperature is right, I take her hand and help her in before I step in behind her. I settle her between my legs and force her to lean back against my chest. This isn't overtly sexual, but I still feel this need for her riding me, and my desire to touch her leads to me stroking a washcloth over her skin and dribbling water over her body.

"That feel nice?"

"Mmm, it does."

"Do you want to tell me about it now?"

She sighs but nods.

"I didn't find out I was pregnant straight away but then I started to feel off, being sick a lot, and I thought I had food poisoning. I went to the doctor, and he did a test and I found I was expecting Isaac. I was terrified but also excited and he told me the morning sickness would ease so I went home."

My gut twists at the image she's painting so far.

"It didn't get better. It got worse and, in the end, I could only keep down water and saltines. It got so bad that I collapsed and they admitted me to the hospital."

I run my hand over her nape, trying to ease the trauma she suffered retrospectively, and know it's a useless gesture.

"The doctor told me I had something called *hyperemesis gravidarum*, which is severe morning sickness and often requires hospitalization for fluids and rest. At about five months, it eased enough that I could function, and I knew I had to contact you but it didn't feel right to just call or text something like this so I got the train to New York. I came to your house to tell you."

My entire body freezes at her confession. "You did?"

She nods but doesn't look at me and I can hear the emotion in her voice. "Yes, I waited across the street for ages and then I saw you come out with Audrey all dressed up like you were going out. You were both laughing, and you seemed so close. She kissed your cheek and hugged you."

My heart sinks as I remember the night vividly. We were attending the Kennedy Foundation Gala, and she'd persuaded me to go with her. "I remember that night, but you have to know Audrey and I've never been like that to one another."

THE CONSEQUENCE

"I know that now, but I was emotional and exhausted, and I was crushed. I thought you'd lied to me about her or moved on and forgotten me, so I went home to lick my wounds and decide how to approach you."

"But you didn't."

"No, I was taken back into hospital as my blood pressure was high and they put me on bed rest for the remainder of my pregnancy."

She tries to look at me and I can see the anguish and fear in her eyes.

"I'm so sorry, Harrison. I should have found a way, but I was a mess and then they told me I had something called HELLP syndrome and I had to deliver early. I was so scared for my baby, I already knew it was a boy and I loved him so much. But I was so weak and they asked if I wanted anyone told if something happened to me. I knew in my heart you'd take care of our child if I wasn't here to do it."

Just the thought of losing her sends a shaft of pain through my chest that's almost staggering.

"I was taken into the OR, but they discovered I was already in labor, and he was born an hour later naturally. After that, it was non-stop. I recovered quickly once he was born but I'd lost a lot of weight."

I hear the smile in her voice now that she's told me what I pray is the worst of it.

"Isaac was a trooper though. He gained weight well and after two weeks they sent us home. I know I should have contacted you then, and really, I have no excuse for not doing so except I was trying to adjust."

I wrap my arms around her and kiss her head, feeling closer to her than any other person on the planet. "I'm sorry I wasn't there."

She laughs humorlessly. "You couldn't have known."

"No, but I should have called and checked in on you."

"Why didn't you call?"

Her voice is small, and I want to be honest but how do I tell this woman that the feelings she evoked in me terrified me to the point I ran away like a pussy?

"It's okay, you don't have to answer."

I can hear the hurt in her voice, and it guts me because I never want to hurt her. I squeeze her in my arms. "It's not that. I just didn't know how. You were so unexpected in my life. I never expected to meet anyone like you, especially someone I'd connect with so fast like we did. The truth is, you overwhelm me in a good way and that scared me."

Silence fills the room as we both process everything that has been said.

"Thank you for telling me."

"Sweetheart, I need to apologize to you. I should have let you explain straight away but I was so determined to hang on to my anger that I was a dick to you."

"You were a bit of a dick."

I burst out laughing at her unexpected sass and my heart squeezes in my chest. I'm not sure what is happening, but it scares me as much as it excites me. This woman could gut me and leave me a broken shell and I'm not sure I'd survive it if she did. There have been so many lies and disappointments in my life, and it takes an effort to open myself up to someone.

"Are the risks high of you being sick like that again?" I hate the thought of her so ill, especially as she's only just recovered from her accident, and wonder if we should wait. Perhaps I can speak to Beck about it.

"A little higher than most but I'm not opposed to having another baby. I want it, I just don't relish the idea of getting so sick again."

"God, I don't blame you, it sounds awful." I'm not sure how I'd cope seeing her like that either.

She turns in my arms, the water sloshing over the side of the tub and presses her body against mine.

"But you'd be there this time, wouldn't you?"

I stroke her wet hair from her face, her big brown eyes sparkling with water on her lashes, and I know I'll do whatever it takes to protect her. "Yes, sweetheart, you never have to worry about me not being there for you again."

"Then I think we should do it."

My heart rate kicks up and I pull her closer so I can reach her lips with mine. "Really?"

"Yes."

"You're something else, you know that?"

"Meh, I'm just me."

"Well, just you is fucking perfect. Can you promise me one thing?"

She cocks her head as her fingernails scrape over my nipple making my dick twitch between us.

"What is that?"

"That there are no more secrets between us?"

I feel her still like she might say something, but she nods. "Of course. A fresh start from here on out."

"Sounds good to me."

I drop my head and kiss her and then proceed to try and make good on my promise to put a baby in her.

18: Norrie

"Here are the newlyweds."

Beck holds up his glass as we join them all for brunch the next morning. Harrison had already picked up Isaac from Heather and has him in his arms as we walk into the dining room hand in hand.

Last night was perfect, we talked, we made love, and we made a plan that excites me. He never declared his love for me, and I didn't tell him, but I still feel like we're moving forward in a positive way. The only fly in the ointment is my lie about Xander. Guilt makes me feel nauseous, but I push it away. I almost told him last night but the timing was wrong, and I'd unloaded so much on him it felt like the wrong time to add, oh by the way my brother is one of Hollywood's biggest actions stars.

"So how was it?"

"Ryker, do not ask my wife about her sex life," Harrison barks at his friend and Beck slaps Ryker upside his head with a shake of his head.

I laugh and look around the table. "Where's Amelia?"

Audrey cuts a hand across her throat but it's too late, the question is out.

"She had to go home, something about a job interview."

Beck frowns as he speaks, and I know he's lying through his teeth but I don't say anything.

We sit and the staff serves us coffee and juice before a huge breakfast buffet is set along the side. Everyone loads their plates and I soak in the atmosphere. These people are richer than gods. They own a sex club but seeing them together, all I see are friends who'd die for each other. The best bit is I'm a part of it. They make me feel like I belong.

It's a loud, lively affair, where everyone is talking over each other but it's full of love and laughter and it makes me see how lonely I was.

Harrison takes my hand. "You, okay?"

He looks at me intently, his eyes searching, and I smile wide and nod. "Just taking it all in."

"They're a lot to handle."

"It's perfect. Thank you for letting me be part of it."

His brow furrows. "You don't have to thank me for being part of my life, sweetheart."

"Maybe but I'm doing it anyway."

He kisses me sweetly and Audrey groans.

"Ugh, get a room you two."

"We have one, but you assholes wanted a big brunch so we left it."

"Yeah, well, we'll be gone soon."

Audrey seems a little out of sorts and I wonder what happened and decide to ask her as soon as we get home. Harrison and I are staying on for a few days with Isaac, but the others are leaving early afternoon.

"This place is amazing, Nora. Did you buy it or inherit it?"

Lincoln is speaking to me and out of them all, he's the one I know the least.

"I inherited it from my adoptive grandma. She died five years ago."

He forks bacon as he looks up from his plate. "Your parents?"

"My adoptive parents died in a car accident and my real parents died in a fire. My adoptive dad is actually the fireman who rescued me."

His eyebrows shoot up. "Really?"

I nod and my emotions are always mixed about this subject. I miss my birth parents, but I hardly remember them and without losing them,

I wouldn't have had my adopted parents or Xander. I probably wouldn't have met Harrison and had Isaac either.

"Yes."

"Wow, that's awful. I'm so sorry for your loss."

"Thank you. I guess I see that everything happens for a reason. Without losing my birth parents, I wouldn't have met my adopted family. And without that, I may not have been with you here today. It all happens for a reason."

"That's an amazing outlook."

I shrug. "We either accept it or wallow."

Harrison kisses my shoulder. "She's an amazing woman."

"She must be to put up with you," Beck interrupts.

I laugh and feel relieved that I've managed to avoid the conversation of family as things move on to talk of work and the Love Books Foundation that Lottie and Audrey run with Lincoln working in the background.

I lean into Harrison. "I'm just going to speak to the girls for a minute."

"Okay, hurry back."

I smile at his words and a warm fuzzy feeling works its way over my body and lodges in my heart.

I excuse myself and go and find Suzie and Kate. They've been running this place for me. I need to take a minute to properly thank them and ask if they're prepared to continue doing so until I decide the future of the lodge.

I should sell but I love this place, and something is stopping me from pulling the trigger on such a big move. It feels final and I'm not quite ready to lose my safety net, not yet and maybe not ever. I think a big part of that is not knowing how Harrison feels about me. His actions say one thing, but he hasn't said the words to me and maybe he never will. Maybe he meant it when he said he can't love me, but hope is a fickle thing and it burns under all the doubt.

"Oh, Nora, I'm so happy for you."

Suzie grabs my hands and squeezes, her face alight with joy. Suzie is older than me by three years and recently got married to her childhood sweetheart, a fireman in the town where we live.

"Thank you, and I don't know how to thank you for stepping up for me."

She waves away my thanks. "Honestly, it's been a pleasure and the extra pay has been great. Me and Jimmy are saving for our first house, and I don't have to tell you how hard that is."

I smile at her exuberance. "That's wonderful. Have you seen anywhere you like yet?"

She goes shy but then pulls out her phone and scrolls until she finds a picture and turns the screen to me.

A gorgeous little townhouse on a new development just outside town is clear.

"It's gorgeous."

"I know but we have a little more saving to do before we can make an offer."

"How much?"

She names a figure and I make an instant decision. "Well, that works out because it matches the bonus I'm giving you and Katie for running this place. I'd also like you to consider taking the full-time manager's position. It will mean an increase in salary too."

Suzie is looking at me with open-mouthed shock before she starts to tremble. "Oh my God, do you mean it?"

I take her hands in mine this time. "Yes of course."

She starts to scream and jump up and down and her excitement is infectious, so I start to laugh with her.

We're interrupted as Harrison bursts into the room like it's on fire. Beck and Ryker are right behind him, all of them looking for the reason behind the noise.

"What the hell happened? I heard screaming."

Suzie marches up to him and throws her arms around a stunned Harrison as I watch with barely suppressed humor as he pats her back, looking awkwardly at me for help.

"Thank you for making my friend happy." She pulls back to look at him. "And you make sure you treat her right or you'll have me to deal with."

The stark warning is hilarious because like me, Suzie is vertically challenged and the thought of her going at Harrison makes me laugh.

Harrison looks at me and smiles. "I'll treat her like a queen."

"You make sure you do because she's special. She just needs to see it. She sits in her brother's shadow and she shouldn't."

Panic ripples through me and I move quickly to get Harrison out of there before Suzie can land me in hot water.

"I think I hear Isaac crying."

I mentally chastise myself for using my son to divert attention but brush it off as Harrison does exactly what I expect and turns on his heel and heads for the dining room.

Back at the table the food is eaten, and Isaac is with his father. Seeing them together I know I made the right decision to marry him. I just hope I don't get my own heart trampled in the process.

19: Harrison

"I'd like to stop by my mom's on the way home if you don't mind?" I glance across at Norrie as we make the drive home from our wedding. My wife looks stunning. Her hair is loose, and she looks relaxed and utterly enchanting. I'm not one for prose and flowery thoughts like this usually but it's the only explanation or description I can come up with. She enchants me, consumes me in a way I never thought would happen.

It's getting harder and harder to ignore the possibility that I might be falling in love with my wife. She turns to me with a tired smile, the dusting of freckles on her nose and cheeks making me want to kiss every single one.

"Okay by me but do you think she'll handle it okay?"

I grimace, my good mood evaporating because she's right. Mom won't handle it well, but it's the only way I can think of to force her to meet my wife and son, and that in itself is depressing.

"Probably not but she needs to meet her grandson."

"Well, whatever you want I'm here for it."

I take her hand and kiss her palm before holding her hand on my thigh as I drive the rest of the way. I've never been particularly touchy-feely but with Norrie, I can't seem to go two minutes without needing to feel her touch or be touching her. The connection is like nothing I've ever felt before. She's the sweet to my salty, the light to my dark, and I'm a better person for being around her.

I pull into my mom's apartment block and the knot of anxiety builds in my gut. This was a mistake but I'm here now and I'm not backing out. I move to open the car door for Norrie, stealing a kiss as I do, and get Isaac from his car seat. This won't be a long visit, but I still grab the changing bag just in case.

I feel Norrie's hand on my back, in comfort and support as we walk up the steps. Norrie takes Isaac as I use my key to let myself in, calling out to my mom.

"Mom, it's me."

"Oh, Harrison, where have you been? It's been days and I need my magazines."

Her voice sounds harried, and I know this is a bad idea. I follow the sound of her voice and find her in the living room in her chair, surrounded by things she's ordered online and never used. She isn't dressed. It's almost two in the afternoon and she's wearing a robe and slippers.

"Hey, Mom." I address her like a skittish colt because that's how she reacts, like an injured animal. Maggie Brooks looks up accusingly and all I want to do is turn and run and get my family out of here before they can see what a screw-up I am. My mom's eyes zero in on Norrie behind me and I see the panic.

"Who is that? Get her out of my house."

"Mom, this is Norrie, my wife, and Isaac, my son."

"Why are they here? I don't want them here." Her voice rises and humiliation washes through me.

I look at Norrie and see the sympathy in her eyes and detest that she's witnessing this cluster fuck. "I wanted you to meet them. They mean a lot to me."

"But I don't want them here."

"Why don't Isaac and I wait in the hall for you?"

I nod at Norrie, humiliation torching a hole through my chest. "Mom, that was rude."

"I was rude? You came into my home with strangers. You know I don't like strangers."

I feel the last vestige of my temper incinerate. "Because you wouldn't fucking meet them."

My mom glares at me with open hostility. "This is your fault, Harrison. You brought them here and forced me to be rude. You always do this, you ruin everything. Your father left because of you, and that girl and her baby will do the same when they see the truth of how selfish you are."

I feel like my heart is being put through a meat grinder as she spits her bile at me. I know she's sick but that doesn't make it hurt less. "And what truth is that, Mother?"

"You're unlovable. You're weird and nobody can love you. That's why people leave you."

If I thought her words before hurt, this just hollows me out until nothing is left. I purse my lips and straighten my spine, not showing her how much her words affect me. "I see. Well, I might as well go then."

I turn and stride to the door.

"What about my magazines?"

"I guess you'll have to find someone else to get it for you since I'm so awful."

I pause as I see Norrie standing with Isaac pressed tight in her arms, a look of horror on her face. Shame makes me grit my jaw as I usher her out and to the car. I don't speak as I drive us home, lost in thought as my brain goes over and over my mother's words. I know in a few days she'll feel bad about what she said and want to make up, but I can't keep doing this.

I owe her a lot but every time she chips away at me in frustration, I notice the distance between us gets bigger and bigger and I have my own family to protect now. I won't subject Norrie or Isaac to that.

"Do you want to talk about it?"

Her words are soft as she reaches for my hand, but I keep my eyes and hands on the wheel. I can't cope with her pity. "No, it is what it is."

"Maybe but what she said was hurtful and untrue."

"Is this us not talking about it?" I snap and Norrie rolls her lips between her teeth and goes silent. *Great now I've been a dick to the one person I don't want to upset.* "I'm sorry."

"It's fine. I get it."

We arrive home and I help Norrie in with Isaac before collecting the bags. I head to my office, wanting the peace to process and decide what I can possibly give my mother going forward. I pour myself a Cognac and toss it back like cheap vodka, loving the burn which seems to fill the space my mother gouged from my chest.

I don't know how long I sit there, but it's dark when a knock interrupts my thoughts. "Come in."

Norrie puts her head around the door and smiles, and it's like the sun hitting my face after a long winter. She's changed into a short, black sequin skirt, her long toned legs ending in fuck-me heels that make my cock instantly harden. A silver cami top shows a hint of her curves, and her blonde hair is down around her shoulders. She looks fucking perfect.

"Hey."

I cock my head. "Are you going out?" Jealousy instantly assaults me, and I have the urge to deny her when I have no right. I don't own her. Nobody could own Norrie, she's too free, and I envy that.

She walks around the desk to me, and I turn my chair so she's standing between my thighs. A vision of her on her knees makes my cock throb with need. I don't reach for her like I want, I remain outwardly unaffected, my mother's words haunting me.

"No. Well, not alone. I thought maybe you and I could go out and you could show me your club."

Her hands smooth up my thighs and I snatch her wrist and pull her forward so she's half leaning, half straddling me. Her gasp of delight feeds my soul and I reach out and cup her breast through her top, the weight in my hand feels perfect. But it's her reaction to me that makes my blood simmer with hunger. "Did you now?"

Norrie bites her lip and I pinch her nipple for teasing me. Her whimper pleases me and I smirk. "And who's looking after Isaac?"

"Amelia is here."

"I see. So you arranged this behind my back trying to manipulate me?"

Her hurt expression makes me feel like shit. She's trying to be kind and I'm being a dick and lashing out at her.

"I wanted to do something nice for you and I thought this would be fun."

I stand abruptly and grip her waist, holding her to me as I down the rest of my drink and slam the glass down on the desk. "We better go have some fun then."

I see her smile. Excitement and apprehension dance in her eyes and I know she's right. This is the perfect distraction after a fucking horrible day. Norrie has never been to a sex club, and I'm filled with anticipation that I get to show her this new experience. Even though I never play at the club, I know there'll be private rooms available so I can fuck my wife until I forget everything but her sweet body.

WE WALK INTO CLUB RUIN HAND IN HAND AND INSTANTLY I SEE THE looks of appreciation she gets from other patrons and even staff members, both men and women. Norrie is a knockout and she has no clue. Her open smile and natural inquisitiveness are like a siren call to other men and I hold her closer, making it clear to anyone watching that she's off-limits to them. We head for the third floor and I wonder if I should warn her about what she might see. But then I remember we talked about the club when we were together the first time and she seemed intrigued even then.

I should make her sign the NDA but if I can't trust Norrie who can I trust? I remember I can't trust my own mother. The thought pulls me up short and she turns to look at me.

"What's wrong?"

"I need you to sign some forms."

"Okay."

I lead her to the office and hand her the standard forms all the floor-three members sign. She adds her name to the bottom. It's the first time seeing her sign Nora Brooks and it makes me pause. This woman is my wife, the mother of my son. I should be able to trust her, especially after what she did with changing his name. That still makes my chest ache when I think about it, and I rub the spot as I watch her. She looks up with a huge smile on her face and I have to look away.

She's too much, too beautiful, too joyful and I know my mother is right in this if nothing else. She'll leave me one day and I must guard against that.

"Ready to have fun." Yes, that's what I need, fun.

Norrie nods and I take her hand and lead her out to the club floor. It's not overly busy on a Monday night but we still have a healthy number of people playing. Two men and a woman are engaged in a domination scene on the stage. One man is strapped to the St Andrews cross, and the other man is on his knees as the woman, a well-known artist, uses a whip on both men. My wife is entranced by it, and I watch her watching the sheer bliss on the faces of the men she must recognize.

To the left, a Shibari master is teaching a class and the woman is bound around her breasts and belly in an intricate pattern that enhances her beauty and pleasure. I'm relieved none of the other owners are playing tonight. I'm not sure how Norrie would take to seeing Ryker with his dick swinging in the wind.

"Do you see anything you might like?"

I look down at her and she's looking around as if her eyes don't know what to look at first. They're languid and glassy, and I know if I reached under that skirt I'll find her soaked.

I step behind her and do just that. She gasps at my touch but settles against me as I swipe two fingers along her wet cunt, slowly pushing into her dripping pussy.

"Hmm, you like this."

"Yes."

"What else do you like?"

"Whatever you want, sir."

Her words make my fingers, which are slowly fucking in and out of her, still. I always knew Norrie had a submissive side, but we've never explored it. "So, you want me to be in charge?"

"Yes, sir."

The thought makes me so hard, but I have rules about playing here and I won't break them, and in any case, I'm not sharing her pleasure with anyone else.

"Let's mingle."

I pull my fingers from her just before she can climax and hear her whimper, so I spin her around and make her watch as I lick the salty-sweet evidence of her desire from my fingers.

"You come when I say you can, do you understand?"

"Yes, sir."

"And drop the sir. You can address me as husband."

I want every man in this room to know who she fucking belongs to, to claim her for all to see.

"Yes, husband."

I nod in satisfaction and lead her to the bar where I order water for us both.

"It's good to see you, Mr. Brooks. We've missed you around here."

I nod at Simon, one of the longest-serving bar staff members. "It's good to be back. This is my wife, Norrie."

He smiles at her, and she returns it, and I can almost see him falling under her spell.

"It's nice to meet you. I'm sorry I've been dominating all of his time but I promise to share in the future."

"Nice to meet you, Norrie." He turns to me. "Now I get it, boss. If my wife looked like that, I'm not sure you'd ever see me again."

I shove down the irritation and nod. "Let's walk around."

"Yes, husband."

I see a few regulars and go over to say hello as they stand drinking a glass of liquor. Alcohol is limited on this floor to two per patron for safety reasons.

"Milo, Franco, it's so good to see you."

Both are rockstars with a persona to play for the world, but the truth is, Milo isn't the womanizer he makes people believe he is. No, he's Franco's Dom and he's devoted to him but they have an agreement that works for them.

Milo reaches out and I shake his hand. "Harrison, long time no see. I hear you have a kid now?"

I nod and smile. "I do, and this is my wife, Nora." I don't make the mistake of calling her Norrie again because that name is for me and our friends, not every Tom, Dick, or Harry, and yes, I see the irony.

Milo and Franco turn their attention to her, and I see both men look her over from top to toe with appreciation evident on their faces.

"You're punching, Harrison. She's stunning. You up for sharing?"

It's an innocent question and one that's perfectly natural in this setting but coupled with the comment about her being out of my league, it rubs me wrong. "No, and I won't ever be so don't ask again."

Milo holds his hands up. "Just asking, man."

I nod and drag Norrie away before she even has time to speak with them. I know I'm acting like a neanderthal, but I can't help it.

"Where are we going?"

I stop and glare at Norrie. My irritation isn't with her but rather with the way she affects others. People love her and react to her in such a positive way, and I know it's only a matter of time before someone steals her away from me. "Did I say you could speak?"

Her head drops and I feel like an asshole. "No, husband. Sorry, husband."

I pull her into a free room, not looking at which one it is but I'm pleased when I see it's a room with lots of mirrors.

I lock the door and reach to loosen my tie. "Undress and lie on the bed."

I go to the other side of the room and collect what I need, watching my wife undress quickly and lie in the middle of the bed. She's a vision but I don't want emotions playing a part in this tonight, mine are too close to the surface.

I place the items on the table beside the bed and watch her eyes go languorous, her nipples beading tight. I unbutton my shirt and shuck it from my shoulders to the floor, unbuttoning the top of my pants next.

"Open your legs and put your arms above your head." She does as I say without question, her trust absolute in this moment.

I quickly secure her wrists, her breasts brush against my chest and she moans, arching toward me.

"Did I say you could rub against me like a cat in heat?"

"No, husband."

"Are you being a bad girl, Norrie?"

"No."

She deliberately withholds my title and I smirk at her insubordination. "Hmm. Someone needs a lesson in manners."

I pull her legs wider apart and see her desire glistening on her thighs. Her cunt is pink and hungry for my cock. I secure her ankles, making sure that it's not tight enough to hurt her in any way. "If you want to stop, just say stop and I will. You don't need a safe word with me, Norrie. Do you understand?"

"Yes, husband."

"Good girl."

I pick up the vibrator I had placed on the side table and she licks her lips. Moving slowly and deliberately, I stand between her spread thighs and take a second to admire how fucking stunning she is like this.

Placing the vibrator against her pussy, I move it so it's coated in her desire before holding it against her clit.

Her hips buck but she's restrained enough to limit her movement and I pull it away. "Keep still."

I do it again and watch her face contort, little hums of pleasure whispering from her parted lips. I reach forward and tweak her nipples until she moans and thrashes her head, trying to chase the orgasm I'm holding just out of reach. As she begins to peak, I retreat, making her moan in frustration. I do this four more times until she's panting and sweating.

"Doesn't seem like such a good idea to defy me now does it, wife?"

"I'm sorry. Please let me come."

"Tut tut. I didn't say you could speak."

My dick could drive nails through a wall it's so hard, but I ignore my own needs and concentrate on her. She goes to speak but bites her lip and I want to kiss her, to bite that pink flesh until she understands who she belongs to.

"Do you want to come, sweetheart?"

She nods.

"Ask me nicely."

"Please, husband, let me come."

I smile and unzip my pants, letting them fall and then I swipe my cock through the wetness on her lips and push inside to the hilt. She's coming before I'm fully inside her, screaming and thrashing and gripping my cock so hard I almost see stars. Her arms rattle the bindings, and I don't think I've ever seen something so fucking erotic in my life.

I fuck her through her climax, leaning down as I do to capture her mouth in a deep drugging kiss, trying to tell her with my body how I feel. In this moment she thinks I'm dominating her, and I am, but she has all the power. She owns me in a way that terrifies me.

I pull out and grab the lube from the side, coating my cock with it before tipping some onto my fingers. I kneel between her thighs and tease my fingers along her back passage, watching her hips thrust up trying to make me fuck her but I want her ass tonight. I want it all. I insert a finger into her puckered hole and pump it a few times, loosening her up, but she's so tight I wonder if we can make this work, but we have before.

I add a second finger as I hold the tip of the vibrator on her clit, trying to make her relax. I can hear the sounds we're creating together, her moans and whimpers, my wet fingers, and the slight buzz of the toy I'm using on her.

When I'm happy she's ready, I pull my fingers away and line my cock up with her ass. I give myself a stroke and slowly begin to push inside her. She's tight, gripping me hard and I hear her breathing speed up.

"Relax, wife, I won't hurt you. You look so fucking good taking my cock in your ass." Her body relaxes slightly, and I push all the way inside, closing my eyes in pleasure as I brace myself on my arms. "Such a good girl."

I begin to move, fucking her slowly as she gets used to the feel of me again. My balls draw up and I feel a tingle in my spine. Every inch of my body is on fire for this woman. I use one hand to release her wrists and she reaches for me, her hands skimming everywhere, and I throw my head back as I speed up. I want to come so badly but I need one more from her first.

I reach between us and push the vibrator into her slick pussy, and she screams. I can feel the climax barreling down on me as the vibration on my cock through the thin wall between her body sends me spiraling. Her body grips me, adding to the pleasure. Fireworks explode behind my eyes as my release hits me and I fill her body with my come.

I sag over her still-pliant body, sweat covering us, and feel utter peace. I know, in that moment, the storm is coming and it's going to sweep us both away because the last time I felt like this was the day my father walked out on us.

20: Norrie

THE LAST TWO WEEKS HAVE BEEN STRANGE. I CAN'T PUT MY FINGER ON what is wrong exactly, but Harrison is different. He blows hot and cold. One minute he's expressing how much he cares with his actions, like leaving coffee by the bed for when I wake up or buying cookie recipe books and leaving them in the kitchen for me to find, and the next, he's hardly speaking two words to me.

I know he was hurt by what his mother said, and quite frankly it's taking everything in me not to drive over to her house and give her a piece of my mind, but I don't. It won't help because it won't change how she is or behaves. I hate that she could wound him like that, reduce such a wonderful, kind, caring man to unlovable when it's the furthest thing from the truth.

I tried several times to bring it up but every time I do, Harrison shuts me down. The only place I can see a piece of the man I love is in bed or with Isaac.

He's still passionate and giving as ever and his hunger for me is boundless. Not a night goes by when he doesn't reach for me and it's not always for sex. Sometimes he just needs me close and it's the one thing I can give him that he'll accept so I try and show him with my actions and body how I feel about him.

I stand at the door to our bedroom and listen through the monitor as he reads the Monkey Puzzle book to Isaac. Harrison is convinced he's a child prodigy, and research has shown that reading to a child from a young age does help. I also think he finds it soothing. My poor man is hurting and wounded, and I don't know how to reach him.

I feel my phone vibrate against my hip and take it out and glance at the caller ID. Xander is calling and I want nothing more than to talk to him but I can't risk it with Harrison home. I send it to voicemail and follow up with a quick text letting him know I'll call him tomorrow.

"Who was that?"

I see Harrison watching me from the door and startle, clutching my hand to my chest as I slip my phone into my pocket. "Jesus, you scared me to death."

"Who was on the phone?"

"My brother sent a text to say he's coming home in a few weeks." That at least is the truth. He's coming home as he has a private premiere for his new movie coming up soon.

"Oh, he does remember you then?"

He pushes past me and I sigh, not wanting to snap at him but I'm not going to be his emotional punching bag either. "Don't start, Harry."

He rounds on me, his eyes stormy. "Start what? The truth?"

"This isn't about my brother. This is about your mother hurting you."

He spins and heads for the bathroom. "You don't know what you're talking about."

I throw up my hands in frustration and follow him. "Of course not, because you won't talk to me about it."

He begins to strip his shirt off and even angry with him, I feel my body respond.

"There is nothing to talk about."

"Yes, there is. She was awful to you, and she hurt you. Why can't you admit that?" Both our voices are raised, and I try to lower mine for the sake of our son. I won't have him witness this.

"Fine, she was a bitch. I'm unlovable. You happy now?" His pants go next, and he switches on the shower and steps in, blocking me out. Anger forces me to close my eyes and count to ten but it does no good.

I open the shower door and see him tipping his head back under the spray like a Greek god, his body chiseled and bronze from hours in the sun with Isaac this summer.

"Why do you always turn everything into a fight?"

He rolls his eyes. "Don't be dramatic."

I huff and barely resist the urge to stamp my foot. "I'm being real. You're the one hiding from your feelings, not me."

"Hiding stuff? That's rich coming from you. You couldn't put your phone away fast enough when I walked into the room. What's the matter, Norrie, bored with me already? Moving on to the next chump?"

I gasp in shock that he'd accuse me of something like that. "What the hell does that mean?"

"You're hiding something from me."

"I told you who it was, do you want to see my phone and check?"

"What I want to do is take a fucking shower in peace without you harping on at me but since I can't...." He snatches my arm and drags me into the shower with him fully clothed and crashes his mouth to mine.

I fight him for a second, but he doesn't give in and soon I'm kissing him back, pouring my own anger into it.

Harrison shreds my top and strips me down and I can feel the desperation in him as my clothes tear and he takes everything he's feeling out on my body. Yet I'm not an unwilling victim, I grasp his cock, stroking him hard as he groans into my mouth. I lift my leg and he boosts me up so my back is to the wall, my leggings hanging from one leg in bits and he thrusts into me hard.

There's no finesse; this is lava-hot passion, and the desperate need to fuck our anger at each other away. His teeth nip my neck and I scratch my nails down his back as he tilts me, his cock hitting that place inside me that makes me see stars.

"This what you wanted all along, Norrie? An angry fuck?"

"Maybe."

He snarls as his head dips, and he pulls my nipple between his teeth and widens his legs to get deeper. "Just fucking ask next time."

"I would if you weren't such a grumpy prick."

The last word comes out strangled as he bites down on my nipple and my pussy clenches around him.

"Such a greedy cunt for my cock."

"Asshole."

"Yes, I am and you fucking love it."

"I fucking love you but God knows why when you behave like such a dick."

His eyes find mine and he fucks me harder, the fire in his expression searing my skin. I don't have time to process because he touches his thumb to my clit, and I climax, pulsing and tightening around him as pleasure bites me hard. I throw my head back, chanting his name over and over as I feel him release into me as he clutches me and shudders.

I don't know what I expect to happen next, but it isn't what he does. He lets me go, opens the door, and steps out of the shower. Grabbing a towel, he swipes it over his face and wraps it around his waist before he looks at me with all the emotion of a dead fish.

"Don't ever say you love me again. I won't have you spitting lies to me in the heat of the moment. I'm not some sucker easily manipulated and you saying you love me won't make me say it back."

I'm not sure he could've hurt me more if he'd physically struck me. I feel vulnerable as he spits bile at me and denies my feelings, accusing me once again of manipulation. I hadn't meant for it to come out as it did, or maybe even at all but it did, and I meant it. I should feel angry or sad but as he turns and walks away, I have the dawning realization that he'll never love me like I love him and it's crushing any feeling out of me. Numbness sets in and I feel empty.

I'd hoped and dreamed that we could make this work, that he'd fall for me like I did him if I could just show him how happy we could be but you can't love enough for two people and make a marriage work. I was kidding myself. I'll never be enough to fix the emotional wounds his parents have bestowed upon him, even if he'd let me try.

I was a fool to think I could be enough. I'm never enough for any man. Every single man I've been with has either cheated on me or used me to get to Xander. Harrison may not have done either of those things, but his behavior hurts the worst.

Because you love him, and you never did the others.

My brain whispers the truth, but I shove it away. I get out of the shower and dry off, silently getting ready for bed and not knowing how I'll face him or what I'll say. Luckily, he's not in the bedroom when I come out and a few minutes later I hear the front door slam.

OVER THE NEXT FEW DAYS, I BARELY SEE MY HUSBAND AND WHEN I do, we're polite and stilted, focusing on Isaac. He comes to bed after I'm asleep and yet each night, he pulls me into the safety of his arms and holds me. I savor the feeling even knowing it's all lies.

I want to talk to him, to convince him but I don't know how to get through to him or even if I want to now. Maybe it's time to cut my losses and walk away, but I made a commitment for my son's sake and that hasn't changed.

How is it only a few weeks ago that everything seemed so perfect, so filled with hope? Audrey and Lottie have called but I've put them off and kept my own council because ultimately, they're Harrison's friends first. Amelia has sent a few texts and I've agreed to meet her for a coffee.

I walk in and almost turn on my heel and leave when I see Lottie and Audrey are there too.

Audrey stands and moves to me. "Please don't go."

I still, frozen in the middle of the busy coffee shop, indecision warring inside me.

"Please, we're worried about you."

I sigh and push the stroller over to the table they've found. Lottie hugs me tight, and I feel tears prick my eyes but have cried enough these last few months. Isaac is asleep so I have a few minutes of respite but also no buffer.

Audrey orders our drinks and a plate of blueberry scones.

"So, what is going on? Harrison is like a bear with a sore head, and you're missing in action."

I shrug. "Nothing. Everything is fine."

Lottie rolls her eyes. "Sure it is because that's the look of a happy woman."

I'm angry enough that some of the truth slips out. "What do you want from me? Yes, my life is shit. Everything is a mess and I feel lost. Is that what you want to hear because that's the truth."

I swipe angrily at the stray tears that betray how much I'm hurting.

Amelia takes my hand and squeezes gently, and Lottie offers me a clean tissue, which I snatch from her hand. "Thank you."

"Why didn't you talk to us?"

Audrey sounds hurt and I look up to see genuine anguish in her eyes. I'd never hurt her intentionally. She took me in and befriended me when she could've left me out in the cold.

"You're Harrison's friends first and I don't want split loyalties or anything I say getting back to him. If I tell you anything, I put you in that position."

"That's my fault and I apologize. I never should have opened my mouth to Linc and believe me when I say it won't happen again."

I shake my head. I'm not angry at Lottie for telling Linc about me worrying about Harrison cheating at the club, not really, and I don't want her feeling bad about it. "No, I get it. He's the man you love, and I understand not wanting secrets. Believe me, I do."

"Maybe but you're my best friends and sometimes it needs to be sisters before misters."

Audrey nods. "I agree with Lottie."

Amelia shrugs. "I have no man, really thanks to Beck running the last one off, so nobody to tell but I wouldn't anyway. You've taken me in too. I've never really had girlfriends before, and I love you guys."

Audrey hugs Amelia, who's closest to her, and I smile as I look around the table, feeling incredibly grateful to these women.

Audrey raises her mug. "Okay let's make a pact. Anything said between us stays between us alone."

"Why are you raising your coffee mug?" Lottie frowns but does the same.

Audrey looks at Lottie like she has two heads. "Because we don't have any Champagne."

I laugh and lift my mug and we all clink. "To friendship pacts and girl squads."

"To friends."

"Right, now spill it."

I spend the next ten minutes verbally vomiting all that has happened between me and Harrison the last few days. Audrey is suitably outraged and threatening to kick his ass but promises she won't say or do any such thing. Lottie is the voice of reason advising me to give it time but Amelia surprises me the most.

"You should leave."

"Amelia!"

She looks at Audrey and purses her lips. "I don't mean forever. I mean take a break, have a few days away. Think about what you want and what you can cope with."

"Isn't that running away?" I nibble on my scone; my appetite has been shit the last few days, but I feel hungry now as if there's room inside me now the weight of it all has lifted.

"Maybe but I'm the queen of running away after all. I did run across the other side of the world because I'm in love with my best friend and he doesn't see me the same way."

I gasp my eyes going wide. "You and Beck? I thought perhaps you were in denial about that."

"No, just me, and I'm very aware. He sees the tomboy who climbed trees with him and nothing more. But that's not my point. My point is you need to give yourself some space to think."

"It might help."

Audrey crosses her long legs and flicks her hair back off her shoulder. "Well, let me tell you from experience in dealing with super rich, alpha assholes. He won't like it."

She's right, he won't but this is about me too. "I'm gonna do it. I'm gonna head home for a few days and give us both some space."

Audrey groans. "This is going to be a disaster."

"Maybe but it can't get worse, can it?"

"Maybe not," Lottie chips in but she doesn't seem convinced. "Now, back to you being in love with Beck."

We all look at Amelia and it's nice not to be everyone's focus for a change.

"Nothing to tell. I love him. He doesn't love me or see me that way, so I'm stuck here in the friend zone. I've learned that it's okay. There are plenty of wonderful men out there and I'm going to find one and live my best life."

"Why did you come back if he doesn't love you?" Audrey knows more about their history than I do, so I listen intently.

"Because I missed home. London is great but I miss my family and Beck's friendship and, if that's all I can have of him, I'll take it."

"Does he know?"

"God no, and he'll never know. He can't. Promise me."

"You guys are killing me today."

Amelia glares at Audrey and I love that she isn't awed by the tough, glamorous businesswoman.

"Fine. Girls' pact in place."

"Well, I'm going home to pack a bag for me and Isaac. Wish me luck."

"Good luck."

I walk out of the coffee shop and make the short journey home. I want to be gone before he gets home and tries to stop me. I get caught up feeding Isaac his lunch. Then my brother calls and we chat for a bit and in the end, I decide to leave tomorrow.

Each day over the next few, I put it off in the hopes that something will get better, but if anything, it's getting worse. He's shutting me out completely, only when he reaches for me at night do we have any kind of intimacy. Even then it's our bodies forming that connection, not our minds.

I put Isaac to bed and read to him like I've taken to doing now Harrison is working late every night and decide tomorrow is the day. I can't take much more, it's killing me.

21: Harrison

I WATCH HER AS SHE READS TO OUR SON AND FEEL A HEAVINESS IN MY chest. I rub the spot to try and ease the knot but it's persistent. Since the shower incident, I've hardly been able to look at Norrie. Hearing her say she loved me filled me with such joy that for a split second I wanted to weep like a baby and tell her I loved her too. Then my mother's words filtered through my mind, and I saw how foolish I was.

Norrie doesn't love me, there's nothing to love. She cares, she's grateful, she's a kind person but love, that big, huge emotion everyone talks about, that people make movies about and write about, isn't something for me.

My own parents don't love me, why the fuck would anyone else? Having Isaac has really sealed that for me. I love him so much it terrifies me. It's like wearing my heart outside my chest on a daily basis. I'd die for him. I don't evoke that emotion in my family, so why would I evoke it in anyone else?

I hear Norrie put on the voices of the characters as she reads and smile to myself. I did something right though. I gave my son a mother in a million. There's nobody I could've picked who's better suited, in my opinion, and that makes me smile sadly. I know my behavior is hurting her, but I don't know how to get back what we had before.

"Harrison, you're home early."

I look down into her beautiful face as she meets me at the door to Isaac's nursery and want to slice open my heart and tell her how much I adore her. How my heart beats for her. How beautiful she is inside and out but I don't do any of that. "I missed you."

I see hope form on her face and want to keep it there, but I need to protect her from hope. It isn't a good thing and hurts and maims you because you let your guard down. She can't love me and I can't let her believe she can because I know one day she'll leave. "Or should I say, I missed your pussy."

Her jaw grits and her eyes drop to my chest, and I let her. It's for the best.

I take her hand and lead her to our room, where I slowly undress her, kissing each and every inch of her skin. Lavishing every emotion I feel on her in the only way I can. I kiss and caress, driving her higher with my mouth and hands, making her climax until she's crying my name on her lips. I quickly undress and crawl up her naked body, kissing her warm skin, and tasting her on my tongue. When I push my cock inside her, it feels like home.

I slowly fuck her, drawing out our pleasure until I can't hold back any longer, and let us tip over the edge into bliss.

Her fingers tighten in my hair and on my back. I hold her close, our hearts beating as one and it feels profound and monumental. I love this woman so much it guts me that I'll never have that back in the same way.

I see a tear slip from her eye and kiss it away. "Don't cry, sweetheart."

"I can't help it. It hurts too much, Harrison. I need to leave."

My stomach rolls and my breathing turns to dust in my chest, almost choking me. I roll away and stand, pulling on sweatpants. Norrie pulls the sheet up around her and watches me pleadingly.

"Leave?" My brain reacts. It's happening already and I can't let her go.

"Just for a few days."

"No."

I can't let her leave me. Hurt that she'd give up so quickly on me lashes my skin and it's a wonder the wounds she's inflicting aren't visible.

"I'm not asking, Harrison. I need some time on my own to think."

I can't believe she'd betray me like this so soon. We've barely begun. I need more time. "Think about what?"

"How we move forward. I can't live like this, Harrison. You never promised me love and I get that, I do. But you promised me friendship and since the other night, you've shut me down, locked me out of your life, and I don't want Isaac around that."

"Oh, you mean you got called out for your bullshit and now I'm bad for our son. Is that it?"

"No, of course not, and whether you believe me or not, I do...."

I hold up a finger. "Don't fucking say it."

"For God's sake. She fucked you up good, didn't she?"

"Don't bring my mother into this."

I've cut her from my life since she was so vicious in front of Norrie and Isaac. Her calls go to voicemail, and I delete them before I even listen to the excuses she makes.

Norrie jumps from the bed and begins to dress, pulling on underwear and jeans and even now I can't help but admire her beauty.

"I'm leaving."

She walks to the closet and grabs a case that's already packed by the looks of it. Another feeling of bitterness washes over me. She had her exit already planned. She never planned to stay. "If you leave this house, you do so without Isaac. He's my son, and I'll have you up on kidnapping charges if you take him."

Her eyes grow wide. "You wouldn't?"

I stalk closer and cup her cheek, half of me wanting to fall to my knees and beg, the other half furious with her for making me the bad guy again. "Want to test me on that?"

"You bastard."

"Maybe so, but I protect what's mine, and you and Isaac are mine."

"I hate you."

I smile without joy and it's almost funny because I find that easy to believe. "At least now you're being honest."

"You don't know what honest is."

"I know this: if you ever try to run from me again, I'll ruin your life."

She crosses her arms and glares at me with hatred. "News flash, asshole, you got your wish."

I turn and walk away, shutting myself away in my office where I get blind drunk. The devastation I feel that she'd leave me, throw away what we had over a misunderstanding, guts me.

Avoidance is the pattern for the next few days as we barely speak, our communication is via text with one-word answers and questions.

The longer it goes on, the more I see her spark dim. Her light goes out and I know it's my fault, but I don't know how to fix it. How do I go back and undo all the decisions I've made and do I want to?

I have a conference next week in L.A. I wasn't going to attend but maybe the week apart will help us reset and give her the space she obviously craves from me. I can't bear to see her like this any longer and I know I have a few very tough decisions of my own to make.

We're eating dinner together, Norrie barely touches her food and I'm chewing but not tasting anything when I tell her.

"I have to go away for a week. Well, five days."

"When?"

"Tomorrow."

"I see."

I look up but her face has no emotion on it. "I expect you to be here when I get home."

Her jaw ticks and her anger makes me hard, makes me want to feel all that passion writhe beneath me.

"Don't worry, Harrison. I won't leave your little prison."

"You may leave whenever you wish, but Isaac stays."

"That's really all I am to you, isn't it?"

"No, you're my wife."

"In name only."

"Which is what we agreed."

Her shoulders sag and I know every time I open my mouth, I make it worse, but I can't stop.

"I know we did. Don't worry, Harrison, I'll be here when you get home."

"Good."

I leave at six am the next morning, kissing Isaac and telling him to be a good boy for his mom. I take a last peek at her in the bed and wish I could just crawl back in beside her and make all the bad stuff go away.

The conference is boring but on the third day, Beck flies out to meet me for the evening. He's consulting on a case out here and it's good to have the company. Not that I couldn't have had loads. I've had four door keys slipped into my hand this week already and I've returned every one of them unused. I have no wish or desire to touch or even look at another woman. Norrie has ruined me for every other woman but her. We text daily about Isaac, but we don't talk about anything else. There are none of the fun gifs or chitchat that would make me smile, yet my heart still soars at the sight of her name on my phone.

"How's the conference?"

"Boring."

Beck looks around the bar, studying the room for a potential hookup and looking as disinterested as I feel.

"So why come?"

"Norrie and I needed the space."

Beck pauses as he lifts his drink to his lips. "Trouble already?"

"We had a fight."

"About?"

I give him a what the fuck look. "I'm not discussing my feelings with you."

"Why? You have someone better to do it with?"

"No, but I don't need to discuss them, I have it in hand."

Beck chuckles. "Looks like it. You're out here miserable and your family is across the country."

"It's fine."

He holds his hands up. "If you say so."

"I do. We just need a little time apart to cool down."

"You did something, didn't you? I fucking told Linc you'd fuck this up."

Indignation snaps my head up from staring at my brandy. "What the fuck? You made a bet I'd fuck up?"

"Oh, come on, Harrison. You blackmail her into marriage and tell her it's about the kid. Then you plan her perfect wedding because you're so far gone for her you can't see straight. She probably doesn't know which way is up. The woman is so in love with you it's painful to watch and you're fucking oblivious to the mixed signals you're sending."

"She's not in love with me."

Beck snorts and knocks back his drink, raising his glass to the passing waiter for another.

"I'm gonna need more alcohol for this."

The waiter brings his drink, and he takes another sip. The man can hold his liquor, that's for sure.

"It's interesting you only heard she loved you but didn't deny loving her. Is that because you do love her or I'm so far off the mark it doesn't matter?"

I roll my eyes and shake my head in exasperation. I love my friends, I do but fuck me, they drive me insane sometimes. "Let's say I do love her. What does it matter? She doesn't love me."

"Did she say that?"

I look away from his knowing expression. "No, she said the opposite. Happy now?"

"Well, I'm a fuck of a lot happier than you are about it. My guess is you threw it back in her face and didn't believe her."

That's exactly what I did but there's no way I'm telling him that.

"Brother, your silence says more than your words ever do. You did exactly that and more knowing you. I expect you spewed venom at her for it and were a dick."

"I don't like lies."

"Why would she be lying?"

I slam my glass on the table between us. "Because we both know it's not true. It can't be."

"Why? Because your dad ran out and your mom is a manic-depressive agoraphobic with a mild personality disorder and doesn't know how to love? Is that what you're basing this on? Because that's some hearty bullshit right there."

"My own parents don't love me. How the fuck could someone like Norrie?"

"Do you love me and Linc and Audrey and Ryker?"

"Don't start that shit. It's different and you know it."

"Maybe how you feel about us is different. Love and passion are different, but we love you. And you can believe that. The difference is we're not a threat to you. Your parents hurt you. They fucked you up and made you feel unworthy and hurt you. Norrie has the same ability if you let yourself believe she loves you."

I don't say anything, trying to process what he's said.

Beck stands and presses his hand to my shoulder. "Wake up, man, before you lose the best damn thing that ever happened to you because you're being a pussy." He looks up and grins at a brunette at the bar. "On that note, I'm going to get my dick wet."

I watch him walk away, turning his charm on the woman at the bar and a few minutes later he's walking out with her.

Is Beck right? Am I denying her because I'm scared? Worse, could I be hurting her because I'm scared? I've been so consumed with myself and how I feel that I haven't considered her and how she feels. The more I think about it, the worse I feel but I also feel braver, stronger. Thinking back on all the moments we spent together, I have no doubt I love her, but can it be true that she loves me? My mother especially has dictated my life for so long and I do owe her but maybe I've paid my dues for her going it alone. Maybe I can be loved by someone with a heart as big as Norrie's.

I go to bed that night with a lighter feeling. I'll take these few days here and evaluate it more. Look at the data and analyze it before I come to a decision on how I'll win my wife back because one thing is for certain, I'm not going to lose her.

I love her too much not to try and fix this.

22: Norrie

I OPEN THE DOOR AND GASP, MY HAND MOVING OVER MY MOUTH BUT then I'm in a strong pair of arms and the tears are running down my face. "Xander! What are you doing here?"

He has a five-day scruff and sunglasses on his face, but his trademark grin and blonde good looks are the same.

"Well hello to you, too."

"Oh, my God. Come in, come in."

He steps into the home I share with Harrison and looks around before he drops his bag in the hallway.

"How did you find me?"

His brow furrows. "Well, I went to the lodge and they told me you were here with your husband."

I see the hurt on his face as he eyes my left hand. "I see."

"Well, that's more than I see."

"Why don't you come into the kitchen. I have a lot to tell you."

He follows me into the kitchen. His eyes move around as he does, taking in the place, and I know he can't fail to see the opulence in this home, no matter how understated.

"Coffee?"

"Please."

Xander hauls his six-foot-four frame onto a barstool, his arm muscles bulging. He's bulked out for this last role, but he's still the same brother who pushed me on the swing. Yet he looks natural here, but he does everywhere he goes. He fits in like a chameleon in a way I envy.

"So, want to tell me what the hell is going on?"

I know I've hurt him by keeping so much hidden and vow to be open with him now, no matter the cost to me. I wring my hands with nerves. "I'm not sure where to start?"

Xander reaches for me and stills my fidgeting, his smile warm even now. "How about at the beginning?"

I push the cream and sweetener toward him and doctor my own drink. "After I left you in New York, I was in an accident. I was hit by a car and spent nearly three weeks in a coma."

Xander jumps to his feet. "What the fuck, Nora? Why didn't someone call me?"

I reach for his hand to temper his reaction. "I had Isaac's father down as next of kin because if something happened to me, then that was the best for him."

"I thought you said he was out of the picture."

"He was but it turns out I was wrong."

"He turned his back on you and Isaac."

I shake my head not willing to let Xander think that of Harrison. "No, he didn't know."

The look of incredulity on his face speaks volumes and I hate that I'm disappointing him.

"You didn't tell him he had a son?"

"No."

"Why not?"

"I didn't want to mess his life up. I thought he'd moved on from us and I didn't want to push Isaac into a situation where he felt like he was an unwanted extra in someone's life."

His eyes run over me as if he's looking for evidence of the accident but outwardly there's nothing to see. "But you're okay now?"

I nod. "Yes, Harrison got me the best care and had me moved to a specialist hospital. I had some weakness in my leg, but physical therapy has helped that a lot."

"So how did you end up married?" Xander sips his coffee thoughtfully, patiently waiting for me to go on.

"Harrison was predictably angry I hadn't told him about Isaac and demanded we get married. He had no intention of being an absent father and I agreed we could make it work."

"Do you love him?"

I blink furiously as hot tears sting my eyes at his question. "Yes."

His arm comes around me and I pull in the familiar scent and let his big arms comfort me. Xander gives the best hugs and I've missed him so much.

"Then why the tears?"

"Because he doesn't love me and doesn't believe I love him."

"Well, he sounds like a fucking idiot if he doesn't love you."

I laugh at my big brother's protective instinct. "He's actually a genius."

"So where is he?"

I pull away and wipe my eyes on my sleeve. "Away on business."

"Is he fucking other women? Because if he is, I'm going to rip his balls off."

I shake my head. "No, nothing like that. We just can't communicate without fighting. He's had a rough time and he doesn't want to believe I can love him like I do."

"Well, that's something, I guess." He shakes his head again. "I still can't believe you didn't tell me about the accident or the wedding." He looks at me with sadness. "I can't deny I'm a little hurt, Nora."

The reprimand is gentle, but it still stings and I deserve it. I should have told him about all of it, I just hate to be a bother to him or anyone else. "I know but I didn't want to upset your creative process. Then you were filming, and I didn't want to be a distraction."

"You're my baby sister, you'll always come before the job. Why can't you understand that?"

"I do."

He shakes his head. "No, Nora, you don't. You spend so much time pleasing others and being so determined not to be a nuisance that you forget how much you're loved. How would you feel if you were finding out all this about me?"

"Hurt."

"Exactly. You need to start being truthful with yourself and putting yourself first for a change. You matter." He pushes my hair from my cheek and kisses my head. "Now, when can I meet him?"

"Well, he doesn't exactly know who you are."

"What?"

"Well, he knows I have a brother called Xander who's an actor, but I might have played it down a little."

"Well, I'm not Xander the actor to you. I'm Xander your brother."

"Yes, I know that, but in the past, it's caused issues for me, so I didn't mention your…" I throw up my hands. "Well, you."

"What kind of issues?"

His face is stormy as he steps back and crosses his arms over his chest. Like this, he's taken on the character he plays in his films, all brooding and dangerous.

"Just guys using me to get to you."

"Why didn't you tell me so I could make their lives a living hell?"

I chuckle and it feels silly now. "They weren't worth it."

"They hurt you. That's worth it." He slings his arm around my shoulder. "We're gonna work on this. But for now, do you have an evening dress?"

I frown. "Yes, probably. Why?"

"I need a date to this private viewing tonight and I choose you, Pikachu."

I shake my head. "I can't. I don't want Harrison finding out we're related on the news."

"He won't. No paps allowed, and you need a night to let your hair down."

"I have Isaac."

"Get a sitter."

"I don't know." I can feel myself waning, wanting to go and forget about the disaster of my life but at the same time, not wanting to rock the boat.

"Please, for me?"

I feel myself cave. "Fine. When is it?"

"Tonight, at seven. So shake a leg."

"Where do you get these expressions from."

Xander throws his arms wide and affects an air of superiority. "I'm an actor, darling. I have a whole repertoire of sayings."

I roll my eyes but I'm happy he's here and that I've got at least a few secrets off my chest. It's made me realize how unfair I've been to Harrison. He deserves better. He's never given me a reason to think he'd treat me the way those other men have. Tarring him with the same brush is no different than him assuming I'm a gold digger, which he's never done.

"Chop, chop." Xander claps his hands with a grin and I shake my head and smile.

"Whatever, just let me get Isaac from his nap and I'll see if I can organize a sitter."

I GRIP MY BROTHER'S ARM AS WE SLIP INTO THE THEATER BY A SIDE door. I'm wearing a floor-length red lace gown that has a Bardot neckline and a fishtail skirt. It's Valentino and one Xander bought me a few years ago to wear to the premiere of his first action movie. I never got the chance because we'd had an incident at the lodge.

I can't resist running my hand over the gorgeous fabric or touching my hair with nerves. I'm here among some of the most beautiful women in the world and I'm a little self-conscious.

"Stop fidgeting, you look beautiful."

I drop my hand and grip his arm tighter, praying I don't take a header in these heels. "I thought you said there would be no photographers." I smile automatically as the cameras flash and Xander turns on his movie star charm.

"No, I said there would be no paps, and that's different. These are here at the request of the production company."

"If Harrison sees these, I'm going to murder you."

"Relax, he won't."

I try and do as he says, taking a glass of Champagne off the tray.

"Xander, good to see you."

A tall man with dark brown hair and blue eyes approaches with his hand outstretched. Beside him is a stunning woman around my age with long dark hair in waves down her back. Both have the same green eyes and high cheekbones. Siblings would be my guess or at the very least, related in some way.

"Nora, this is my friend, Ethan Masters, and his sister Serenity." He turns to them as he finishes shaking Ethan's hand "And this is my baby sister, Nora."

I meet Ethan's eyes and see the appreciative look he gives me before he dips his head to my hand. "A pleasure."

Serenity leans in and gives me an unexpected air kiss and I immediately like this girl. I see no artifice or malice, which can sometimes be the case, only open friendliness.

"Lovely to meet you, Nora."

"It's great to meet you. Are you both actors too?"

Ethan laughs. "God, no. I own the Manhattan Cleavers."

"The hockey team?"

"You know hockey?"

His eyes twinkle and a smile tugs at his lips. He's devilishly handsome and he knows it. If I wasn't head over heels for Harrison, I'd be attracted to this man. But no matter what, Harrison is the man I love and he's my husband.

"A little, yes, but I'm afraid my allegiance lies with the New York Howlers."

He slaps a hand over his heart and fakes pain. "You wound me."

"All right, brother, dial back the charm. This one is clearly taken."

"Then I guess I'm destined for a broken heart, sister."

"I'm sure you'll live."

"Tell us about you, Nora? Xander is very tight-lipped about his family."

I glance at Xander who's looking around the room for someone before turning back to Serenity. "Well, there's not much to tell. I run a lodge in the Catskills, I recently got married, and I have a six-month-old son."

"Wow, that's a lot and here I am trying to get my life together enough to find a permanent place to live."

"But you're an actress, that must be so much fun."

"Not as much as you think. Lots of auditions and rejections and being told to lose weight and dealing with pervy directors and handsy actors. But other than that, I love it."

We both laugh at the obvious opposition between her description and reality.

A light flashes and I look at Xander. "What is that?"

"Time for us to find out seats."

I can feel the nerves thrum through him as we make our way to the VIP seats with the other members of the cast and crew. Serenity has a small part in the movie but is killed off pretty early in the film.

I watch with awe and pride as my brother transforms into his character. Only minutes in and he's no longer Xander, he's a superhero trying to save the world.

Later, as the credits roll and a huge cheer goes up in the auditorium, I join in as Xander blushes to the roots of his hair.

Out in the foyer, people jostle to come over and congratulate him and I stand back with utter pride on my face and in my heart. He's worked so hard for this and he got what he wanted. He even overcame his early struggles with determination and grit.

When the crowd thins, I move closer and throw my arms around him, hugging him tight and he returns my embrace, almost crushing me in his big arms.

"I'm so proud of you."

I lean back and look up at him and that's when bulbs start flashing and a microphone is thrust under Xander's nose.

"Xander, you're live on Movie Scoop. Can you tell us who this woman is and what your relationship is to her?"

I feel panic hit me, but it's overshadowed by anger that this man would ambush my brother on his special night. Before I have a chance to respond, the man is dragged out by two burly security guards.

"I'm so sorry, Nora."

"Don't worry. I'll handle it if it's a problem."

"I'm sure Harrison doesn't watch Movie Scoop, although I can't guarantee that story won't make the networks."

"Xander, don't worry."

He looks furious and the night is dimmed for us both, so an hour later we head home. I pull out my phone and check for messages and see fifteen missed calls from Audrey and Lottie, and the last two are from Harrison.

Dread makes my stomach sink as we approach my home and I see the horde of paparazzi outside.

"Oh shit."

23: Harrison

I GRAB MY CARRY-ON AS THE SEAT BELT SIGNS TURN OFF. I'M EAGER TO get home and see my wife and see if we can fix what I broke. A few days to process things and think has done me good and for the first time in a long time, I can see clearly. I love Norrie and there's a chance she loves me too. I'm still slightly stunned by that notion, but I can't deny her actions or her words might just be true.

I'm hurrying through the departures when my eye catches on a TV screen. I pause, the breath knocked from my lungs as I stare at my wife looking like a fucking vision in another man's arms. Other passengers bump into me and curse but I'm rendered immobile by what I'm seeing.

I can't hear the words as the TV is muted but it keeps repeating the footage. Norrie hugging this man and gazing up into his eyes with a look of absolute love. It's like being stabbed in the heart. I'm bleeding out in the middle of the airport, and nobody can see because it's invisible, and yet it's the worst thing I've ever felt.

The headline catches my eye.

Mystery Woman in the Arms of Playboy Movie Star.

Something about the man is familiar and I think I've seen him in a few movies but right now, I want to rip his heart out and feed it to him.

"Harrison."

I turn at the sound of Beck's voice. "Beck, what are you doing here?"

He looks up at the screen and grimaces, but he isn't shocked.

"Did you know?"

Beck steers me toward his car. "Of course not, and we don't know anything yet. There could be a simple explanation."

"You mean other than my wife might be fucking some movie star the first chance she gets?"

"Yes."

I get in the car, and he jumps in the driver's seat of his Porsche and heads toward my home.

"And where the fuck was my son while she was out fucking some rich prick?"

"Isaac is with Amelia."

I glare angrily, all hurt buried under the burning anger I feel toward Nora. I know at some point the pain and betrayal will return and take my legs from under me, but for now, the anger and bitterness are preferable.

"Is she in on this?"

Beck shoots me a look of warning. "We don't know what this is, and Amelia is the one who called me when the paparazzi turned up outside your door."

I clench my fist. "They're at my home?"

Beck rolls his lips between his teeth and nods. "Yes, but she just sent a text to say Nora is home and the guy is with her and refusing to leave."

"Put your fucking foot down, Beck."

I seethe as he gets me home in record time, but the front street is a writhing mass of people and cameras, and we have to park down the street.

"Have the security company we use for the club send some people over."

"Lincoln already called them and they're on their way."

We sit and look at the crowd thankfully unnoticed for now, but we don't have long before some asshole with a camera spots us.

"So, what's the plan?"

I point at the people fighting to get a picture. "Well, I'm not walking through that. Let's walk around the back and go in through the garden."

Beck and I jog around the back of the row of homes. Luckily it's clear for now but it's only a matter of time. These people are like leeches and Norrie has shoved us straight into the middle of this nightmare with her behavior.

I unlock the back gate using the security code and thank God she'd had enough sense to set the alarm. Lights are on as we approach, and I can see my wife looking stunning in a red dress as she buries her head in the asshole's chest.

I see red, pushing through the door angrily as they jump apart.

"Harrison!"

She gasps but I'm focused only on him, and he knows it. I swing and my fist lands on his cheekbone with a crack. He staggers back but only a fraction. The guy is big and yet I feel a rage that makes me believe I could take on the world and win.

"It's not what you think, buddy."

I move to hit him again, but Norrie squeezes herself between us. I glare at her lying, deceitful face, hating that my heart still yearns for her.

"Don't fucking tell me what I think and we ain't buddies just because you're fucking my wife."

He straightens and we're both around the same height, but he outweighs me by probably twenty pounds in muscle.

"Xander!"

Beck's shocked voice reaches me and I turn to see him looking stunned behind me. I look between the two men and suddenly I know where I remember him from. It's not just movies, it's the club. He's a fucking member.

"Beck?"

"What the hell is going on here?"

"Harrison, let me explain."

I point at Norrie. "I don't want to hear anything you have to say."

"Don't talk to her like that."

Xander steps up to me and we're chin to chin, two men simmering with adrenaline and rage.

"She's my wife. I'll do whatever the fuck I want."

"Yeah, well, she's my sister and I say you need to shut the fuck up."

"Sister?"

I glance at Norrie who's wringing her hands and looking between us. "Norrie, is that true?"

She nods and I notice her mascara has run. It hurts me to see she's been crying but I harden my heart to it. She still lied to me.

"So Xander Reynolds is your brother, and you didn't think to mention it to me?"

"I…"

Even now she can't say the truth.

"Get out, all of you." I point to the door. "I said out."

"I'm not leaving you with him like this, Nora."

She moves to Xander and touches his arm. I grit my teeth. Even knowing who he is to her, I can't shake the feeling of betrayal. Her brother isn't some two-bit jobbing actor, he's the biggest name in Hollywood right now. "I said get out of my house, right now."

I grit my teeth as I speak, trying to control my temper remembering at the last second Isaac is in the house somewhere.

"Harrison, please. Xander is just trying to protect me."

"Fine, you can go too. I don't want someone who can lie so easily in my life."

Her face loses all color and I have a moment's thought that I'm making a huge mistake, but I brush it off.

"You don't mean that."

"But I do. We both know this marriage was a mistake. We can't even be civil half the time and clearly, I don't mean enough to you that you'll let me into your life. So yeah, I mean it. Go."

"Harrison, what are you doing, man?"

I turn to look at Beck who's watching me intently, a look of worry on his face. "What I should have done weeks ago. Calling time on this mistake." I see Norrie straighten her shoulders and lift her chin, even as tears sparkle on her long lashes.

"So once again you're pushing me away without giving me a chance to explain?"

I stride to her quickly and see Xander move but Beck grabs his arm.

"He won't hurt her."

"He already is, asshole."

I ignore them both and concentrate on her, looking for something I can grasp onto.

"You promised me on our wedding day that there were no more secrets. Yet here we are in this mess with fucking cameras outside my home while our son sleeps upstairs. Tell me again why I should let you explain."

"I'm sorry."

"Not good enough, Norrie. I trusted you and you let me down."

She huffs out a breath, clenching her fists by her sides. "Now who's lying? You never trusted me. You've been waiting for me to give you a reason to run since the start. You don't trust anyone, Harrison, and it's sad because you'll be a lonely old man when you could've had everything you ever wanted."

I grip her neck gently, the silky skin so smooth against my fingers and I wonder if this will be the last time I get to touch her like this. "How do you know what I want, Norrie? We obviously barely know each other." I glance back to see Xander and Beck in a heated conversation of their own.

"I do know you, Harrison. I know you love our son and would do anything for him, and I know you love me and it terrifies you. I also know the damage your parents have done. I made mistakes, big ones but at least I'm not afraid to say I love you."

Her words are like tiny blades against an open wound. I drop my hand as if her skin burns me. "Isaac stays here when you leave."

Panic washes over her face. "What? No."

"Yes, Norrie, and if you cross me on this, I'll make you regret it." I stride away from her, shove past Xander, and head for the office where I keep a stash of my favorite Cognac. I pour a glass and my hand shakes, making the amber liquid slosh over the sides.

I hear the door open but don't turn from where I'm watching our security team disperse the journalists hounding our door.

"Harrison, you can't expect her to leave without Isaac."

"Why not? He's my son too."

"I know but you're doing this to punish her and, believe me, when you calm down, you're going to regret it."

I spin on my heel. "Why the fuck does everyone seem to know what it is they think I want or need or will feel?"

Beck steps forward and grasps my neck, putting his forehead to mine. "Brother, I know you. We've been through a lot, and I know the man you are and he wouldn't hurt someone he loves, no matter how angry he's with them."

"I don't love her."

"Yes, brother, you do. That's why this hurts so fucking much."

I feel the truth behind his words and he's right. He does know me and no matter how angry I am, I can't hurt her anymore. "Fine, she can take Isaac, but I want to know exactly where she is and I want a security detail on them until this clusterfuck dies down."

"Good decision."

I grunt as Beck walks out to deliver the news to Norrie. I sit in my chair as I listen to the sounds of people in the house. Twenty minutes later, I hear the front door slam and the shouts begin. I can't help but watch out of the window as Norrie and my son are whisked away and out of my life. An emptiness settles over me as I see the car turn the corner, taking them away, and I have the strongest desire to run after them and bring them home.

The door clicks behind me and I see Beck, Linc, Ryker, and Audrey standing there.

"What are you all doing here?"

Ryker lifts a bottle of whiskey in the air. "Family doesn't leave when the shit hits the fan."

A warmth spreads through my chest and suddenly that lonely feeling isn't so oppressive. "What about you, Audrey? You're Norrie's friend now."

Audrey is wearing jeans and a hoodie sans make-up, her hair in a bun, and not many people get to see this side of her.

She moves toward me, shaking her head. "I'm her friend, and I'm yours too, but you need me more right now. So, are we drinking or not?"

"Damn right we're drinking."

Ryker raises his glass with a smirk. "Then when he's good and drunk, we can explain to Harrison what a dickwad he's being."

24: Harrison

I WAKE AND GROAN AT THE STIFF FEELING IN MY NECK AND REALIZE it's because I've slept sitting up in the rocking chair in Isaac's nursery. Last night's events spill over my brain and I wince at the slight headache in my temples.

Thank God Lincoln had the sense to cut me off before I got too wasted, but I clearly had enough to knock me out. I stand and move stiffly to the crib where my son sleeps, lifting his blanket and bringing it to my nose. His familiar baby scent hits me, washing detergent and baby powder. I feel a pang in my chest, missing him already, and pull out my phone just so I can see his face on the screen.

It's barely six and I know my body has woken out of habit, ready to start the morning with Isaac but I sent his mother away and now my home is a shell. Trudging into the bedroom, I grit my jaw as her scent lingers in the air. She's everywhere I look. Her things crowd the surface of the dresser, and her dresses and clothes hang beside mine in the closet.

I take a shower and, even here, our last encounter fills my mind. The way she responded to me, the words she said, the sounds she made when I was inside her. I try and imagine a time when she wasn't in my life, and I can't. Norrie is so full of life that she imbues that on everyone she meets but I can't get past the fact she lied to me.

I dress in sweats and a tee, ready to hit my home gym and sweat some of the liquor from my pores.

"Hey, we're heading out. Do you need anything?" Audrey is standing at my bedroom door looking worse for wear.

"No, I don't think so. Are the journalists still there?"

"A few but Xander Reynolds has called a press conference for later today so they're camping out at his hotel."

My stomach knots as I sit heavily on the bed. "What about Norrie and Isaac? Are they safe?"

"Yeah, I had them stay at my place last night and my security won't let anyone near."

I'm grateful I have friends who step up for me. "Are you going to see her now?"

Audrey nods. "I am."

I open my mouth but what can I say? What is there to say?

Audrey sighs and steps into the room. "Harrison, you know I love you and your mom, but she's fucked you up. I know she's sick, but she's also selfish and self-centered at times. You've spent years trying to prove to her that you're worthy of her love and sacrifice, and that's not how it's meant to be with family."

She crosses her arms as I remain silent.

"Your dad left because he was a dick, plain and simple. Maybe they had problems in their relationship but that wasn't caused by you."

"Why are you saying this now?"

Audrey sinks onto the bed beside me. "Because Norrie made mistakes, but she's not malicious, she's scared too. Do you have any idea what she's been through in her life?"

"Of course I do."

"But do you know how much she keeps her own wounds hidden so as not to be a burden to others? She didn't tell her own brother about her accident because she didn't want to bother him. Who does that?"

I shrug, having no answer for her.

Audrey pats my arm and leans her head on my shoulder. "Just think things through and decide if you really want to throw everything away without a fight."

Audrey leaves and I spend the rest of the day working out until I can barely stand. Then I work, trying to get some emails answered in my office but I can't concentrate and by mid-afternoon, I give up and head to the bedroom. I haven't heard from Norrie and I don't expect to either, but I miss her texts, even the ones that are only one word. I wander aimlessly into the closet, drawn to her things, my fingers moving over the scarves and sun dresses. Each one holds a memory, and in every one, she's smiling.

I miss her and I don't know what to do about that except put one foot in front of the other.

I watch the news that night with a TV dinner of noodles, which I don't taste, and see Xander Reynolds on the screen. Grabbing the remote, I turn up the volume.

"I'm angered and disappointed that the media saw fit to sneak into a private event and photograph a private moment. My sister, Norrie Richards, has no desire to be in the life I live and therefore I ask that she be left alone. Being the family member of an actor as a member of the public isn't easy, and I've done my utmost to protect her. On this occasion, I failed. Now, if anyone has any questions about the movie, I'd be happy to answer them."

"Xander, Xander."

Journalists call his name, and he points at one of them. I have to admire him for protecting Norrie and the way he commands the room, but I still hate that he brought this to us. Is this why she lied to me about who he was or at least misled me?

"Isn't your sister married to the billionaire Harrison Brooks?"

Xander grits his teeth. "You people are not hearing me. My sister is off-limits. Now, any other questions?"

I want to fist bump the air but at the same time I want him to answer and say yes, she's married to Harrison Brooks. Norrie is my wife, but I gave up the right to claim her when I threw her out of our home. I close my eyes wondering what the fuck I've done. I love her and I threw her away, not once but twice, and I need to fix myself before I can know for sure I won't ever hurt her again. I dial the number I know by heart and wait for the person to pick up.

"Hey, I need to see you."

I STARE AT THE DOOR FIGHTING MY INSTINCT TO TURN AROUND AND run, but I need to do this so I can move on. I haven't stopped thinking about what Audrey said about my mom and I need to confront it if I stand any chance of moving on with my life. Beck gave me the number of a support group for family members dealing with personality disorders and it's been eye-opening to realize I'm not alone in feeling like I do. They've also helped me to see that removing myself from the situation isn't selfish, it's sometimes the only thing you can do to keep yourself healthy.

I've begun journaling, which felt silly at first but purging all of my thoughts onto paper has helped me see how damaging they were. I know Norrie journals, and I found them in the closet under her shoes. It's tempting to read them but that would be a breach of her privacy and I won't cross that line. If she ever wants me to read them, I will and I hope mine will help her understand me better.

I knock and wait on the threshold wondering if she'll even answer the door. I wait and half of me hopes she doesn't, but the other half knows I need this. A lock clicks and I hear a shuffling before the door cracks open a touch.

"Harrison? Why didn't you use your key?"

My mother looks the same as always. Her life within these four walls is so insular that she has no concept of the outside world now or how her actions and words affect people.

"Can I come in?" I ignore her question about the key.

"Yes, of course."

I follow her in and sit at the kitchen table as she moves around making tea.

"Mom, will you come and sit down. I want to say something and then I'll leave."

"Okay."

She sits meekly and I know today won't be one filled with bile and hate, but compliance and understanding.

"I know Dad leaving us hurt you. I know this wasn't the life you planned, and I'm not the son you wanted but none of that is my fault. I didn't make Dad walk out. I didn't ask to be born and I'm worthy of love. I deserve it and I shouldn't have been made to work for it all my life. I know that now because I'd never make my son work for my love. It's unconditional and absolute."

Her lip wobbles and she reaches for my hand. "I'm sorry for what I said, Harrison. You're a good boy and I do love you."

I hear her words, but I don't know whether to believe them and that's the crux of my problem. I've spent so many years hearing her say this and then taking it back when it suits her or she's having a bad day. That's why I threw it back in Norrie's face like I did.

"I believe you do in your own way, but I'm here to tell you I won't be coming around anymore, not until you get some help. I need to look out for my family and to do that, I need to look out for myself and that means protecting myself from you."

"But what will I do?"

I stand and lean down to kiss her cheek, so many warring emotions in my head but the biggest is love for Norrie and my son. "You'll manage, Mom."

"But, Harrison…"

I walk to the front door feeling freer than ever before turning around a look at the woman who gave me life. I know I'll always love her, but I can no longer let her use me as her emotional punching bag. "I love you, Mom."

I sit in the car and it's like a weight has lifted from my chest. I start the car and hope the second part of my plan works because I'm going to win my family back if it takes me the rest of my life.

I pull up at Audrey's home where I know they're still staying and park my car. It's been fourteen days, and I miss them so much it leaves a hollow ache in my chest. Audrey knows I'm coming but she also warned me Xander is here and I'll need to get past him first.

I don't mind that. I owe him an apology too.

I head up in the elevator using the code Audrey gave me. When the doors open I take a deep breath and step out.

"What the fuck do you want?"

25: Norrie

"Nora, are you here?"

I swipe at my tears as Audrey yells up the stairs of her swanky condo.

"Up here." I'm proud of how steady my voice sounds considering I spent half the night crying.

Audrey walks into the room and she stinks of booze. I wrinkle my nose as she sits in the chair in the room I'm using for now.

Audrey tries to take a whiff of her own breath and grimaces. "I smell that bad?"

"Yeah, pretty bad."

"I'll take a shower in a minute, but I wanted to check on you."

"I'm fine."

"Of course you are. Your life is imploding but you won't say that because you don't want to be a bother."

I roll my eyes. "You've been talking to Xander."

"No, I have eyes."

I stand and march to the window looking out over the view of the city. "It's not a crime not to want to put people out, Audrey."

"True, but it's a crime that someone as wonderful as you thinks she has to be less, and puts her own needs last all the time."

I want to ask after Harrison, but I bite my tongue. I'm not sure I want to know right now. Audrey and the guys spent the night with him, and Lottie and Amelia stayed here with me. It was the right thing, and he was clearly hurt but once again he proved that when the going gets tough, Harrison pushes me away.

"Where's Xander?"

"He's holding a press conference to ask them to leave me alone."

"You think it will work?"

"He does and he knows them best. Although it won't happen straight away. They need a new bigger scandal to focus on first."

"Why didn't you tell us?"

I thought this over all night and decided only the truth will suffice. "Ever since Xander hit it big, I've had to deal with people using me to get close to him. Boyfriends, friends. Even guests at the lodge would pretend to like me but all they wanted was access to him. I got sick of being second best all the time, so I started keeping it a secret. Then I knew if people stuck around, it was because of me."

"That makes sense in the beginning, but why not say anything after you knew us, especially to Harrison?"

I sigh and flop on the bed, exhausted from hardly any sleep last night. Isaac was restless, sensing that something was up, and I kept replaying things over and over in my head.

"I don't know. The longer I didn't say anything, the harder it got until I was in too deep. Then we started having problems and it was the least of my worries."

"Well, you're a pair. Him with his mommy issues, and you and your abandonment ones."

"I don't have abandonment issues."

"Woman, you're a walking case study."

"Rude."

"But true and I get it. Shit, you've lost more than most in your life than a lot do in an entire lifetime. I'd be surprised if you didn't have issues."

"It doesn't excuse Harrison's behavior though."

"No, it doesn't. He was a dick and I think if you give him time, he'll see it."

"I'm not sure I want to give him time. He hurt me and honestly, as much as I love my son, I'm not sure I can be with a man who doesn't love me or trust me."

"He loves you, honey."

"Actions, Audrey. They speak the loudest."

"I know."

She grips my hand and then hugs me tight. I'm hurting but I know how lucky I am to have her and Lottie and Amelia and even Suzie.

Xander calls around after the press conference, which I refused to watch, and he brings pizza and mojito mix.

Amelia and Lottie turn up too and we spend the night watching movies and stuffing our faces. I smile, I laugh, but inside I'm ravaged with guilt and wretchedness. I miss him, his arms around me, his scent, the way he makes me feel safe and beautiful, and special.

He's the person who hurt me and yet it's his arms I want to make it all better. How messed up is that?

Around nine, I'm exhausted from trying to be upbeat and say good night. I lie in my bed and let the tears come. The release is cathartic in some ways. I cry for my birth parents, my adoptive parents, and my nanna who taught me so much. I cry for what could've been and I cry for myself, letting the emotion drain me until I have nothing left inside me.

∼

"WHAT THE FUCK DO YOU WANT?"

I hear Xander's tone change and move from my spot at the kitchen island where I'm making up bottles for Isaac. My heart stutters as I see Harrison looking at me.

"Harrison?"

"Norrie, I need to talk to you."

He rushes toward me with a look of panic on his face and then he sees his son and a smile so big it could diminish the sun breaks across his face.

"Hey, buddy." He lifts him from the play mat where he'd been playing with his toys and hugs him close, kissing his head and making him giggle. "I've missed you so much."

My heart feels like it will melt but I can't allow that, so I cross my arms over my chest. "What do you want, Harrison?"

He moves toward me and I stand my ground, not wanting to show weakness when all I want to do is throw myself into his arms.

"Can we talk?"

"No."

"Yes."

I glare at Xander speaking for me and reiterate my answer. "Yes, let's sit down."

"Xander, you and I are going to take your nephew for a walk in the park and see if we can rustle up some new rumors about you."

Audrey takes charge of my brother and I almost feel sorry for him but not enough to step in and help. I stay silent as I watch them leave, Xander hoisting Isaac's bag over his shoulder and Audrey clipping Isaac in the stroller.

"Oh, to be a fly on the wall for that one."

I smirk but remember he's here to talk about us and probably custody and access. "Let's sit." I lead him into the living area and take the chair as he sits in the corner of the couch. "I don't want to involve lawyers unless we have to, Harrison."

"Lawyers?"

I frown. "Yes. I assume this is about custody?"

Harrison jumps to his feet and comes over to kneel at my feet, taking my hands in his. "God, no. I don't want a custody fight, Norrie."

Relief almost overwhelms me, and I sag, dropping my head. "Thank God." But then I furrow my brow. "Then why are you here?"

"I want to apologize. I was wrong on so many counts. Wrong for forcing this marriage, wrong not believing you when you said you loved me, and wrong for not trusting you enough to listen. But most of all, I was wrong to walk away from you last year because you're the love of my life."

I snatch my hands away, not wanting to ignite hope when he could take it away again. "Why are you saying this now? What changed?"

"I did. I realized I've been blaming you for my parents' mistakes. I let the damage they caused ruin my future with you and that stops."

"Harrison, you can't just say that to me and expect me to put myself and our son through that risk again. You hurt me."

"I know I did and for that, I'll forever be sorry. I never meant to hurt you. I love you and it terrified me. You were right about that. I joined a support group for families dealing with mental illness and it's helped. I've also written in this journal and I want you to read it."

He hands me a brown leather-bound journal and I take it with shaking hands.

"You don't have to read it now, but when you're ready. If you can find it in your heart to forgive me, I promise I'll never let you down again. I love you so much, Norrie, and every day without you is torture that I deserve, but it's hell on earth."

"You love me."

"I love you so much. I love your smile, your laugh, and the way you bite your lip when you're thinking. The way you keep baking those damn cookies even though they never go right but most of all, I love the way you love our son and me."

"You believe me?"

"I always did deep down but I was scared. The journals will explain more but the highlight is I spent years trying to earn a love I never should have had to. My mom would say she loved me and then the next breath, she'd tell me I was unworthy. I'm not blaming her. She's sick but it still did damage, and losing you made me see that."

I reach for him, cupping his face. "I'm sorry you went through that and I'm sorry I lied and withheld the truth."

Harrison's hands cover mine. "I get it, Norrie. Nobody made you feel like number one, and they should have. I'll spend my life making you and our son, and any more children we might be lucky enough to have, a priority in my life."

"I love you, Harrison Brooks."

"I love you, Norrie Brooks."

I don't wait a second longer or draw out this reunion. I know in my heart this is us now. I push off the chair and kiss him, taking us both to the ground in my desperation to feel him again.

His mouth commands me, dominates mine, his tongue stroking inside as we tear at each other's clothes in a desperate bid to feel skin. He's warm under my hands as I yank his shirt from his pants. He shivers as my fingers touch his abs, working over his skin. We separate long enough for him to pull my shirt over my head and then his mouth is on my aching nipple, and he's suckling as I squirm, my pussy drenched with need.

"Harrison, I need you."

"I know, sweetheart."

I reach for his pants and unzip them, grasping his cock and stroking from root to tip and hearing him groan.

"So fucking good."

He thrusts into my hand as he draws my yoga pants down my legs and then he's there at my entrance, pushing inside me. I moan and he catches it in a kiss as he holds me close with no space between us and I wrap my legs around his hips, meeting him stroke for stroke.

"Don't ever leave me, Norrie."

"Never. Oh God, that feels so good."

His pelvis hits my clit with every stroke, and I can feel my body climbing that peak, building until every inch of me is primed. My pussy flutters around him and it's like an avalanche of pleasure washing over me.

I cry out his name like a prayer. "Harrison, oh God. Oh God."

His hips speed up and slam into me so hard that we move up the rug where we landed. I love that he's so blown away with need he has no control, that he doesn't look at me and see someone who's broken.

"Norrie." He stills and then I feel him come, his climax extending mine until he collapses against me kissing my neck, my cheek, my lips.

He lifts up and looks at me with so much adoration and love, it's blinding.

"I fucking love you, Norrie Brooks."

"And I love you, Harrison."

We don't hear the elevator so wrapped up in our bubble.

"Oh my God, put some fucking clothes on."

Harrison lifts his head to look at Xander as I bury my head and giggle. I'm covered head to toe, but it's still embarrassing getting caught in a compromising position by your big brother.

"How about you give us a minute, dickhead."

"Fucking my sister on the floor? Disgusting."

We hear his voice get softer as he walks away grumbling.

"Shut it or I'll revoke your membership at the club."

"Asshole."

Harrison laughs and it's the first time I've seen him so free, and I can't help but join in. "He isn't really a member, is he?"

"Yeah. About that NDA."

I swat his bare ass and he flexes inside me, and I realize he's still hard. "Really?" I wriggle beneath him, and he flexes his hips again and I whimper.

"What do you expect? I've been without you for weeks."

"Whose fault is that?"

Harrison growls and nibbles my neck. "Mine but I did do something right."

"Oh yeah, what's that?" I run my fingers over his back.

"I knocked you up."

"That you did."

He drops a kiss on my lips. "Best thing I ever did."

"I agree."

"Are you two decent yet?"

"No!"

"No!"

We burst into fits of giggles as the door slams and we get busy.

Epilogue: Harrison

"Norrie, I'm home!"

I dump my jacket on the back of the chair as I loosen my tie, my eyes moving around our home looking for the love of my life.

"In here."

I follow the sound of her voice, a smile twitching on my lips. I turn the corner into the living area and there she is. Like it always does, my breath catches in my chest at the sight of her. She's the most beautiful woman in the world to me. Always has been and always will be but like this, she's otherworldly.

She walks toward me with her arms outstretched and I reach for her, bringing my hands to clasp her lower back as her body molds to mine. Dipping my head, I kiss her upturned lips and smile as my son or daughter gives a kick I can feel through both our bodies.

Norrie grins. "We missed you."

"I missed you all too."

I rub my hand over her huge belly and bend to speak to our unborn child. "Stop kicking your mom so hard." I can hardly conceive of the love I feel for a person I've never met. But each morning I wake with wonder as I watch her grow and change, relishing every second that I'm privileged enough to witness it.

EPILOGUE: HARRISON

You would've thought conceiving would be as easy the second time as the first, but it wasn't. The first year was hard on Norrie and she fretted that perhaps she'd done something, but Beck reassured us that it was different each time. Just as we made an appointment to see a specialist, this little one decided to join the party.

"Dadda, Dadda."

I grin as I crouch to receive a hug from Isaac as he throws himself at me. Scooping him into my arms, I blow raspberries on his neck, thinking that the sound of his giggles is one of the purest in the universe.

Isaac is two and a half now, and any day now he's going to become a big brother. I, for one, am terrified. When Norrie told me she was pregnant, I cried like a baby, I was so overjoyed. But watching her get so sick each day to the point she was hospitalized again, I can't say I'm keen to do this again.

I adore my family more than life but watching her so weak and barely able to keep plain pasta down was horrific.

"He wants to show you the new truck Uncle Xander bought him."

"Xander is home?"

Xander and I had gotten off to a rough start, to say the least, but we have common ground in our love for Norrie and Isaac, and that was enough to forge the bond to a point where I now consider him a brother. Plus, the fact he's in a relationship with one of my best friends makes it impossible to avoid him.

"Yes, they wrapped up filming last week."

"Cool."

"How was your mom?"

The subject of my mother is still fraught but she at least apologized and has met Norrie and Isaac, although I'm careful to make sure I'm around when they interact. I love my mom and we have a tentative relationship again now, but I won't think twice about cutting her out of it to protect my wife and children. They are, and will always be, my priority.

"Okay. She has some new online game she's playing, so she seems content."

EPILOGUE: HARRISON

"Good...ooof."

Norrie bends and grabs her tummy and instant panic ripples through me. I take her arm and guide her to the couch. "Are you having contractions?"

Norrie blows out a breath and slowly straightens. "I've been having strong Braxton Hicks today."

"Are you sure they're Braxton Hicks?" I learned they were like fake contractions and it was the body's way of getting ready for birth.

"They must be. We aren't due for a week."

I bug my eyes at my wife. "Norrie, how far apart are these fake contractions?"

"About five—"

She doesn't get to finish her sentence because another hits and I have my answer. There's nothing practice about this. "We're going to the hospital."

"But what about Isaac?"

My heart is racing so fast inside my chest but outwardly I'm calm. "We can get Xander or Lottie to meet us at the hospital and take him." I'm already pulling out my phone and sending the text to the group chat.

HARRISON: IT'S GO TIME!

BECK: JUST HEADED INTO SURGERY. KEEP ME POSTED AND GOOD LUCK.

LINC: LOTTIE AND I ARE LEAVING NOW.

LOTTIE: LINC, CALL RYKER.

XANDER: OMG

AMELIA: I'M SO EXCITED.

AUDREY: I'VE CALLED AHEAD AND ALERTED THE DOCTORS

RYKER: CAN WE WATCH THE BIRTH?

HARRISON: FUCK NO!

NORRIE: HARRISON, MY WATER BROKE.

I glance up and see Norrie standing in a pool of water looking at me.

RYKER: GROSS

AUDREY: GROW UP RYKER

EPILOGUE: HARRISON

I slide my phone into my pocket and race to my wife, guiding her to sit on the stairs as I clean up the mess from the floor. Isaac runs around the corner and stops dead in his tracks as he looks at his mother.

"Mommy have an owie?"

Norrie smiles and strokes his face, pushing any sign of pain away to protect him. "No, sweetie. Mommy is just getting ready to have your baby brother or sister."

Isaac claps and I can't help but reflect on how lucky I am in that moment.

Six hours later, I'm not feeling so lucky and I vow that we're never having another baby.

"That's it, Nora, push."

I clasp Norrie's hand and she squeezes my fingers so hard I'm sure they must have snapped hours ago. When we reached the hospital, she was early stages so she held off on the epidural saying she could handle it. Over the next few hours though, she progressed so fast that she completely bypassed the point she could have one.

"Arrgggghh."

Norrie turns puce red, sweat pouring from her and I've never loved her more. Women are fucking rockstars.

A cry pierces the air and I look down through blurry eyes filled with wonder to see my baby being born.

"It's a boy."

I blink and look at Norrie, who looks almost angelic with joy as she sags back against the bed exhausted from pushing for two hours. Our son is placed on her belly and she immediately reaches to snuggle him and bring him to her breast. It's a moment I'll never forget and one so humbling I can hardly breathe.

"Would you like to cut the cord?"

The doctor hands me the special surgical scissors and with shaking hands, I cut the cord.

Norrie looks up at me with a beatific smile and I kiss her, placing my arm around them both. "I love you so much, Norrie."

"I love you, too."

Her eyes move to our son again and she pulls the sheet back and counts his fingers and toes, and we spend a few minutes marveling at this miracle.

"Go, let them know."

"I don't want to leave you."

"They're just outside the door and I want Lottie to bring Isaac in so he can meet his brother."

I kiss her lips and then kiss my son's head, a lump in my throat. "I love you."

"We did good."

"You did amazing. I just did the fun parts."

"No, Harrison, you were the one holding my hair, taking care of Isaac, and loving me every single day."

"And I'll love you every single day until the day I take my last breath, and then I'll love you in the afterlife."

Her grin makes my chest tighten but her words make me hard.

"You're so getting lucky in about six weeks' time."

"Can't wait."

My lips find hers again and then I move away, stopping at the door to watch her looking down with so much motherly love that my heart feels like it won't fit in my chest.

I pull open the door and there are all my friends, even Lottie is here with Isaac asleep on her lap.

"Well?" Audrey demands.

"It's a boy."

A whoop fills the room and then congratulations and hugs and questions about Norrie and the baby are thrown my way.

"He was seven pounds, nine ounces, and we're going to call him Finley John James Brooks."

I see Xander nod, his emotions choked at the revelation that we named our son after his father, Norrie's adopted father, and her birth father.

"Can we see them?"

"Yes, but give us a couple of hours with just us and Isaac first, then

EPILOGUE: HARRISON

you can visit." I lift my sleeping son from Lottie with a thank you and head back into my wife and Finley.

We're a family, not just the four of us but everyone in this room and I'm just sorry it took so long for me to see it.

Beck barrels around the corner, looking harried and still wearing his scrubs. "Did I miss it?"

Amelia takes his hand as Xander takes the other, the three of them forming an unlikely bond but one as strong as any I've seen. But that's their story to tell and I'm just happy to live my own.

∽

This is the happy ever after for Harrison and Norrie. If you want to read what happens to Beck and Amelia, you'll find their story in *The Unexpected*, releasing May 2023.

Books by L. Knight

KINGS OF RUIN

The Auction

The Consequence

The Unexpected

About the Author

Lia Knight is a romance author of billionaire romance with lots of angst, and heat. Her heroes are super rich, demanding and know exactly what they want, so when they set their sights on the heroines in these books you know the chemistry will explode your kindle. Having written over forty books under a different pen name she wanted to give those rich, bossy heroes fighting for a story a chance have their say and find their HEA.

When she isn't writing she is binging Yellowstone, The Big Bang Theory, and Bridgerton from her home in Hereford in the UK.

You can contact me at: lknightauthor@gmail.com

Join my Facebook group to get all the latest updates: https://www.facebook.com/groups/KnightsDelights1

Printed in Great Britain
by Amazon